THRILL

THRILL

Robert Byrne

Carroll & Graf Publishers, Inc.
New York

First edition 1995

Carroll & Graf Publishers, Inc.
260 Fifth Avenue
New York, NY 10001

Library of Congress Cataloging-in-Publication Data

Byrne, Robert, 1930–
    Thrill / Robert Byrne. — 1st ed.
        p.   cm.
    ISBN 0-7867-0199-4 (cloth)
    I. Title.
PS3552.Y13T47   1995
813'.54—dc20   95-8851
                                                    CIP

Manufactured in the United States of America

1   2   3   4   5   6   7   8   9   10

For my brother Bill

A certain amount of danger is essential
to the quality of life.

Charles Lindbergh

THRILL

CHAPTER ONE

Ruby Glouster hesitated. Should she walk all the way around or take the shortcut? Night was falling fast and she was already late. She could save several minutes by following the plank walkway that passed beneath the tracks and through the forest of white wooden columns. It was strictly against park regulations to cross under the roller coaster during operating hours, but she had done it dozens of times.

There was a double column of people waiting to take the last rides of the evening. Thrill sure packed them in, despite its reputation as the roughest ride in the country . . . or maybe because of its reputation. Ruby walked to the front of the line, pushed through a door marked "Employees only," and skipped up a short flight of stairs, her long ponytail bouncing behind her. She was an energetic woman with an athletic figure and a tanned face that looked far younger than her thirty-five years. Her most striking feature was her brown eyes, which were large and lively and which—a man she once dated told her—served both as skewers and heat lamps. Her eyes were narrow now, reflecting the discomfort she felt at the prospect of crossing under the coaster when the sun was down and the train was running.

On the end of the launching platform above her was the control booth. Mark, one of the teenage operators, called down to her.

"You're late, Ruby! We want to get out of here."

"Chill out," she called back. "In five minutes I'll have the sky filled with thunder and lightning . . . and you can quit watching the clock." Even though they were only ten feet apart, they had to raise their voices to be heard over the park's background din: calliope music from the merry-go-round, demented cackling from Laughing Sal at the Fun House, the roar of machinery, and the screams from nearby rides like the Octopus and Loop the Loop.

"Wanna meet me after? I'll show you some *real* fireworks."

Ruby wrinkled her nose. "I'm old enough to be your mother. Take a cold shower. Think about sports."

She swung her legs over a low barrier and stepped onto the walkway that led into the shadows under the coaster's tracks. The first rains of fall had soaked the bare ground enough to let the side-by-side planks yield slightly under her weight, but no water oozed over the surface as it would later in the winter. She hesitated, making sure that a train wouldn't be launched directly over her head, then hurried quickly into the labyrinth. Light from the darkening sky cast a pattern of shadows on the damp and glistening ground, but in the gloom it was hard to make out details, which made the footing treacherous. She had progressed no more than ten feet, stepping carefully, when the floodlights came on. "Damn!" she said aloud. Now the shadows were cast upward onto the spiderweb of columns, beams, and braces, while the walkway almost disappeared in blackness. That's what she got for running so far behind schedule. In the distance was the slowly turning Ferris wheel, another relic of an earlier age; seen through the latticework, the wheel's lights seemed to blink on and off. The scene was surreal, something from a nightmare . . . and in fact it would be the stuff of her nightmares for months to come.

She walked as quickly as she could. Her goal was to make it to the far side of Thrill, just a hundred yards away, without twisting her ankle or breaking her neck. She would be at the edge of the bay then and could walk to the end of the pier under better lights and with bettter footing. She would make sure that Soo Kim, or Koo Sim, or whatever the new technician's name was, had the fireworks wired up correctly and would supervise him as he set them off. As a nightly ritual, three low-level rockets and three high-level aerial bombs told the world that the park was closing. Since this was Sunday night and the end of another week, Ruby usually threw in a few extra effects. Tonight she planned to send up a half-dozen barium chlorate and copper carbonate stars, using four- and six-inch mortars to get them up to 150 feet. She had given the Korean, whose official title was Pyrotechnical Apprentice, Class B, detailed instructions, and she would be interested to see if he had followed them correctly.

Why did she feel so uneasy? Because she always did when she was someplace where screams would go unheard. What could happen? Was somebody lurking in the shadows? The posts were too

2

thin to conceal a mugger or a rapist, though it was so dark now at ground level they would hardly need anything to hide behind. Was the whole spindly pile of pick-up sticks going to come crashing down? Not likely.

She heard a familiar sound, the metallic clank-clank-clank of the train being hauled to the top of the first hill. Her step slowed; she didn't want to be alongside the track when the train hit the valley at top speed. She stopped and waited. There it came from far overhead, a sinuous black shape that rocketed down the slope with a roar, making the ground tremble like eight-point-five on the Richter scale. She grimaced and covered her ears with her palms, only partly succeeding in blocking out the thunder and the screams of the riders.

Quickly the rumble fell to a whisper as the train headed down the line. Ruby jogged forward, touching the columns on each side with her hands to keep herself centered on the walkway she could no longer see. She crossed under the track at Banshee Curve, so called because of the way riders tended to scream at that point, and was well past it when the train streaked through. It was a cat-and-mouse game Ruby was playing with the train, first waiting and then hurrying, always managing never to be underneath the track when the train was passing overhead.

It was amazing, the stuff that fell from Thrill. Fountain pens, purses, billfolds, and hats were to be expected, but some things Ruby picked up in the daytime almost defied explanation, like a pair of pantyhose, a pool cue, and a set of false teeth. Leon, the park's chief mechanic, had a cardboard box full of odds and ends that no one claimed, including knives, guns, and at least fifty earrings.

One more checkpoint and she would be in the clear. Ahead and high above her was a cruel twist of track called Lurch, where the train came around a curve and plunged almost straight down, gaining speed and turning hard right and hard left before straightening out and rising again. Most of the wrenched necks and bruises claimed by Thrill took place there; riders braced themselves against a force from one direction and then were hit from the opposite side. Ruby stopped and watched. The train dropped and threaded its way through the tight curves, twisting like a snake trying to shake off its skin, flashing with a strobe-light effect in the lights and shadows.

When the train was gone, Ruby advanced again. Something liquid hit her face, drops of water or . . . Good God, had one of the passen-

3

gers lost control of his bladder? Had a startled sea gull unloaded on her? She touched her cheek . . . her fingertip came away so covered with red she thought for a second she had cut her finger. Her forehead felt slippery, and when she held her hand to the light it looked as though she was wearing a red glove. She raised her arm to ward off what had become a shower, and what she saw in the scaffolding overhead made her heart stop. A body was draped across a wooden beam, the motionless body of a girl with arms and legs projecting at grotesque angles, a girl apparently thrown from the train and broken open so badly that blood was pouring from her.

Ruby tore her eyes away and ran sobbing and gasping toward the pier, wiping the blood from her eyes and mouth, falling heavily on the walkway when her legs turned to rubber.

She was a senior at Sonoma High named Holly Sonnenvold, a vivacious girl and a daredevil. Her friends weren't surprised that she wanted to ride Thrill, the creaking and dilapidated wooden roller coaster that for thirty years had served as test of courage. They were surprised when she jumped aboard the empty last car when the lap bar was already down and the train was rolling. She managed to wriggle under the bar—she weighed less than a hundred pounds—not realizing that the platform attendants had left the last car empty for a reason: previous riders reported that something was wrong with the lap-bar latching mechanism. Holly was laughing and bouncing up and down in her seat during the train's slow climb, a motion that no doubt contributed to the final failure of the lock. At the top of the hill, just as the train left the hoisting lugs and was rolling across the flat section toward the main drop, the lap bar broke free and rose to its full open position above her head. The train nosed over the edge and began accelerating, the lead cars dropping out of sight one after another. Holly started screaming then, flailing about for a handhold, when it was too late to avoid disaster.

Park officials speculated that Miss Sonnenvold didn't jump out when the train was still at crawl speed because she didn't realize the seriousness of her predicament. They also pointed out that her blood-alcohol level was 1.0, well above California's legal limit.

4

By grasping the side edge of the car with one hand and the front edge with the other, she managed to hang on through the first descent and the so-called "Banshee" curve. A friend in the car ahead twisted in his seat and tried to give her a hand, but she was beyond his reach. He watched her fight a losing battle against centrifugal force and her own terror.

On the sharp twists called Lurch, Holly Sonnenvold was thrown out. She traveled approximately fifteen feet before striking a timber cross beam. Wounds were opened in her neck and stomach, and her body became snagged on broken X-braces thirty feet above the ground. If she hadn't been killed by the impact, the county coroner stated in his report, she would have died from loss of blood before rescuers could reach her.

Her blood fell like a curtain on a low section of track, and from there to a walkway on the ground. Twenty seconds after the accident, the train returned from the far end of its run and passed directly below the body, where it was caressed from front to back by a fine and ghastly rain. When the train finally rolled to a stop at the platform, every rider's face and clothes were flecked with red.

CHAPTER TWO

Hunched in front of a computer screen was a square-shouldered, square-faced man with a full head of wavy black hair. He was wearing blue jeans and a short-sleeved sport shirt. A sweater was draped over the back of his chair. He had kicked off his shoes. Even though he was only thirty-four years old, the pattern of creases at the corners of his blue eyes were deep, especially when he smiled or laughed, neither of which he was doing at the moment. He was squinting and he was frowning, for he had lost the will to continue.

On the screen was a diagram of a bridge pier resting on a cluster of H-piles. Design problems that involved finding the greatest strength for the least cost were not without intellectual interest . . . but not today, not when you'd rather be skiing.

His eyes wandered to the window of his office. Ten stories below on Michigan Avenue was the old limestone water tower, a fanciful turret inspired by a medieval castle and his favorite piece of architecture in all of Chicago's Loop. It was easy to imagine a knight in armor defending it against a snorting dragon.

He wished he was the knight. Or the dragon. Anything but a designer of foundations. It depressed him to think that his life was turning into an endless series of abutments, prestressed concrete-bearing pads, and building excavations that had to be stabilized with tie-backs, dewatering, slurry, and grout. He had an urge to throw his computer out the window and watch it smash on the sidewalk like one of David Letterman's late-night stunts. No, somebody might get hurt.

His thoughts turned to one of his favorite fantasies, the one in which he stomped into the president's office and shouted, "No more frigging foundations! I quit! I'm going to follow my bliss and become a ski instructor, or open a ski shop, or lead tours to the slopes of Switzerland. Anything but design foundations! I don't care if trains and trucks cross rivers on piers superbly designed by McKenzie and Son. As far as I'm concerned, the world would be a better place if trains and trucks couldn't get across rivers at all.''

That was a bad idea, too, though thinking about it cheered him up a little. If he made a speech like that, the old man would cut him to ribbons. "I see," he would say in his patrician and precise way. "Have you thought this through? Who will hire a ski instructor who has broken his leg three times? How do you think your skis got to Chicago? They got here by truck or train, with many bridges to cross along the way. And what about your engineering education? Is that to be sluiced down the sewer like a piece of effluvia from the treatment plant?" They would argue about it, getting further and further from the point, as they had so many times in the past.

The intercom on his desk crackled. "Jack, would you come up, please?" It was McKenzie of McKenzie and Son. When McKenzie spoke, the Son responded.

"Be right there, Dad."

Jack left his office and strode purposefully to the foyer, pausing to tell the receptionist that he was off to see the Wizard. "If I'm not back in half an hour, Mary Lou," he said ominously, "suspect foul play. Wait two days, then drag the lake."

Behind her was a wall chart with every employee's name. She lifted a tab that changed the status of *John McKenzie, Jr.,* from IN to OUT. Under the column *Will Return At* she inserted a question mark. Then it was back to the crossword puzzle in the *Tribune.*

Jack bypassed the elevator and sprinted up the stairs, taking the steps two at a time, pumping himself up for a confrontation. The father would have to be told that the son was tired of the whole idea of foundations and wanted more excitement in his life, even if it meant sluicing his education down the sewer. He realized when he reached the upper landing that he needed a plan, a way of making his discontent sound reasonable. Thirty-four was too old for a seven-year itch and too young for a midlife crisis.

John McKenzie, Senior, a stern man with an office to match, was at his desk paging through a set of what he sometimes called "blueprints," even though engineering drawings hadn't been blue since ancient times. Prints were white now, the color of old snow, though not, of course, as white as fresh powder. On the walls were photo-

7

graphs of warehouses, bridges, and grain elevators, all of which rested comfortably—one could almost say arrogantly—on McKenzie and Son foundations. Part of Jack's problem was that everything he had done in the last five years, including his very best work, was buried. At least structural and mechanical and aeronautical engineers could *see* the results of their efforts. They could walk up to buildings and slap them with their hands and say "I designed this. It will last as long as civilization." Satisfaction like that was denied to foundation engineers.

"Sit down, my boy," the president said, not looking up. "How are you coming along with Pier Three?"

Jack sat down and sighed. One of his father's weaknesses—or was it a strength?—was that he seemed to know exactly what his scores of employees were doing at all times. Did a good job of it, too. There wasn't a designer in the company who didn't feel that if the slightest error was made, day or night, John Archibald McKenzie would miraculously appear and say in his intimidating baritone, "Well, well, Carstairs, what's this? Forgot to convert meters to yards, did we? That will never do."

"Well?"

"Fine, Dad. It's a little hard to concentrate just before a vacation."

"Fine? Is that all? Not a lot of specific information in 'fine.' "

"I'm looking at steel rather than concrete at the moment, maybe a group of ten H-piles with the four at the corners twenty degrees off vertical to resist lateral forces."

The elder McKenzie nodded. He turned one of the large sheets and examined the next one with interest, pushing his glasses tight against the top of his nose with his middle finger, a characteristic gesture. His bushy black eyebrows seemed wilder than usual. There was a time in Jack's childhood when he was afraid of his father because he thought those eyebrows were tarantulas.

"Tough to get a pile driver in there, though," Jack said. "The river bank is steep. Might be better to go with mass concrete block with a few mats of number 12 re-bar. Pump the mud in. Probably would be cheaper."

The father looked at the son pleasantly. "A barge-mounted pile driver could be used. The contractor has one."

"I'm happy for him." Nothing had changed. Nothing Jack said or did could be allowed to stand without criticism or amendment.

8

"Work up a couple of designs and let me have a look. We'll make the final decision together."

"Okay. Then I'm going on vacation. I'm burning out on this stuff. You've got to get me some superstructure work to do. Foundations are eating my brain."

Jack hated to hurt his father's feelings. He was a great guy, was John Archibald McKenzie, in a lot of ways. "A credit to his community, a professional respected by his peers the world over, a loving husband and father," in the words of a citation awarded by the American Society of Civil Engineers. It was true, even the loving father part. He expressed his love by letting his son share with him the responsibility of choosing the final design for the pile cluster under Pier Three, but not by letting him choose it all by himself. His vision was to one day hand over the company reins to his son, a priceless gift he had once received from his own father. It was hard for him to imagine that the beneficiary of his largesse might have a vision different from his own.

"I'm going to have to take you off the bridge project."

"Thank God!"

"I want you to go to the Coast for a week or so. Finish up the roller coaster job."

"What happened to Ray Schuler?"

"Gallstones."

"Can it wait till I get back from vacation? There's still snow in the Canadian Rockies."

"Did you say vacation? You just took a vacation."

"That was a year ago, Dad."

"I haven't taken a vacation in five years. Ten, maybe."

"It's a disease. You should see a doctor."

Jack covered his eyes and rubbed his forehead with his fingertips. There went skiing for the season ... unless he flew to Argentina or some damned place. The South Pole was probably open year round. There was a larger problem, too. Jack considered engineering to be a good job, his father thought of it as life itself. It was a difference in outlook that kept their relationship under constant tension.

Jack had majored in engineering at the University of Illinois because at the age of eighteen he wasn't articulate enough to counter his father's main argument: "If I'm going to spend the money and you're going to spend the time, you might as well major in something

9

that people will pay you for when you get out. You can read poetry and listen to music and that sort of fluff later. You don't need teachers for that."

Jack graduated "cum minima laude," as he liked to put it, failing to match the straight A average his father recorded thirty years earlier. That was disappointment number one. Disappointment number two came when Jack spent a year in Alpine ski resorts supporting himself by bussing dishes and teaching English. He showed no signs of wanting to begin his engineering career until an ultimatum arrived from Chicago.

Jack joined the family firm at last at the age of twenty-four and put in five years of solid work. John McKenzie, Senior, watched his progress closely. Just when it looked as though Junior had joined the adult world, he walked out and became a ski instructor at Cochiti Hills in Colorado, which soon became famous as the only ski resort in the modern era to go bankrupt. Following that, Jack spent a year chained to a drafting table in Ohio helping Zephyr Dynamics design amusement park rides. When his mother died, he dutifully came back to McKenzie and Son, and his father's hopes were rising once again. Maybe the boy had finally settled down and put foolishness behind him.

"The coaster, which is called Thrill, is in a park called Wildcat Mountain."

"On San Francisco Bay. Ray mentioned it to me."

"San Pablo Bay, to be exact."

"Excuse me," Jack said with a hint of sarcasm. "We certainly want to be exact."

"I don't know what else Ray mentioned to you, but let me remind you that last year a girl was thrown from the coaster and killed. The State of California shut it down—it has a history of accidents, I gather—and forced a redesign. Slow it up, make it safer, the park was told, or tear it down."

"I read about it in one of the journals."

"It's an old, ramshackle wooden monster like the ones I used to ride as a boy."

It was hard for Jack to imagine his father riding a roller coaster or doing anything that involved physical exhilaration. Engineering was both his profession and his hobby, and when he wanted to relax on weekends he wrote essays about it.

"I was looking at the plans when you came in. The company doing the work is called Speedtech, the original builder of the ride, with help from the park's technical people. The State requires an independent review of the new design and we were retained to make it, as you know. We've completed the work of double-checking the design calculations, and Ray was putting the report together when this gallstone thing flared up."

"Poor Ray." Northern California. San Francisco. There were worse places to spend ten days when the humidity was rising in Chicago.

"Somebody has to visit the site, check the quality of the construction, and plug the requisite paragraphs into the general report. Ray kept putting the trip off, and now there's no more time left. On July 2, we need a man to appear before a state committee in Sacramento and testify that everything has been done according to accepted professional standards, provided that is the case. You know the routine. Speedtech is located at the south end of the bay, the park is at the north end, and Sacramento is an hour and half to the east, so it's all quite convenient."

"I have a nonrefundable plane ticket to Calgary."

"You'll be reimbursed for that."

"What about Aronek?"

"George's wife is about to give birth. You're the only other man in the firm with roller coaster experience."

"Such as it is."

"The ride opens on the Fourth of July, a Friday, two weeks from today. You can finish Pier Three over the weekend, study the coaster plans and specs on Monday, and leave for California on Tuesday."

Jack sighed hopelessly. "Okay, Dad, I'll do it. I don't have a wife who's giving birth and I don't even know where my gall bladder is."

"As I said, the report is practically done. We just need you to plug in the paragraphs about the field inspection."

"I'll go."

"You're always complaining about not getting out in the field enough. Here's your chance. It's a piece of cake."

"I said I'd go. Actually, it sounds interesting."

Wheels in Jack's mind were spinning. He would stay an extra week in California and look into some other career possibilities. He had been wondering for a long time if he would be happier in envi-

11

ronmental engineering, or possibly the growing specialty of failure analysis. Many of the best-known companies in those fields were headquartered in California. He'd check them out.

"Good," his father said. "There's just one thing."

"Oh?"

"I hate to mention it because it might lead to one of our little acrimonious discussions. There's a lot of ground we don't have to go over again about, well, points of view, the rewards of the engineering life, how society is counting on us, what your mother—bless her memory—and I want for you and the company . . ."

Jack pursed his lips and waited.

"Wildcat Park is owned by an old friend of mine named Wilson St. James. Inherited it from his family. We were second lieutenants together in the Korean War. Haven't seen him in forty years, but we exchange Christmas cards, or used to. When the state required peer review, he suggested me. That's how McKenzie and Son got the job. I should take the assignment myself and spend some time with Wilson, but on July 2 I'll be in Rio at the International Foundations Conference."

"So what's the problem?" Jack saw his father push his glasses against the bridge of his nose even though they didn't need pushing. That was a bad sign.

"Wilson St. James is a meticulous, fastidious sort of person. Spit and polish. By the book. We were friends in the war because we shared many of the same values."

"What are you driving at, Dad?"

"He came to McKenzie and Son because he knows that I put a high premium on old-fashioned integrity and professionalism. Now he'll meet my son, and, well, I think he'll be . . . he's liable to be—"

"What? Disappointed? Appalled?"

"No. He'll be . . . put off by the way you dress."

"By the way I *dress?*"

"Blue jeans don't project the right image. Will is a man of the old school. A military man."

"These are designer jeans. They set me back a hundred and fifty bucks."

"I want you to wear your dark suit."

"My dark suit."

"With a white shirt and tie. You are representing an old-line com-

12

pany. A company with a conservative reputation. You should look the part."

"All right, Dad, I'll take some suits. I was saving the dark one for funerals."

"And get a haircut, please."

"A *haircut?* Am I in a time warp here? Didn't we have this conversation when I was in high school?"

"It's down to your collar."

Jack stood up, walked around his chair, and sat down again. He needed a break from the office, he wanted to go to California on an assignment that promised to be a breeze, and he wanted to get away from his father. Before speaking, he waited until the impulse to unleash a string of expletives had passed.

"I'll dress your way and I'll get a haircut. I'll represent the company the way you think I should. I'll go to California and be the Dudley Do-Right of engineering."

He didn't add that it would be the last time. He was going to bail out of McKenzie and Son. The Son and McKenzie just weren't meant to work together. The Son was going to strike out on his own even if it meant selling redhots from a pushcart.

CHAPTER THREE

S hortly after midnight, a ten-year-old Buick was traveling slowly east on the desolate stretch of California Highway 37 that skirted the north shore of San Pablo Bay. Fog was blowing across the roadway in such thick sheets that the headlights penetrated no more than a hundred yards ahead. The driver, who was dressed entirely in black, gripped the steering wheel tightly and peered through the windshield. When the car was crossing the Golden Gate Bridge forty minutes earlier, a mountainous wall of fog rolling in from the Pacific cut the bridge in two. The south tower was clear, the north tower was shrouded and invisible. At midspan, two hundred and fifty feet above the water, the roadway seemed to come to an end as if it were a springboard.

A bad night for driving, a perfect night for trespassing.

A mile past the turnoff to the town of Sonoma was the approach road to the amusement park. A floodlit sign announced that the park was closed and gave its summer hours as ten in the morning to ten at night. The car turned and proceeded ever more slowly for a quarter of a mile. Near the first parking lot, which was dark now and empty, the car pulled onto the shoulder and came to a stop behind a clump of scrub oak and manzanita. After several minutes, the door opened and closed. The driver, carrying a small leather case, trudged diagonally across the parking lot, leaning forward into the cold fog, which moved across the expanse of asphalt like gray smoke. The park's night lights were a ghostly glow in the distance. To the south, it was impossible to tell where the pavement ended and the water of the bay began.

On reaching the park's perimeter fence opposite the roller coaster, the intruder paused and stood still, listening. The wind moaned and whistled in the white columns and beams of the coaster's underpinnings, but there was no sound of alarms or human voices, nothing to indicate that anyone or anything had noticed the arrival of an uninvited visitor.

The perimeter fence was only a month old and a formidable barrier: ten feet of heavy-gauge chain link topped by a roll of razor wire. The fence it replaced was a joke, with several ruptured seams through which it was easy to squeeze. A hundred thousand dollars had been spent on the new fence in an effort to stop a wave of vandalism and malicious mischief. The intruder had to laugh at the waste of money. The new fence had served its purpose for only a few weeks. Now there was a better way to pierce the park's defenses, one that wouldn't be discovered in time.

At the southeast corner of the parking lot, a double row of tapered steel columns extended at right angles to the fence. The columns looked to be about a hundred feet tall and supported two back-to-back billboards. One sign described the attractions of Wildcat Mountain Park, the other carried a montage of patriotic images, including an enormous likeness of the Statue of Liberty's face. At ground level was a locked grillework cage, whose door yielded to a home-made key. A steel ladder led from the cage to a platform between the signs. Straight up the ladder rose without a landing or an offset till it reached the top. Horizontal hoops circled it every five feet, but aside from those there was nothing that would break a climber's fall.

There were a hundred and fifty rungs, and they were cold to the touch even through gloves. On a windy night, the higher one climbed, the more the structure trembled and swayed, and the louder grew the wailing of the wind. At the top, in the narrow passageway between the signs, the wind strained against the billboards as if they were sails. Flaps cut in the canvas of the signs to reduce the force of the wind fluttered and slapped like the wings of startled birds. Gusts created such severe motion that it was hard to keep one's balance without hanging on to the hand railings and dropping to one knee.

At the end of the passageway was a door that opened onto a painter's catwalk. The doorway was slightly higher than the crests of the roller coaster, the tracks of which twisted and turned like a snake coiled on a pillow. Across twelve feet of empty space and at the same elevation as the catwalk was the railing of the crow's nest, an observation deck that had been built as part of Thrill's reconstruction.

15

Using a small flashlight, the intruder checked the rolling gangplank that had taken two weeks to build. Materials had been hauled up from the parking lot with the help of an electric winch. The gangplank was eighteen feet long and was made of two-by-fours spaced two inches apart and held together by cross-bolts. Skate wheels spaced three feet apart along each edge made it easy to roll the walkway forward, even though it weighed two hundred and ten pounds, not counting a counterweight of bricks. It took only a minute to roll the gangplank through the doorway until the far end rested on the railing of the crow's nest. At the most unstable position, just before landing, the gangplank was cantilevered twelve feet into space, with six feet still inside the passageway. To keep the gangplank level as it advanced toward the crow's nest required a counterweight weighing a hundred pounds. A stack of bricks served nicely.

Once it was in position, crossing it on a windy night would be a daunting prospect for a normal person, but not for one with no fear of heights and little fear of death. Ten stories below the center of the temporary span was the chain-link perimeter fence. A body falling on the fence from such a height would likely be cut in two.

Ten minutes after reaching the crow's nest, the figure in black was in the coaster's control booth on the loading platform and plugging a cable into the computer's RS232 port.

Soon the managers of the park would have to find a stronger term than malicious mischief.

As usual on a week night, Eunice Carver, a dispatcher for the Muskegon, Michigan, Yellow Cab company, and her husband Eldon, an auto mechanic, were arranged in their matching Barcaloungers in front of the television set. Mrs. Carver was aiming the remote control and pushing the channel selector repeatedly—grazing, she called it— trying to find a program that would keep her awake until it was time to go to bed. Mr. Carver was engrossed in a copy of *Coaster World*. He had started it the moment he got home, ignoring the rest of the mail, kept his nose in it all through dinner, and found his way to the lounge chair like a zombie, never speaking or lifting his eyes from the pages. She admired his concentration. As a test, she paused on an old war movie and turned up the volume. Bombs, artillery, and John Wayne barking orders failed to penetrate the invisible shield that surrounded her husband. She pushed the Mute button and watched him over the top of her glasses. Even the sudden silence made no impact. It was amazing, really. When he was devouring his favorite magazine it was as if he had lost his hearing . . . and his brain. She wondered if she should divorce him.

"If I left you," she said, "would you care?"

Just as she expected: no response.

No, divorce would cause more problems than it solved. Eldon Carver was a good husband in many ways, better than the half-dozen other men she could have married and better than the hopeless male chauvinists and sports nuts most of her friends were stuck with. An example of his essential decency and fairness was that he let her have the controller when they were watching TV, a position of power no wife she knew enjoyed.

"I've got it," he announced, closing the magazine and slapping it on his knee. Eunice winced, startled. "Cancel all other plans. We're going to California on our vacation!"

"Let me guess," Eunice said, pretending to think hard, "there's a new roller coaster you want to ride."

"You got it, hon! A legend, in fact, that's been shut since last fall. Thrill is the name. It's got some new features that sound cool. It opens on the Fourth of July."

"I thought we were going fishing in Florida."

"I never made the reservations," he said with a grin.

Mrs. Carver shook her head tiredly. "I might have known. Where did you get this need to tie your insides into knots?"

"I'm the Coaster King, sweetheart, it's expected of me. Besides, as you always say, I'm abscessed."

"Obsessed. Where are you going to put another badge, on your forehead? There's no more room on your jacket."

"Wrong!" He bounded to the hall closet and returned with a jacket covered front and back and on both sleeves with patches, pins, and decals dating back ten years. The jacket was proof that he had been aboard either the first or last runs of the season on nearly every major coaster in North America: The Beast at Kings Island, Ohio; Thunderbolt at Kennywood, Pennsylvania; The Big Bad Wolf at Busch Gardens, Virginia; Twister at Elitch Gardens, Colorado; a dozen rides called Cyclone in honor of the much-loved granddaddy at Coney Island; Le Monstre in Montreal; The Viper in southern California; scores and scores of high-speed rides east and west, north

17

and south. But not Thrill in northern California. It was a defect in his record he had to correct.

The panel of judges assembled by *Coaster World* had good reason to name Eldon Carver Coaster King for the previous year; not only had he ridden more coasters than anybody else, he had taken more rides. Once he arranged with a park's management to stay aboard for half a day, racking up fifty consecutive rides. Feats like that had earned him a scrapbook full of newspaper clippings and appearances on a dozen television news shows in the Midwest. While still far from matching the records of earlier Coaster Kings, he could stand tall and proud among them.

"Look," he said to his wife, lifting the left sleeve of his jacket and pointing to his armpit. "Virgin territory all the way from here to my wrist. Room for another twenty pins and patches."

"Wonderful," she said.

"Cheer up, Eunie! Wildcat Mountain Park is next to California's wine country! It's beautiful around there. We'll visit San Francisco, just like you always wanted."

Eunice sighed. It was impossible for a person without any obsessions or even a strong sense of purpose in life to withstand the energy and intensity of a true fanatic. "All right, California it is. While you're breaking your neck, I'll shop till I drop in San Francisco and get drunk on a fine California wine."

"You'll take at least one ride, won't you? If I can get us seats on the first train?"

"Why not? Whatever you want, Eldon. We'll spend our vacation hanging around amusement parks. It'll be just like our honeymoon."

CHAPTER FOUR

Well, it's not Disneyland, Jack thought as he walked across the lot toward the entrance, threading his way between the cars moving bumper to bumper toward the exits. He had been to Disneyland and remembered the way an army of uniformed and well-scrubbed youngsters snatched up every scrap of trash as soon as it hit the ground. Wildcat Mountain's standards suggested that maybe the groundskeepers were on strike. At the base of the chain-link fence was a line of debris—styrofoam cups, food wrappers, advertising leaflets, napkins, newspapers—blown there by the prevailing wind from the ocean. Was that a coil of razor wire at the top of the fence? That was more appropriate for a medium-security prison than an amusement park.

Dominating the entire near side of the park was the roller coaster, a gigantic advertisement for itself that could be seen for miles. A bank of floodlights made its maze of white columns and braces stand out starkly against the darkening sky. It was as big as an aircraft carrier, and it loomed taller and taller as Jack approached.

Far to the right at the corner of the parking lot closest to the bay were tall steel stanchions supporting two large billboards. Floodlights made the message on the near side easy to read:

WILDCAT MOUNTAIN PARK
Fun for the whole family
Since 1936
Home of the greatest coaster of them all—

THRILL

If size were the only criterion, Thrill may well have been the greatest of them all. It was silent now, "closed for remodeling," a tattered banner announced, but looking at its hills and valleys, its dips and curves, it was easy to imagine the screams of riders and the roar of steel wheels.

It wasn't the tallest structure in the park. That honor went to the Ferris wheel, the top of which looked down on the coaster's highest peaks.

Jack was wearing a dark suit and had to be careful to avoid getting run over. At least half of the cars in the lot were either backing out of parking spaces or jockeying for position in the exit lines. In the glare of massed headlights, the surface of the pavement looked rough and pitted. He leaned down and ran his fingertips across the asphalt, then paused to scribble some observations into a notebook.

"Needs better housekeeping. Signs, inc. elevated billboard, show effect of salt air. Bituminous binder eroded from aggregate in Parking Area 3; needs repaving or patching and seal coat. No prking attendant on duty at 9:00 pm. on a Tues. night. Traffic heavy leaving lot; control needed at exit gate and at Hwy 37."

Laughter, shouts, and honking horns made Jack wonder if beer was sold right up to closing time. The park could be liable if one of those fun-seekers had an accident on the way home. He made a note to mention the possibility in his report.

Jack had decided that even though this was the last assignment he would ever accept from his father, he would represent him as well as he could. He would be thorough, he would be professional, he would dress like a dork.

Once inside the park, Jack was reminded of why he had never liked them. Assaulting his ears were tinny music, crying children, and the clatter of mechanical equipment. Assaulting his nose were the smells of food he hated: caramel apples, cotton candy, and corn dogs. Business seemed to be good; plenty of customers, most of them under the age of twenty-five, were strolling on the sidewalks, lined up at food booths, and allowing themselves to be flung about on rides called SuperSnake, Whirl-A-Gig, and Octopus. He shook his head at the spectacle of people subjecting themselves to wildly changing centrifugal and inertial forces. They seemed to be enjoying it; the screams were definitely of delight rather than terror. When those happy screamers were infants, Jack wondered, did they like being tossed into the air by their fathers?

20

The Ferris wheel, that's about as far as he cared to go in the thrill-seeking department, and he spent several minutes watching the ponderous revolutions of Wildcat Mountain's version, called Big Daddy. It was a big daddy, all right, at least a hundred and twenty feet in diameter. It was constructed like a bicycle wheel with small-diameter spokes rather than heavy radial beams. The open gondolas appeared to be made of wicker, and when the wheel stopped to take on or discharge passengers, they rocked back and forth as gently as porch swings. Near the top were two teenage girls in halter tops who looked down at him and waved. He waved back, and they laughed. They probably thought he was a preacher or a school principal, dressed as he was in a suit and tie. He looked as out of place as they would in an engineering office.

Jack made a leisurely circuit of the park, pausing only at the Midway to watch people try their luck at games of chance and skill. Over the public address system came the announcement that the park was closing in thirty minutes. "Willie the Wildcat hopes you had a great time and hopes to see you again soon. Have a safe trip home." The voice should have told departing patrons to take their garbage home with them, for there was no more room in the trash barrels, all of which were filled to overflowing and standing in little islands of debris. The walkways were mine fields of gum, candy, and melting ice cream.

"Hey, Professor, try your luck!" It was a woman's voice, and at first he didn't realize it was directed at him. "Yes, you! Don't look so surprised!"

A woman in a visor and a Wildcat Mountain change apron was standing in a booth idly tossing a basketball up and down. Before he could decline the invitation, she fired the ball to him. He had to react fast to catch it.

"Six shots for a dollar. Make four, you win a prize. Five, you get something from the top shelf. Six, you win a stuffed panda that was smuggled out of Tibet by freedom fighters."

"No, thanks, I haven't played basketball in ten years."

She refused to take the ball back, pointing instead to the backboard and basket, which hung on a pole at temptingly close range. "Do you mean to tell me that you can't throw the ball through the hoop? Even I can do it." As proof, she took another ball and tossed up a hook shot, which settled in after bouncing several times.

21

Jack looked at her more closely. She wasn't a high-school kid with a summer job; she was somewhere between twenty-five and thirty years old. She was one of those great-looking young women who looked good even in work clothes and under fluorescent lights.

"Come on," she said, "I dare you." She had good bones in the face and a smile full of straight white teeth. Jack needed a stuffed panda about as much as he needed a plastic flamingo. On the other hand, she wasn't wearing a ring on her third finger. "Okay, I'll give it a try. Here's a dollar. Hold my coat."

Jack had once prided himself on his accuracy as a free-throw shooter, but despite concentrating and trying his best, he made only two shots in his six attempts. The ball was hard and the rim was attached rigidly to the backboard; the result was a liveliness that made it hard to score if the ball hit the rim.

"Gee, that's too bad," the woman said with mock sympathy, "you lose. Care to try again?"

"Only if I can have a different ball. A soft one, like the one you used."

She looked at him narrowly, then reached under the counter and handed him a ball that was spongy to the touch. "Anything you say, Professor. You're pretty smart. The minute I saw you I said to myself, hey, there is one smart guy."

This time Jack made four out of six and was rewarded with a small plaster statue of Bullwinkle the Moose. "Thanks," he said. "Do you have permission for this from the creators of Bullwinkle?"

"I knew it! You're a cop, aren't you? You're going to throw me in jail!"

"No, I'm not a cop. Your secrets are safe with me."

"A narc, then. An FBI agent. An accountant?"

"I look that bad, eh?" He should never have listened to his father on how to dress. He felt his face reddening. A young woman was looking at him the way she might look at a museum display of eighteenth-century costumes.

"You look bad, but it's nothing that couldn't be fixed. Does everybody in Chicago dress like you and cut their hair so short?"

Jack's jaw dropped. "How'd you know where I'm from?"

She smiled at his reaction. "I read minds."

"Come on, how did you know?"

"I'll tell you for another dollar."

"You were talking to Van Zant, that's it. He told you I called from the airport and was on my way."

"I haven't talked to him today."

"I don't believe you."

"You have to believe or the magic won't happen. Try to send your name to me by ESP, a message from your tiny brain to my big one." She closed her eyes and screwed up her face. "I'm getting an M! Good! You're doing great! I see a C. I see a K. McKenzie! John McKenzie!" Her eyes popped open. "Am I right?"

Jack laughed and put on his coat. "Van Zant told you. You can't kid me."

"No he didn't. Honest. I work alone. Now try to send me your profession." She concentrated again. "I'm seeing something and it looks like an E. Starts with an E. You're an egret? No. An electrician? A eunuch? No, sorry. I've got it! You're sending it loud and clear. You're an engineer! Yes! You work for your father. Something to do with foundations. You sniff out foundations the way pigs sniff out truffles."

"I'll have to tell Van Zant not to talk so freely. What does he look like? I'm supposed to meet him in a couple of minutes at the entrance to the roller coaster."

"I'll tell you for a dollar."

Jack opened his billfold. "What's your name?"

"Ruby."

"What's your phone number?"

"You don't want it. I live with a circus strong man and a lion tamer."

He handed her another dollar and smiled. "There's plenty more where this came from . . . if you play your cards right."

She put the bill in an apron pocket. "Leon is a fat guy who looks twelve months pregnant. Wears his belt underneath his stomach. In the back he's got the most fantastic plumber's butt you ever saw." She held one hand above the other to indicate the length.

"Thanks. I like you, Ruby, because you know what's important in life. Money."

"I like you, too, Professor. You blush easily."

Jack walked away, waving good-bye over his shoulder. Was he blushing? If he was, how could she tell in such dim light? It was a reflex that used to plague him as a teenager. He thought he had gotten

23

over it. Maybe the inappropriateness of his clothes was bothering him more than he realized. The people around him on the sidewalk were generally dressed in shorts or jeans, message T-shirts, athletic shoes, and baseball caps turned backward.

He should have known better than to wear a suit and tie to an amusement park. What could he be but a preacher, a mortician, or a government agent? Well, an engineer. Nothing to be ashamed of there. Despite occasional complaints, Jack McKenzie was glad he was an engineer. He was grateful to his father for forcing him to major in one of the technical professions rather than in some- thing soft and spongy like liberal arts, or, his favorite, "general studies."

Even though he could be happy as a ski bum, he liked engineering, especially civil engineering, which gave him an understanding of how civilization worked he would otherwise lack. There is satisfaction in knowing why buildings, bridges, and planes don't fall down, where electricity comes from and how it gets to your house sockets, how your car engine and television set work, why the earth doesn't fall into the sun, how to figure out how thick floors have to be to support the weight of, say, a soprano. The answers most of his friends would give to such questions were comical in their fuzziness. You almost had to feel sorry for them. They could listen to a song recital in blissful ignorance, never once wondering why the soprano didn't suddenly drop into the boiler room.

John Archibald McKenzie the elder carried it too far. He thought of the engineering professions as a kind of priesthood. Engineers had knowledge that gave them almost godlike powers. They could create powerplants, dams, bridges, skyscrapers, planes, cars—the list was endless—and because of that they had enormous influence over the course of human affairs. He had heard his father's lectures many times at the dinner table. The whole of western civilization was, his father intoned, jabbing his fork for emphasis, a creation of engineers, and without engineers to keep it going, mankind would be plunged into unimaginable misery. Most of the world's problems aren't the result of too much technology, he argued, but rather not enough, or the wrong kind.

Now you take pollution. Environmentalists blame it on technology, but the true culprit is government and the short-sighted know-nothings who run it. The world would be a lot better off if more engineers ran for office. Leaving the field to lawyers is plainly an unmitigated disaster.

Jack's reveries were interrupted by a gruff voice.

"You McKenzie? You looking for me?"

CHAPTER FIVE

The claim that Leon Van Zant wore his belt under his stomach must be based on an assumption, Jack thought when he saw him at the entrance to Thrill, because his belt, if any, was hidden from view under the overhang. The man's midsection strained at his shirt and seemed ready to burst like an overripe melon. He was dressed in blue denim from head to toe, with permanent sweat stains under the arms. He didn't look friendly.

"Mr. Van Zant?" Jack asked, extending his hand.

"Yeah." Van Zant shook Jack's hand perfunctorily. A toothpick migrated from one side of his mouth to the other.

"Nice of you to meet me on such short notice. My plane from Chicago was late, so I had to drive directly from—"

Van Zant looked at him sullenly. "You're the new wise man from the East? Another detective checking up on us. Don't you think we know what we're doing?"

So that was the problem. "I'm sure you know what you're doing. I'm here to finish the report our Mr. Schuler started, say what a great job everybody is doing, and go home. It makes the state look as though it's protecting the public."

"This whole outside expert thing pisses me off. Waste of money."

"Yes, I suppose it is. But what are you going to do? That's politics for you."

"You got any complaints, you take 'em up with Speedtech. They're the subcontractor for the design and construction. I'm just a maintenance man. But I know more about this damned coaster than any man alive."

"I plan to talk to the Speedtech people."

"Whaddya wanna do, walk the line?"

"Maybe part of it. It'll help me get oriented."

26

"I been working late every night. Opening day for this baby ain't that far off." Van Zant's eyes, deep set in his round face, wandered down to Jack's left hand, which was holding the statue of Bullwinkle. A slight smile revealed a couple of missing teeth. "I see you've met Ruby. You musta made a good impression, because she let you use the soft ball."

"She knew my name. Did you tell her?"

"Me? No. Ain't talked to her in a couple of days."

"But you're the only one who knew I was coming tonight."

"So she read your mind. She useta tell fortunes for a living."

"You didn't tell her?"

"Swear to God. Maybe she picked your pocket and looked at your driver's license. Useta pick pockets for a living, too."

"Hmmm."

Van Zant slapped a flashlight into Jack's hand. "Here, you'll need this. Follow me."

Jack followed him up a short flight of steps to the launch platform. He let his left hand drop to his rear pants pocket to check on his billfold—it was still there, and the pocket was still buttoned. Ruby would have to be an impossibly gifted pickpocket to have sneaked a peek at his billfold . . . still, that was easier to believe than that she could read his mind. Maybe she overheard Van Zant or the park manager, St. James, talking about him.

A string of yellow-and-green cars were standing on the track. The cars looked banged up. Several of the padded lap bars were ripped and stuffing was hanging out.

"Are the trains going to be replaced?"

Van Zant seemed irritated by the question. "The wheels and axles are brand new. A ride that looks like it's ready to fall apart helps get people in a screaming frame of mind. Fact is, these cars are safer than baby strollers."

At the end of the platform was an elevated enclosure. "That there's the control booth," Van Zant said. "A broad sits in there and when the computer says okay, she pushes the launch button. The computer does the thinking. If there's a break in the track, or if the previous train is stalled somewhere down the line, or if all the lap bars and shoulder restraints aren't down and locked, the computer won't let anything move. Have you worked around coasters before?"

27

"For a year, with Zephyr Dynamics. I helped design and install Maelstrom in Sandusky, Ohio."

"Maelstrom? That's all steel. Not the same. Wooden coasters, like my friend Thrill here, are a whole different ball game."

At the end of the platform the tracks tilted steeply upward. Jack knew that the slope of the first hill was thirty degrees, but climbing it on foot made it seem twice that. Boards were nailed across the catwalk at one-foot intervals to provide footing, and a quarter-inch cable draped between wooden uprights served as a handrail. Floodlights on the ground made the shadows underfoot impenetrable. As the men gained height, Jack tried not to look down, keeping his attention instead on Van Zant's substantial rear end, which shifted oddly back and forth with each step he took. Being at least seventy-five pounds overweight didn't seem to slow him down.

"Steel coasters are all right, I guess, and if this park had five or ten million bucks to spare I suppose we'd have one, but for me they don't have no soul, know what I mean? They're higher, they're faster, they can do loops, they can do corkscrews, but they're not as scary. Steel pipe rails, steel pipe supports, plastic wheels, they take the noise and the shaking out of it. Nothing like screaming wheels and a lot of vibration to make the young broads twist and shout."

Van Zant stopped and aimed his flashlight between the tracks. "You can see the haul chain. Because of the slow speed, it takes only a seventy-five horse motor, which isn't much when you think that a ten-car train loaded with fatsos can weigh six or seven tons. Slow on the way up, that's what you want, real slow so there's time for the victims to get nervous and realize how high they're getting. There's a lot of psychology that goes into it. See the ratchet dogs alongside the rail? They bump against the axles and make the clunk-clunk-clunk sound typical of your old-style coaster. If the haul chain breaks and the train tries to roll backward, the dogs catch and nothing can move."

"Yes, I know. I've studied your plans and specs, and, as I said, I've had experience with—"

"Working on a steel coaster and reading books about coasters and looking at plans is not going to do you a whole hell of a lot of good when it comes to these old wooden mothers. Each one has its own personality. They're a hands-on sort of thing. Experience, that's what counts."

"Still, the engineering principles are pretty much—"

"Yeah, let's not forget the engineering principles."

Halfway to the top, they paused on a small platform to catch their breaths. Van Zant surveyed the colorful scene spread out beneath them and pointed out the administration building, the maintenance shops, and the park's main attractions. The Ferris wheel seemed almost close enough to touch, and in one of its swaying gondolas Jack could see a couple kissing. In the parking lot, auto taillights formed several red lines that merged at the single exit. He peered over the edge of the wire handrail at the ground five stories below. His stomach felt uneasy.

"Excuse me, but is there any particular reason why we have to climb all the way to the top? I'm not dressed for it and it's getting late. I haven't checked into my hotel yet."

Van Zant cast his beam at Jack. "Don't like heights? You're in the wrong kind of engineering. You should be in mining." He smiled, as much at Jack's discomfort than at his own remark. "We'll take the transverse . . . cuts off about half the line."

At that moment, a bomb exploded high overhead; Jack winced and ducked his head. He looked up and saw red streamers form a flower that quickly faded. Two more star bursts followed, as bright and brief as bolts of lightning.

"Fireworks," Van Zant said, spitting. "Means closing time. Your friend Ruby is in charge of the fireworks as well as the Bullwinkles."

The transverse was a catwalk that crossed the width of the coaster and provided access for painters and inspectors to areas not adjacent to the tracks. It was supported by the latticework and in part by cables that formed swaying footbridges, not the kind of solid footing that would ease the vertigo of a man with a touch of acrophobia. There were steps and ladders, too, some leading up, some leading down. Away from the perimeter, the shadows deepened, and Jack's sense of height faded somewhat. He kept his flashlight and his eyes on Van Zant's shoes.

The smell of fresh paint was strong. Van Zant reeled off statistics on the number of gallons that were applied as part of the rehabilitation, the number of painters, the number of painter-hours, the number of brushes they wore out. "On an old wooden coaster like Thrill," Van Zant said, strolling along unconcernedly, "woodpeckers can be your best friend. That's right! If you're in charge of maintenance, you watch for wood-

29

peckers because they'll lead you to rotten spots you didn't know existed. That's the kind of stuff you won't learn from books. College may be a fine thing, but I don't think I missed nothing. I've met some real assholes with degrees hanging off the ends of their names.''

"So have I.''

"People call me a glorified mechanic. That suits me fine. Mechanics make the world go round.'' Van Zant paused and pointed his flashlight into the blackness below. A section of track came into ghostly relief. "You see how the track down there looks rusty for twenty feet or so? That's because it's the top of a rise. The train is coming over the top and moving fast. The riders feel negative g's and so does the train, which tries to rise off the tracks. The wheels under the track hold it down while the upper wheels aren't even touching, see, and so don't do their normal polishing job.''

"Interesting.'' Jack tried to sound as if he meant it, which wasn't easy when his stomach was threatening to roll over.

"It was right about here that Thrill almost killed me. Yep. I was walking the line one morning before the park opened—I walk it every morning during the season, the whole three thousand feet, looking for anything that needs fixing—and some idiot launched a train. Sneaked up behind me and knocked me down. If my clothes had snagged, I'd be a dead man today. As it was, I got scars all down my left side. I'll show them to you when we get back to the trailer, if you want.''

"No, that's okay.''

"In one way, coasters are delicate little mothers. When the train hit me, it didn't lose much speed, but it was enough so it couldn't make the last hill. It rolled back and forth and settled in a valley. We had to use winches to haul it back to the platform. Same thing happened one time when a rider dropped a sweater on the track.''

As the two men penetrated deeper and deeper into the structure, the labyrinth of angled white braces caught by their flashlight beams formed receding triangles and trapezoids in all directions like images caught between opposing mirrors. Through it all snaked the steel rails, dipping, climbing, and doubling back as if searching for a way out, which is exactly what Jack wanted to do. The farther they got from the floodlights, the darker it got, until finally it was like groping through a cave.

After several minutes of hiking and climbing, they arrived at a

30

platform sixty or seventy feet above the ground. "Here's something you have to see," Van Zant said, shining his light right and left. "Crash Landing, we call it. Have you met Ernie Krevek yet, the guy who designed Thrill in the first place? No? He hates this new feature. Calls it an abomination. I think it's gonna be a big hit."

Van Zant found an electrical panel and threw a switch. Fluorescent lights came on, revealing a fifty-foot-long tunnel. He pointed out movie projection equipment, loudspeakers, track hinges, and hydraulic rams. "The train stops in the tunnel, see, and pictures flash on the walls that make the riders think the ride is collapsing. They hear sounds of steel and wood ripping apart, and the rams let the track pivot downward a couple of feet in a series of lurches. It'll scare the bejeezus out of them."

"I don't doubt it."

"Then the train rolls out the far end and doubles back to the platform. We'll have some full diapers, I guarantee it. Now, this ladder here, it leads up to an observation platform, what we call the crow's nest. Shine your light up there and you can see it. The state made us put it in. Whenever Thrill is running, we got to have a man up there as a monitor. If anything don't look right, passengers are acting goofy or what have you, he can shout at them through the sound system, or call a doctor. Sounds good, but it's mostly a waste of money. It'd make more sense to have the monitor look the other way, toward the billboards, and watch the parking lot. Now that would be helpful, because we could catch some of the punks who break into cars."

Jack had seen the elevated billboards from his car when he arrived. On the sign facing the park, which rose above him now, was a painting of Thrill with hills of exaggerated size and steepness, flanked by an American flag, the Golden Gate Bridge, and the face of the Statue of Liberty. From a distance, semicircles cut in Liberty's face looked like pockmarks; now Jack could see that they were flaps to reduce wind loads. Being so close to the sign reminded him how far above the ground he was, how queasy he felt, and how much he wished he was in his car and on his way to his hotel. He shouldn't have driven directly to the park from the airport.

"Look, I don't feel so hot. Do you mind if we . . ."

Van Zant stuck his flashlight in Jack's face again. "You all right? You look ready to puke."

"Something I ate, I guess."

"We'll head back. Don't want you puking on the woodwork just after it's been dolled up."

They went down a flight of stairs, across a swaying footbridge, and into another tunnel. The walkway there was between the tracks and there was no handrail. The air was stuffy, and heavy with the smell of paint. Jack stepped carefully, beginning to feel a little better now that they were headed toward solid ground. In the distance he heard a faint rumbling.

Van Zant was explaining features of the remodeling. "Crash Landing takes about thirty seconds, so to keep the ride from taking too long we took out about a thousand feet of track. Krevek hit the ceiling when he heard that. Said it was like having his cock lopped off. What a character! You ought to go down to Speedtech in San Jose and talk to him."

"I intend to." Jack frowned in the darkness. The rumbling was getting louder, and he thought he could feel a faint vibration.

"His problem is that he thinks Thrill is a national monument or religious shrine or some damned thing." He pointed his light at his feet. "Lowest point is right here. The train comes off the second hill and dives into this tunnel. Makes the riders think they're going right into the ground. Inside a tunnel like this, the screaming is magnified, which helps."

Strange, Jack thought as he trudged grimly along, that the designer of a roller coaster is considered a success if he makes people scream. Engineers in any other branch of the profession, those who design buildings or bridges or dams, for instance, are failures if they make people scream, and are often treated as criminals as well.

The rumbling got louder, faded, then grew again. "Mr. Van Zant, are any of the rides still running?"

"Mister? You're a formal sort of fella, aren't you? Call me Leon."

The noise grew. The walkway was trembling.

"Krevek makes good use of tunnels on his rides, yes, he does. One of his trademarks. The element of surprise. Wham! You're in a tunnel. Wham! You're out again."

Jack clapped a hand on his shoulder. "Listen," he said, almost shouting, "is that a train coming?"

The boards beneath their feet were shaking unmistakably.

"No trains are coming," Van Zant laughed, then turned serious.

32

There was a loud roar when what must have been a train passed directly over their heads. Van Zant's eyebrows shot up. "Holy shit," he said, "come on!" He ran like a jackrabbit toward the end of the tunnel, Jack McKenzie close on his heels, their bobbing flashlights casting wild shadows on the walls. At the exit, the tracks rose steeply; the two men climbed the ramp far enough to be able to look back over the top of the tunnel. There was no doubt about it: something was loose on the rails and was threading its way through the course at high speed. Directing their beams into the blackness, they caught a glimpse of a shadow rushing from right to left, then turning sharply and reversing direction. It disappeared, then reappeared at the top of the hill that plunged into the tunnel they had just come through. It was an empty train whose wheels squealed and screamed like a hundred terrified passengers.

"Jesus Christ," Jack heard Van Zant breathe, "it's after me again . . . I can't believe it . . . it never gives up." He pointed to the edge of the structure. "Jump! It's only five feet down . . ."

Van Zant scrambled with surprising agility over the handrail on the opposite side and began sidestepping across a beam like a window-washer on a sill. "Jump, for God sakes!"

Jack stood on the edge of the cross ties and looked down. It was impossible to see the ground immediately below because of the glare of a floodlight, but a short distance away he could make out a sidewalk bordered by lawn. There was no way to tell if the lawn continued under the floodlight and to the edge of Thrill's supports. Over his shoulder he saw the train plummet down an incline with the roar of rolling thunder and disappear into the far end of the tunnel.

"Jump!" he heard Van Zant shout again.

There was no time to think. Jack stepped off just as the train burst from the tunnel with the sound of an explosion and a blast of wind. As he fell, he felt the train rush by behind him.

The five feet turned out to be closer to ten. Even though Jack dropped straight down feet first and was prepared to crumple on impact, he wasn't prepared for such a distance nor for the pond he landed in. He hit two feet of water and three feet of soft mud with a tremendous splash. Despite flailing his arms, he lost his balance and felt water close over his head. A family of ducks quacked in protest, and with a noisy flapping of wings relocated themselves farther along the shore.

Jack straightened up, dripping like a piece of seaweed and drenched from head to foot. He moved his arms and legs—nothing was broken. It was hard to walk with his legs gripped by mud up to his knees, but he managed to take several steps forward and climb onto dry land. He was surrounded by a terrible odor, and from the waist down was covered with a greenish muck.

He lifted his hands and looked at the slime in dismay. His anger would have to wait until his stomach calmed down and he could figure out a way to clean up and change his clothes. He leaned over, his hands on his knees, and wondered if he was going to be sick. The rumble of the runaway train faded in the distance.

A female voice said, "What's wrong? What happened?"

Jack looked up and saw the shadowy figure of a woman walking quickly toward him across the grass.

"A train got loose . . . I had to jump."

Leon's voice came from somewhere overhead: "Hey, you all right?"

"I think so," Jack called back. "How about you?"

"Fine. Ruby? Take care of what's-his-name, will ya? He fell in the drink. I got some work to do here."

"Sure thing, Leon." The woman came closer. "Why, it's Professor McKenzie! I thought you looked familiar. Are you hurt?" She squinted at Jack in the dim light.

Jack shook his head, waiting for his breathing and his stomach to calm down. He slowly flexed his arms and legs and arched his back. "I'm okay."

"You're not okay," she said, stepping back and wrinkling her nose. "You smell like duck poop."

CHAPTER SIX

Jack McKenzie always tried to present himself as a man of reason, a self-assured professional who could be trusted to find the best solution to any problem. His father taught him early on that engineers, not just doctors, should cultivate a soothing manner, a way of carrying themselves that implied total mastery. When people need an engineer, they want technical competence, yes, but they want steel-hard integrity and strength of character as well. Project those qualities, his father advised. Practice the knowing nod and the faint smile of indulgence. Because you can always consult handbooks and specialists later, there is never a need to betray the slightest uncertainty. The client will feel better and the job will flow more smoothly if the engineer is perceived as being all-knowing and infallible.

But what if you are drenched from head to foot and half covered with mud? How do you radiate confidence and sang froid then? Jack turned his palms up helplessly. "I'm your blind date," he said.

Ruby Glouster laughed. "I've had worse. A train got loose? How could that be?"

"I don't know, but I intend to find out."

"That damned ride is cursed. I wish they *would* tear it down."

In the glow of an overhead walkway light, she looked beautiful. She had discarded the Wildcat cap and change apron and was wearing black slacks, a white blouse, and a red jacket that matched her lipstick. Her brown hair, inconspicuous in a ponytail when he saw her before, was loose now and cascading onto her shoulders like a silken waterfall. The mad thought came into his mind that it would be wonderful to be married to her and trying hard to start a family.

Jack looked down at himself and made a face. "What a mess! Is there a place I can go to clean up? I have luggage and a change of clothes in the trunk of my car. I can't check into a hotel looking like this, trailing pond scum."

"*It Came From Out of the Swamp.* Come on, we'll use my pickup truck."

To avoid ruining the truck's upholstery, Jack rode in back and was bounced around like a tennis ball as Ruby drove first to his car to get his garment bag, then to the opposite side of the park and into a corrugated metal building containing an armada of vans, tractors, and electric carts.

Following Ruby's directions, Jack stood in a corner of the garage where the concrete floor sloped to a drain. She put on a yellow rain slicker and picked up a hose. When she turned a wall valve, the hose writhed in response. "This is where we wash vehicles," she said. "A steam cleaning is what you really need, but this will do. Leave your shoes and jacket on for the moment."

Jack felt he was in good hands. Ruby was organized and decisive. She knew how to size up a problem, choose a solution, and carry it out without a lot of hemming and hawing, much like, well, an engineer. She wasn't an engineer, though, she told him; she was in charge of games of chance and fireworks. "Fireworks and games of chance," she said, adjusting the jet, "sounds like the battle of the sexes, doesn't it?"

The stream of water raked him from shoulders to shoes as he slowly turned in a circle. The mud melted away.

"Okay, off with the jacket and pants and shoes. Engineers wear shorts under their clothes, don't they, like regular people?"

"You're enjoying this, aren't you? I'm not."

"You beat me out of Bullwinkle. This is my revenge. By the way, where is Bullwinkle?"

"Must have dropped it when I jumped. Sorry."

They stood for a moment looking at each other. Ruby handed him the hose. "Okay, Mr. Modesty, you do the rest." Pleated against the wall was a canvas curtain suspended from a curved overhead pipe. She pulled it halfway around to give him some privacy.

Jack stripped, wrung the water from his slacks and shirt, and finished washing the slime from his skin. From a janitor's closet, Ruby got a couple of towels and a plastic trash bag for Jack's wet clothes. She spread a towel on a bench and opened the garment bag. "Nice

36

threads you have," she called through the curtain. "You must make big bucks."

"I deserve a raise. Say, do you want to change places? Let me wash you down? The cold water is invigorating."

"No, thanks. Nice of you to ask."

Ruby turned away while Jack dried himself and dressed.

Van Zant arrived on an electric cart when Jack was buttoning his shirt and Ruby was handing him his socks. "Well, well," Van Zant said, pulling to a stop, "I see you two are friends."

Jack was all business. "Did you find out what happened?"

"So you decided to freshen up a bit before retiring, is that it? And this nice lady is helping you? She's never helped me like that. I've been after her for years and she's never even wiped my nose."

"Not that it hasn't needed it," Ruby said.

"You're one fast operator, McKenzie."

"How come you're so cheerful? We almost got killed."

"Wasn't even close." Leon took the toothpick from his mouth and flicked it toward a trash barrel. "Thrill is full of surprises, that's all, always has been. I should have kept my guard up." Leon leaned forward on the steering wheel. "You sure you aren't hurt?"

"I'm sure. Don't worry, I won't sue. Did the train cause any damage?"

"Nope. It got back to the platform with no problem and was waiting for me. I kicked it a few times and blocked the wheels with sandbags."

"There better be a good explanation for how it got loose."

"Somebody on the day shift left the computer on, I found out that much."

"What about the launch button? You said it had to be pushed."

"That's what I thought. Must be bugs in the software or bats in the belfry, some damned thing. We'll check it out, you bet. Thrill just has it in for me, for some reason."

"Me, too," Ruby said. "Kill, it should be called, not Thrill." She pushed the curtain back to the wall and began coiling the hose.

Leon waved a hand dismissively. "She had the bad luck to be walking under the track when the girl got thrown out last year. She caught a little blood." He lowered his voice to a whisper and added, "Don't bother trying anything with her. It's not worth it, believe me."

37

"Oh? Thanks for the advice. I'll factor it in. Listen, until you can explain exactly how the train got loose, Thrill is going to stay closed."

Leon drew a sleeve across his mouth before answering. "I didn't know you were giving the orders around here."

"I have what you might call veto power. The state will keep you shut down until I give the green light." He sat down and pulled on socks and shoes.

Stressing every word, Leon said, "Thrill is going to open on the Fourth of July."

"Maybe, maybe not."

"Don't get in my way, jerkoff."

Ruby clapped her hands happily. "Are you going to fight? Do I have time to get my camera?"

Van Zant turned his cart toward the open garage door at the end of the building. "I better scram before I hurt somebody."

"I'll be in your office at eleven tomorrow morning," Jack called after him.

Van Zant muttered something and sped away, the whine of the electric motor quickly fading.

Ruby watched Jack with her arms folded and a look of amusement on her face.

"Well! You're some tough guy, aren't you?"

"I almost got hit by a train, so I'm not myself. I was hired to do a job, and I'm going to do it. Then I'm going to go into a different line of work entirely. Carnival con games, maybe. Or fireworks. Could I interest you in going out for a late dinner?"

"I'm not hungry."

"A drink, then?"

"I want to go home and sleep."

"Some other time?"

"Maybe."

"Are you married?"

"Not that I know of. Do you cheat on your wife?"

"Never had one. Came close a couple of times. It would be nice if I could see you under circumstances that are a little more ... conventional. I usually make a better first impression. I want you to tell me how you knew who I was. Look into the future and tell me if you see us together in a restaurant."

38

She smiled but didn't reply.

"Our mutual friend said I shouldn't try anything with you, that it wouldn't be worth the trouble. What do you suppose he meant?"

Without altering her bemused expression, she said, "Leon is a dangerous scumbag. If I were you, I'd try to keep on his good side."

"Too late, I'm afraid. Which is too bad, because I need his help to do my job."

"What *is* your job?"

"To make sure the roller coaster is safe to reopen."

"Ha ha. Lots of luck."

Jack stuffed his wet clothes into the plastic bag. "Can I trouble you one more time? Take me back to my car?"

Ruby climbed behind the wheel of her truck. "Get in. This time you can ride in front."

Jack's hotel reservations were at the Holiday Inn Marin in Terra Linda, fifteen minutes south on the freeway. He spent the driving time planning his next steps. First thing in the morning he would inspect Thrill in the sunlight. At ten o'clock he had an appointment with Wilson St. James, the park's general manager, at eleven he'd talk to Van Zant. The next day he would drive to San Jose, at the south end of the bay, to meet Jeremy Allbright, the man who ran Speedtech. Maybe he would be able to talk to Ernest Krevek and get his opinion of the ride's safety. Tonight's close call would be a major topic of conversation.

Then there was Ruby Glouster. It would no doubt be worth it to cultivate her friendship ... if she would give him a chance. She almost certainly knew where the bodies were buried at Wildcat Park. Besides, she was an intriguing woman, both good-looking and humorous. Even wearing rubber rain gear in the garage, washing him down, she looked good. It's a good thing the water was cold, he thought, or he might not have been able to conceal his interest in her.

After a few minutes of driving, a feeling of tiredness closed around him like a cloak. He opened the windows and let the cool wind hit his face. To keep his mind alert, he calculated what the state was giving him by letting him use the freeway all by himself. For a minute he saw no other car. At sixty miles an hour, he covered one mile. To simplify the arithmetic, he assumed that one mile of freeway cost ten million dollars to build. What was it worth to have exclusive use for one minute of something costing ten million dollars? If the interest rate on borrowed money was ten percent, you'd have to pay a million dollars to borrow ten million dollars for a year. When you're sleepy, it isn't easy to multiply three hundred and sixty-five days by twenty-four hours by sixty minutes and divide the result into one million dollars. Jack frowned, thinking hard. The answer was a little more than two dollars. You could borrow ten million dollars for one minute for two dollars. In other words, California had just given him the equivalent of two bucks. Not much. The state could keep its money.

At the hotel, he checked in and found his way to his room in a trance, barely able to stay awake. He closed the door behind him, dropped his bags, and collapsed on the bed. Before turning in, he intended to make a list of everybody he wanted to see and make further notes on his preliminary observations, almost all of which so far, with the exception of Ruby Glouster, were negative. He fell asleep immediately, fully clothed and with the lights blazing.

Leon Van Zant made a phone call from his house trailer. He knew St. James wouldn't pick up the phone at midnight, but at least he'd get the message on his tape first thing in the morning. He waited for the beep, then began talking in an irritated tone:

"Willie, this is Leon. Who is this snoop McKenzie you've saddled me with? He's worse than the last guy from Chicago. He's here an hour, we have a little accident, and already he's talking about delaying the opening. Is that what you want? I thought we had an agreement. Get him off my back, will you?"

In the corner of the garage, beyond the Buick and the Cadillac, was the weapons cabinet, the steel doors of which swung silently open. The light revealed a shotgun, a high-powered rifle, a revolver, a five-gallon can of gas, and two hand grenades. There were three hand grenades a week earlier, but one had been detonated on the beach at Point Reyes to make sure it was live and to time the delay between the release of the catch and detonation. Five seconds.

Maybe the weapons wouldn't be needed. Maybe the high speed wreck would take care of everybody. If not, well, then extra measures would be taken. There was the escape across the gangplank to think about, too. The rifle would come in handy then to shoot out floodlights and make everybody take cover. The plan wasn't designed to be a suicide mission, though there was always the possibility.

The plan. Was it just an idle dream? When the time came, would the nerve and will be there? Pacing through the dark house all night, chain smoking, drinking beer, watching old movies on television, dreaming of revenge and retribution, that was in the past. Now there was a plan to carry out. There's nothing like having a goal and working toward it to give your life a structure and a focus. Merely belly-aching about something all the time without doing anything about it can drive a person crazy.

It was exciting to see the weapons. So still and quiet they were, and so deadly, like venomous snakes dormant in the coolness of the night. They needed only a caress to come to life.

It was enough to gladden the hardest heart and make the adrenaline flow.

CHAPTER SEVEN

At the south end of San Francisco Bay, on ten acres of what was once a walnut orchard, was the headquarters of the Speedtech Corporation. Several of its buildings looked so much like hangars that motorists on Highway 101 assumed that they were part of the nearby San Jose Municipal Airport. Most of the property was given over to the "back lot," where roller coasters, the company's main product, were assembled and tested before being shipped. It was on the back lot that ideas for new rides were tried out, sometimes on scale models, sometimes on full-size mock-ups with engineers and secretaries as the first passengers.

Speedtech's physical plant revealed that the company was growing faster than planned—several army surplus prefab buildings provided temporary warehouse space, the accounting department was housed in a group of mobile homes, and parked cars lined the approach road because the parking lot was too small. It was up to Jeremy Allbright, the company president, to put the best possible light on the situation in his meeting with a young pinch-faced woman officer from California Commercial Bank. Allbright leaned over his desk and with the aid of a map pointed out the company's facilities, at the same time delivering a narrative designed to stress the point that the company was struggling with boom-time growth, not poor management. He had told the same story and recited the same facts when he visited the bank's main office in San Francisco, but of course the bank had assigned a loan officer who was new to the case and had to be coached from scratch.

Allbright was a portly plum pudding of a man with a forehead that rose all the way to the top of his head and a complexion the color of ham. His small, dark eyes stood out like cloves. The banker, by contrast, was small and slightly built. She had a pale, waxen face

42

that made Allbright think of department store mannequins and bowls of artificial fruit. Her hair was close cropped and she wore no makeup . . . as if hoping to be mistaken for a man.

Having to deal with such a cold fish irked the Speedtech president. He thought that in view of his company's perfect credit record his request for a loan ought to go through with little discussion and certainly without an investigation. But no, the bank had sent a pompous nitwit to check up on him as if he was trying to pull a fast one. He had half a notion to take his business elsewhere. If California Commercial wouldn't give him five million dollars on the strength of his signature, then by God he would find a bank that would.

"I walked around the grounds earlier," the banker said, "and as far as I could determine, the assets indicated on the map do in fact exist as shown. Whether they are sufficient to collateralize a loan of the size you have applied for will of course depend on the appraisal. The structures are, as I'm sure you are aware, rather less than first class. The company's cash stream as sketched on your application strikes me as a little too volatile for comfort, but probably sufficient to handle the payback, though there again verification would be necessary from our auditors. I gather you need the loan because you intend to move your operation to . . . Nevada?"

The flavoring she put on Nevada made it sound as though mental health might be a problem. Allbright tightened his fists to keep himself in check. "We are sitting on land that is worth a lot of money. At the same time, home prices around here make it hard to hire and keep the people we need." He spoke slowly and distinctly, as if addressing a freshman class that had been held back a year. "In Nevada, there is no state tax, land is dirt cheap, and you can buy a nice house without selling any of your children. We want to move as soon as possible, but we want to get top dollar for our property, and that may take a bit of time. Which is why we need the money. To tide us over. Call it a bridge loan . . . to be paid off in full when the land sells."

The banker made a notation in her leather organizer and nodded as if to say, "A likely story."

Who was this kid, anyway? Her card was still on the desk where she had placed it with delicate fingers. Allbright snatched it up. Kali L. Delareaux, Loan Officer. Kali? Not even an American name! In her case it should be spelled collie.

43

"The California real estate market is not as robust as it once was," Kali L. Delareaux said in her clipped, precise manner, "as I'm sure I don't have to remind you. Now then, about the problem you've had with the coaster at Wildcat Mountain. Thrill, I believe is the name."

"Problem?"

"It killed a girl last year."

"She killed herself, is more like it. Blood alcohol over the limit. Jumping up and down in her seat. We don't do the maintenance and were completely exonerated. Even the park is off the hook because they managed to settle out of court with the parents. Of course, my heart goes out to the family."

"The ride has a history of accidents, from what I read in the paper."

"What paper, the *National Enquirer?*"

"I mentioned it to your receptionist while I was waiting to see you. She thinks the ride is haunted."

"Oh, she does, does she? For your information, Darlene is the one who is haunted. I hope it doesn't handicap her too much in her search for a new job."

The banker's lips turned up ever so slightly. It was, Allbright guessed, a smile. Allbright wasn't smiling, he was glowering.

"My concern," Loan Officer Delareaux said, "or I should say my bank's concern, is that if there are any further problems of an accident nature, the state will close the ride down, thus impugning the integrity of your company with a possibly crippling effect on sales."

Allbright took the three measured breaths recommended by his therapist. He explained that even if the worst should happen, even if the first train on the Fourth of July tore the ride completely apart and turned it into kindling, it would have no significant effect on sales. "The industry knows that Thrill is a very old wooden coaster of a type we don't even make anymore. We now make steel rides exclusively. Besides, nothing is going to happen when Thrill reopens. The redesign and reconstruction are being done by our best people ... and, may I say, with the best outside consultants." Allbright opened a drawer and fished a letter from a folder. "I got word today from the owner of the park that John McKenzie of Chicago, just about the top engineering mind money can buy, has arrived to review the design and construction in detail to make sure nothing is overlooked."

44

Delareaux extended her hand for the letter. "May I?"

Allbright handed it over. "Believe me, everything is being done to the strictest standards. Climbing out of your bathtub in the morning is going to be a lot riskier than riding the new Thrill."

"I take showers. Why anyone would want to sit in a tub of dirty water is beyond my imagination." Delareaux fell silent and read the letter, then placed it on the desk. "*Senior* is not here. *Junior* is here."

"So old man McKenzie sent his only begotten son! What's the difference? They'll be in constant touch by phone, fax, Fed Ex, and E-mail."

"You don't know if he is only begotten. He could have a sibling. Which is not the point. The point is that another accident would be devastating."

Allbright was beginning to feel that Ms. Delareaux would be much improved by a pie in the face. "Keep one thing in mind," he said in tones of controlled exasperation, "we've got forty coasters around the world operating trouble free, and orders for a dozen more in the five- to ten-million-dollar class. Trouble with one ancient ride won't have any effect even if there is any, which there won't be. I'll be riding the first train, that's how sure I am. I invite you to join me."

The banker gave no indication of being impressed one way or the other with Allbright's arguments. "Another concern," she said, "is that the new version will not be popular. There is opinion that the thrill has been taken out of Thrill, that it will be—I don't want to put too fine a point on it—dull." She seemed pleased by her word choices.

Allbright grabbed the edge of his desk. "What opinion? Whose opinion?"

"Your Mr. Krevek, for one. He told me that the—"

"You talked to him? You're quite the researcher, aren't you?"

"We were standing by the coffee urn a few minutes ago. He is such a strange-looking bird that I couldn't help recognizing him. He thinks the ride will put the aficionados to sleep and they'll stay away in droves. He said the mixture of styles is a crime and an abortion."

Allbright dragged his hand down his face, then explained that Ernie Krevek, Thrill's original designer, treated his creation like a personal Mount Rushmore. "He refuses to work on the redesign and never misses a chance to criticize what we are trying to do, which, after all, was more or less imposed on us by the State of California.

You probably noticed that the man is a few shingles short of a roof. He's . . ." Allbright checked himself. If he called Krevek crazy, then it was evidence of bad management that he was still with the firm, while if he was sane, his opinion would have to be given some weight.

"Nevertheless . . ."

"The old buzzard was a genius in his day," Allbright said, searching for middle ground, "but his day has past. He should have retired long ago. Yesterday would have been good. The new Thrill will have a visual effect at the end that will be a sensation, you'll see. Ernie will have to admit he was wrong or go into seclusion."

"Nevertheless," Delareaux said, rising and primly placing her organizer inside her briefcase, "we intend to wait until, say, the end of July to process your application. We want to be sure that, A, the new Thrill is safe, and, B, the public likes it." She extended her hand as if it should be kissed.

Allbright stood and managed to shake hands without breaking anybody's fingers.

There was no denying that Ernest Krevek was a strange-looking bird. With his shock of gray hair and his thin neck and face, he in fact resembled a bird, white-plumed and with devil's brows and piercing eyes. He even had a birdlike way of sitting at a drafting table, the heel of one shoe hooked on the footrest of his stool, the other planted on the floor at the end of a pipestem leg. It was possible to imagine him in a shallow swamp somewhere, taking one careful step after another, looking for grubs to snap up, and more than one sketch suggesting exactly that had appeared on the company bulletin board.

Krevek was one of the few Speedtech engineers who had an office with a door that closed automatically, a necessary feature because he tended to whistle, mutter, and shake his foot while he worked. Many of the draftsmen in the central bullpen wore earphones and listened to music to block out the noise. His work, increasingly in recent years, tended to be of little value to the company, consisting of endless pencil layouts and details for the sort of coasters parks didn't want anymore: complicated wooden tangles that would be hard to build and costly to maintain. His last few designs, in fact, wouldn't have been accepted even in the Golden Age of wooden coasters in the 1920s; Allbright stored them in a cabinet he called The Nut Bin. Riders on those ferocious contraptions would be turned into bags of broken bones. Krevek seemed to have lost all interest in pleasing commercial clients and was putting on paper ideas for rides that pleased only himself; they were more like elaborate instruments of torture than amusement devices.

Allbright knew that if Krevek wouldn't retire voluntarily he would have to be forced out, yet he hesitated taking that step. He and Krevek had started the company together, and many of the older man's early rides were beloved classics. He was a legend to coaster buffs, and it gave Speedtech prestige and a link to the past to have him on the staff. At one time he was good PR. But my God, he was becoming more and more of a liability. Shooting his mouth off to a loan officer was the last straw. Something had to be done.

Allbright marched into Krevek's office with both of his chins thrust forward. "What you said to the woman from the bank was inexcusable," he said, trying to keep his voice down. "The new Thrill is an abomination and an abortion? Jesus Christ, Ernie, what's the matter with you?"

Krevek was sitting at his desk carefully sharpening a row of drafting pencils with a penknife. Electric sharpeners, he often said, were technological overkill. He didn't look up. "That reminds me," he said, "I've got to put a lock on that door."

Allbright threw up his hands in frustration. "We used to be a team! We used to work together! Now all you do is tear me down and tear the company down. It can't go on. It's got to stop."

Krevek stopped whittling and raised his eyes. "You think I should be your enthusiastic supporter, after what you did?"

"What did I do? What did I do?"

"You okayed the destruction of Thrill. That was my signature ride, the ride that made my reputation. It was an almost perfect design, the pacing, the surprises, the way the suspense grew. It was a poem." He put down the knife. "Chopping it up and tacking a cheap movie onto the end makes me sick. Physically sick. Only my innate sense of decency stops me from throwing up right now."

"Change it or see it torn down, that's the choice we had."

"You didn't fight. You caved in. The price was right, so you agreed to take one of the world's great coasters and turn it into a kindergarten toy."

47

Allbright shook his head in dismay. "That's really how you look at it, isn't it? You're not just trying to make me mad. Well, I'm not going to go through the whole argument again. We get nowhere and we end up shouting. The point I came in here to make is simple. You've got to rejoin the team. If you refuse, then please take the retirement package we offered you, which is extremely generous. Never mind how long we've been together and how much you've done for the company and so on and so forth. Your attitude, your complaining, your badmouthing, it's just impossible, Ernie, can't you see that? No company president in his right mind would put up with it."

Krevek smiled. "That leaves you out then, doesn't it? No, Jeremy, my friend, I'm not going to retire and disappear into the night. That would be too easy for you. You've got to suffer a little."

CHAPTER EIGHT

G etting chased off the coaster by a runaway train was bad, learning that he was expected to ride it on opening day was worse. What Jack thought was going to be as relaxing as a vacation was threatening to become the engineering assignment from hell. The shock came at breakfast, half an hour before his first meeting with Wilson St. James. He was idly leafing through the local paper, the Petaluma *Argus Courier*, when his eye fell on an article under a two-column headline:

CHICAGO ENGINEER CHECKS
COASTER DESIGN, CONSTRUCTION

Final engineering approval of Thrill, Wildcat Mountain's hardluck roller coaster, is expected soon, according to the park's manager, Wilson St. James.

Computer analysis of the new sections is nearing completion by McKenzie and Son, Civil Engineers, Chicago, Illinois. John McKenzie, Jr., a senior associate of the highly regarded firm, is expected on the site today to begin what St. James calls "a detailed inspection of the project. We have an obligation to the riding public where safety is concerned and we take that obligation seriously."

St. James was pleased that a midwestern engineer was brought in to make the final examination of the trouble-plagued ride. "He can operate above the fray, so to speak," the park official said. "He has no connection with the various local organizations and agencies that have made their positions clear and who are unwilling or unable to change or to negotiate without preconceptions. I am confident that John McKenzie will find that the new Thrill is completely safe so that we can return a great recreational resource to the people of the North Bay."

McKenzie and Son is the compromise firm chosen after negotiations among representatives of the park, the State of California, the County of Sonoma, and Speedtech Corporation, which designed and built the coaster in 1954 and is handling the current work.

The article went on to review some of the projects designed by McKenzie and Son in language lightly rewritten from the company brochure. It was the article's final paragraph that made Jack straighten and almost drop his fork:

Park officials yesterday released an updated list of dignitaries who will be aboard the coaster's first run on July 4th. Among them are park manager Wilson St. James, park chief maintenance engineer Leon Van Zant, the mayors of Petaluma, Santa Rosa, Sonoma, and Novato, Barney and Eunice Carver, representing the National Union of Thrill Seekers (an organization of roller coaster enthusiasts), Speedtech Corporation's chief field engineer Carl Ott, and John McKenzie, Jr., of McKenzie and Son.

"I got quite a jolt this morning with my ham and eggs," Jack told St. James in his office. "According to the local paper—"

"Thank God you didn't get hurt last night! That would have been a public relations disaster."

Jack removed the newspaper from his briefcase. "I was surprised to see my name—"

"It's unbelievable! A train has never gotten loose before, and I've told everybody involved to make damned sure it never happens again."

"Glad to hear it. Did you see the article in the morning paper? For some reason it says that I'm going to be aboard for the inaugural run."

"Leon should have his head examined for taking you out on the line at night . . ."

It took five minutes to divert St. James from the points he wanted to make. He apologized over and over to Jack for the scare he was given, told him how angry he was when he heard about the accident from Leon, assured him that he would receive every assistance in his review of the project, and asked him not to say anything to the press, which would ruin everything a lot of fine, hardworking people had been striving toward for many months, namely, the reopening of a ride that was completely safe and an asset to the community.

Wilson St. Jame was a large, rumpled man who waved his hands when he talked and whose glasses magnified eyes that already dominated his face. He wasn't what Jack's father led him to expect, an old-fashioned conservative who would be put off by an engineer in jeans. He was wearing jeans himself ... and a sport shirt with a nautical theme open at the collar. Smoke curled from two cigarettes, one in his hand and one forgotten in an ashtray. There was a yachtsman's cap on a nearby chair and a life preserver hanging on the wall. In the corner was a large ship's anchor that seemed to have been silver-plated. His desk was a mess ... like his park. This was not a man who held fastidiousness and self-discipline to be primary virtues.

Jack calmed him down by assuring him that apologies weren't necessary, that he quite understood that accidents sometimes happen—especially when a project is still under construction—and that he had no intention of talking to the press.

"If I have to later," Jack said, "I'll make plenty of noise, but not now. About the list of names ... my name has to be taken off. Riding the coaster wasn't in the job description I got from my father."

St. James looked at him pleasantly, still not hearing. "Your father," he said. "Haven't seen him in thirty years. How is the old coot?"

"Fine. He sends his regards ... and his thanks for recommending us."

"God, it seems like a thousand years ago. He was a hard-assed ramrod in those days. Everything by the book."

"He says the same about you."

St. James chuckled. Ashes spilled unnoticed down his shirt. "I guess I had him fooled. The real me is the wreck you see before you. Years of lassitude and gin have done their work. You look dismayed, as your father would be. You remind me of him. Same square shoulders. Same tight collar. Same level gaze. Let me compli-

51

ment you on how calm you seem after having to jump into the duck pond.''

"Last night I was mad as a wet hen. In fact, I *looked* quite a bit like a wet hen." Jack shifted in his chair. "May I ask you something? You were in the Army with my father, yet your office suggests another branch of service entirely."

St. James laughed heartily. "I can understand your confusion! Simple explanation. Fifteen years ago I decided to be myself instead of what I was pretending to be. Money let me do it more than courage or principles. I threw away my tailored suits, I took up drinking and smoking and carousing, and I just plain started enjoying life. You might say I came out of the closet. Hell, I came out of seventeen closets! Name a closet, I came out of it. I was a big embarrassment to everybody at first, still am, I suppose. I hated embarrassing the Army, though, which I greatly admire. This would be a better country if the Army was running it. I grew up in the Army; I was an army brat. So I went navy, so to speak. I get a kick out of embarrassing the Navy. Bought a sailboat. I love it! Do you sail?''

"No, I ski." It must be California, Jack thought. Nobody in Illinois would spill his most intimate secrets to a complete stranger.

"Ski? Too strenuous. I sail. And I drink. Usually I don't sail, exactly—I sit on my boat and drink. If you want to go for a cruise on a beautiful, twenty-seven-footer, just say the word. I spend most of my time bobbing on the bay."

Jack cleared his throat. "Mr. St. James, you still haven't answered my first question."

"I haven't? What question?"

"How did my name get on the list of people who are going to ride the coaster? Who gave the paper my name?"

"Great article, wasn't it?"

"Who gave them my name?"

"I did."

"Don't you think you should have checked with me first?"

"You weren't here. The reporter asked if you would be aboard. What could I say? That in your professional opinion the ride was safe enough for other people but not safe enough for you? That would do a lot for our credibility."

"We have a problem. I'm not going to ride."

52

"Of course you are! You have to!"

"I don't like roller coasters. I don't like the height. I don't like the motion."

"You just told me you skied."

"Skiing is different. I'm in control when I'm skiing."

"Relax, my boy. You'll enjoy it! Especially the new version, which is more or less for children, like a merry-go-round."

Jack ground his teeth. He was trapped. He wondered if his father had set him up as another test of his character.

"Twenty seats on the train," St. James went on jovially, "and you know how many applications we got? Fifty! It's amazing how many people want the honor of the first ride . . . and the publicity."

"I'm not one of them. I don't think I can do it."

"Of course you can do it! If you back out the papers will crucify us."

Jack lowered his head into his hands.

St. James walked around his desk and slapped him on the back. "It'll be fun! Trust me!"

One end of the storage shed was filled with coils of rope and cable, barrels of lubricating grease and diesel fuel, tools hanging from pegboards, and boxes of spare parts. The other end served as Leon Van Zant's office. His battered wooden desk was surrounded by overstuffed filing cabinets, a table covered with stacks of manufacturers' catalogs and technical manuals, and a shelf displaying a row of bowling trophies, the most recent one ten years old. Pinned to the wall on each side of the single window beside the desk were *Penthouse* centerfolds; scribbled across the chest of one Pet of the Month in a masculine hand were the words: "To Leon—You're the biggest and the best!"

"Yeah, yeah," Van Zant shouted at the ringing phone, turning away from the doorway. The floor creaked when he walked across it, the chair creaked when he lowered his bulk onto it, the desk creaked when he leaned forward on his elbows.

"Yeah?"

"Leon? Wilson."

"Hey, how ya doin'?"

The connection was terrible. It griped Van Zant that his boss always called on a speaker phone, a car phone, or a radio phone of some damned kind from his boat, never just a plain ordinary phone. Oh, no, he was too much of a big shot for that.

"McKenzie says he's meeting you at eleven. He's on his way. Be nice to him."

"I can't do that. He's one of those college pricks you know I hate. Never been around a wooden coaster and already he's threatening to hold up the opening. Where does he get that shit?"

"Maybe he gets it from almost getting killed by one of your out-of-control trains."

"That was nothing! The guy's a sissy! Get him ten feet off the ground and he turns white. I'm supposed to do what he says? Gimme a break."

"A train running around on its own is not nothing. It's ridiculous, is what it is. It's inexcusable. Listen to me, Leon. If anything like this happens again, it's going to be your ass. Got that?"

"It wasn't my fault," Van Zant said in a subdued tone of voice. "Ott thinks somebody monkeyed with the computer. Maybe the same guy who was sneaking in before we put up the fence."

"It's possible. I've told Costello to step up security. I don't care if we have to guard Thrill around the clock, this endless bullshit has got to stop."

Van Zant had a notion to hide under the coaster for a few nights with his shotgun. When he saw the vandal, he'd blow his fucking head off. That would stop the bullshit.

"Remember, we need a glowing report from McKenzie."

"Pay me what he gets and I'll write a report so glowing you can use it to read a newspaper."

"I'm sure that's true, which is why it wouldn't be worth a nickel."

"What about our deal?"

"It stands. Thrill opens on time, you get a bonus of two thousand dollars—*provided there are no injury accidents of any kind.* You've got to realize that safety is just as important as the schedule. Another accident and it's all over. The state, the public, the law suits, the insurance companies will put us out of business."

"You didn't say there was going to be a spy looking up my butt, and that I'd have to make him happy."

"It has to be that way. Show him your lovable side."

On the corner of the desk was the remains of yesterday's lunch, a half-eaten apple. Van Zant picked it up and hurled it against the opposite wall. "This fries my balls."

"I'll sweeten the pot. If McKenzie says in his report that your maintenance program is adequate and that Thrill is entirely safe, you get another bonus."

"I can't stand the guy."

"That's beside the point. Butter him up. Win him over."

"I can't. I'd rather kill myself. How big a bonus?"

"Another two thousand."

Van Zant sighed. Life was hard. "Okay, I'll do it."

"Let me tell you a little secret. Success in business is mainly a matter of being nice to people you can't stand. Remember that."

"What about people you want to strangle with your bare hands?"

"Are we agreed?"

"Yeah. McKenzie has a new friend."

Van Zant hung up and sat with his arms on his desk and his jaw muscles working. He hated what he was going to have to do, but money was money. Four thousand bucks would finance a weekend at Caesar's Palace with the best hookers in the joint and a chance to strike it really big in the casino.

He watched the wall clock. Eleven o'clock. Just as the second hand swept past twelve, there was a rap at the door and the sound of the engineer's voice.

"Mr. Van Zant? Anybody home?"

"Yeah, yeah, come in."

He would have laid two to one odds that the shmuck would show up *exactly* at eleven. He was just the type to let himself be ruled by the clock. What a way to live! McKenzie probably ironed his underwear, too, and shampooed his hair every day, and never used a toothpick twice. Look at him, wearing a suit and tie like some kind of funeral director!

"Good morning, Mr. McKenzie! How are ya? Nice suit! You look sharp!" Van Zant hoisted himself to his feet and removed a bucket of bolts from the chair beside his desk and dusted off the seat with a rag.

His visitor sat down. "This is a place where work actually gets done," he said. "Reminds me of my office in Chicago."

"I'll bet it does! Ha! That's funny! It looks like a tornado went through here, doesn't it? But I know where everything is." Van Zant

55

didn't like the way McKenzie was looking around. He acted like a cop surveying the scene of a crime, looking for things that didn't add up. Maybe he *was* a cop. One thing his roving eyes didn't rest on were the *Penthouse* centerfolds. Great gobs of pubic hair a foot from his head and he didn't notice! The poor bastard must be sexless. Probably was raised by nuns.

"Good view of Thrill from here," McKenzie said, looking through the window. "Looks peaceful. Not as ominous as it does at night."

"Sure, she's peaceful. You just gotta treat her with respect. Say, I want to apologize for what happened, ruining your clothes and all, and for getting mad in the garage. I was out of line. Let's forget about it, okay?" He forced a smile.

"Okay with me. We have to work together."

"I'm your man!"

"What did you find out about the train?"

Van Zant explained that Carl Ott had isolated the computer as the culprit. "He's still fooling with it, trying to figure out exactly what went wrong."

"I'll talk to him after lunch. For the time being, the train should be disabled so it can't move. Derailing the first car would do it."

"That would do it all right."

"It might be a good idea to require launch signals from two different operators as well as the computer."

"That would be a little clumsy, but, hey, if that's the way you think it should be, let's go for it." Jesus Christ, Van Zant said to himself, this turkey is going to be a worse pain in the ass than he thought.

"Maybe there should be no electrical connection at all between the computer and the launch system. Use the computer only to answer questions: Is the track clear, are all the shoulder restraints down and locked, that sort of thing."

"Good idea!"

"I want to review the design and construction of the new features. Sometimes what's shown on the drawings isn't what's built in the field. Do you have a set of plans and specs? In Chicago, I didn't have them all."

"For the new stuff only. You're going to review everything all by your lonesome? Big job."

"I'll make spot checks. The major work has already been done by my company. What about the original sections of the ride? Do you have those drawings?''

Van Zant shook his head. "You're talking forty years ago. Speedtech might have a set.'' There was something about McKenzie that set Van Zant's teeth on edge, and it wasn't just that the engineer was searching for mistakes. Was it his suit? His flat stomach? The way he wanted to put his soft hands and clean fingernails on Ruby? If there was any justice in the world, Van Zant thought, keeping a half-smile on his lips, he would be allowed to grab McKenzie by the lapels and throw him off a cliff.

"Before anybody rides, the train should go through to the end a few times with sandbags as passengers and accelerometers on both the first and last cars. I want to know the G forces at every point the direction changes, both horizontal and vertical.''

"Standard practice. Talk to Ott.''

"What about Ernest Krevek?''

"Old Ernie? He'll mess with your mind. He hates the whole idea of fiddling with his baby, won't have anything to do with it. He used to phone me damned near every day, asking me to do what I could to stop the project. I told him, hey, I just work here, I don't call the shots.''

McKenzie wrote something in a notepad.

"Now, Mr. Van Zant—''

"Call me Leon. Not even my probation officer calls me Mr.''

"Leon. At some point I want you to explain your preventive maintenance program. How you stop accidents before they happen.''

"Whenever you want. I'm at your service.'' Just when it looked like McKenzie was in fact an engineer and not a cop, he brings up preventive maintenance . . . and in a tone of voice that made Leon's fists tighten. Was McKenzie implying that a better maintenance man would have spotted the defective lock? Okay, so maybe he rarely checked the locks, that didn't make him to blame for the girl's death.

By the time McKenzie left, Van Zant was seething. The hardest thing he had ever done in his life was smiling good-bye at McKenzie and telling him what a gas it was going to be to work with him. Four thousand dollars wasn't enough for such aggravation, and he wondered if he could hold St. Jimmy up for another thousand or two.

57

CHAPTER NINE

Ruby Glouster's office was neat, bright, and cheerful. There was a vase of cut flowers on her desk, lace curtains on the windows, and colorful prints of Paris and Rome on the walls. The overall effect was more feminine than Jack expected for a woman who drove a pickup truck with chrome wheels and mud flaps. She herself was more feminine than he remembered. She was wearing a touch of makeup, that must be it. Her hair was spread across her shoulders and looked as soft as a pillow.

She was cutting a coupon from a magazine called *Concessionaire* when he came in. "Hello, Professor. You look nice and dry for a change."

"I came to ask you to lunch."

"You don't think I'm fat enough?"

"You're perfect."

"You're blind. I'm carrying five extra pounds, maybe ten."

"That's your opinion."

"It's the opinion of my slacks, which resist going on in the morning."

"Then come for the simple human companionship."

She studied him. "You're forgetting the circus strong man, who will pound you into the ground like a stake."

Jack shrugged. "I'll take the risk. The woman at the information booth told me the park has no 'circus strong man.' "

"Clarissa gave a correct answer? That's a first. Look, just because I've seen your shorts doesn't mean I want to have lunch with you. Why do men always think that the next day?"

"Whew! You're tough! Just give me a yes or no."

She stood up and gave him a smile wider than any he had seen so far. "Yes. We'll dine at the Wildcat Chuckwagon here in the park. The burritos aren't half bad."

The Chuckwagon was one of ten fast-food restaurants in a circus tent arranged around a central seating area. There was sawdust on the floor and the air smelled of french fries, hamburgers, and chow mein. Ruby and Jack carried their orders from the counter to one of the few remaining clean tables. Even though the park had only been open for a couple of hours, most of the tables were either occupied or littered with paper plates, napkins, and plastic forks. They sat down as far as they could from a disheveled mother with a clutch of whining children.

"You should have let me buy," Jack said when they were settled. "I owe you something for helping me last night. I wanted this to be my treat."

"No thanks, I've fallen into that trap before. Once I'm in your debt you'll want to do some disgusting thing to my person—survey it or measure it, or whatever engineers do." She watched his reaction, then laughed. "You embarrass easily. It's an endearing quality. Do you have any others?"

"Not that I know of."

"You have some bad qualities, too. One is that in ten days you are going back to Chicago."

"Don't be so sure."

"Another is that you dress funny."

"A suit and tie is the engineer's uniform. I thought women liked men in uniform."

"Only if they are carrying tools or guns. Professor, let's get to the point. You asked me to lunch because you want information, not because you think I'm such a knockout. You want me to tell tales on the people that I work with every day, after which you'll say good-bye and go back to your cronies at the Illinois Athletic Club, leaving me here as the resident fink."

"Leon was right. You *are* a lot of trouble. All I want you to tell me is how you knew my name and occupation when you first saw me. Who tipped you off? How do you know I'm a member of the Athletic Club?"

"I read minds. I tell fortunes. I used to do it for a living. My mother taught me: the late, the great, Madame Zeno. She was famous. She was so famous she was arrested a dozen times. She gave it up

59

to run the midway games at county fairs, and finally here. I inherited the business from her."

"And your father?"

"Another one with a gypsy mentality, even though he was Norwegian. He had the fireworks concession, and I used to help him. When he got blown up, I took over. That's the big picture. The details are boring."

"How do you know so much about me?"

"It bothers you, doesn't it?"

"It does. Who's your informant?"

"I work solo. I'll show you. Give me your palm."

Jack extended his hand and watched with amusement as Ruby studied it. She frowned and shook her head, widened her eyes in mock horror, then squinted as if the signs were hard to read.

"What do you see?"

"It isn't good. I see traces of soap from the Holiday Inn. I see dark specks that could be duck poop. I see grease from a leaking burrito." Jack tried to pull his hand back, but she hung on. "I see that you like the way the Japanese build cars, so much that you recently bought a Mazda. You're thinking of trading it in for an American car for reasons of patriotism. Not a big car, though. A mid-size or even a compact, because of the better mileage. You want an air bag. You'll put a first-aid kit in the trunk."

"That is absolutely amazing!"

She let go of his hand. "Am I right?"

"Almost a hundred percent! How do you do it?"

"You have no idea?"

"None whatsoever. I'm impressed."

"You're easy. My mother and father could have taken you for a bundle. They always said that scientists and engineers were the easiest to fool. Their minds are logical and they have little experience with cheating. I guess because nature doesn't cheat. People cheat. Not me, though, not anymore. I'm an honest woman now and I sleep like a baby."

"How the hell did you know that I keep a first-aid kit in the trunk of my car? Will you tell me that, at least?"

"Yes. At dinner Saturday night. I'll let you pay."

"You are full of surprises."

60

Ruby glanced over Jack's shoulder and a look of pain came over her face. "Oh, no! Here comes bad news."

Jack turned and saw Leon Van Zant waddling toward them carrying a heaping tray of food from The Chinese Kitchen.

"Well, well," Van Zant said, joining them. "You two are getting awful chummy, ain't you?"

"Dammit, Leon," Ruby said, "have you got no manners at all?"

"Don't get on your high horse, sweetheart. Where's Action Jackson? Don't you usually eat with him on Thursdays?" He took a swig from a bottle of Dempsey's Ale, smacked his lips, and banged the bottle on the table. With a jab of his hand he picked up a forkful of chow mein. "Hey," he said to Jack, "I didn't know you were free for lunch or we could have gone together."

Ruby stood up. "I've got to get back to work." Before turning away, she leaned toward Leon and said in a forced whisper: "Why don't you leave me alone?"

"Where ya goin', honey?" Van Zant called after her. "Did I interrupt something? Like a tender moment?"

Jack had to hurry to catch up with Ruby, who was walking with determined strides, her fists clenched. "Sometimes that guy drives me absolutely fruitcake," she said. "Whenever I try to spend time with somebody, he watches me like a hawk, as if it's his business who I see and who I don't. I'm sorry, but I had to get out of there before I blew up."

"Who's Action Jackson?"

"A salesman I sometimes eat with. Leon threw that in to discourage you. Look, I'm going to say good-bye for now. I don't want you to see me in this mood. It can get ugly." She managed a brief smile and squeezed his arm. "Sorry I give you such a hard time, but a girl has to protect herself. There are a lot of weirdos in the world. You might be one."

As the afternoon progressed, Jack got more and more irritated at the prospect of riding Thrill and the way he had been forced into it. He found a phone booth and called Chicago.

"Dad? Jack."

"Hello, Junior. How are things in sunny California?"

"Foggy. Glad I caught you before you leave for Brazil."

"I leave tomorrow. How's the project going?"

"It's looking more like a can of worms than a piece of cake."

Jack told his father about the runaway train, the rundown condition of the park, his uneasy relationship with Leon Van Zant, and his meeting with Wilson St. James. "I hate to tell you this, Dad, but your old army buddy has gone navy. Has a sailboat. Wears a captain's hat. On the plus side, I just had a session with Carl Ott, the Speedtech engineer in charge of the field work. He's tops, and I've no doubt at this point that the coaster is sound. What worries me is management. I think St. James is looking forward to retirement and is letting things slip."

"That's not your concern, but I don't suppose it would hurt to make a few general comments in your report. I can't get over what you said about Wilson. It must be drink. He had a problem with that in our army days."

"Ott told me there's a lot of opposition to the coaster. There's a protest group that formed after the girl was killed last year, there's an environmental outfit that wants the park to revert to wetlands, there's a traffic study that predicts gridlock if the coaster is a hit."

"Again, no concern of yours. Stick to the technical aspects."

"One piece of good news is that I met an interesting woman. I'm going to do my best to leave her pregnant with my child."

"I don't appreciate that kind of humor, Jack."

"I know. That's why I said it. Dad, did you tell anybody that I would ride the first train?"

"Not that I recall."

"But you knew I would be expected to, didn't you? And that it would be impossible for me to refuse?"

"I knew it was a possibility. Are you telling me you are afraid to ride a roller coaster?"

"I'll ride the damned thing, don't worry, but I don't want to, and I wish you hadn't put me in this spot. I know why you did it. You're still testing me to see if I measure up. I guess you can't help it. I'm always on probation."

"That's not true."

"Yes it is, and I'm afraid it always will be. I've been thinking that I should do something on my own. You were running your own company at my age."

There was a moment of silence on the line. Jack could imagine his father pushing his glasses tight against the top of his nose. Then, "This is not something we can work out on a long-distance call."

"You're right, Dad. You're always right."

Jack hated to admit it, but he *was* afraid to ride a roller coaster. Skiing was far more dangerous, yet it gave him no sense of fear at all. Skiing was exhilarating, and he could fly down the slopes with happy abandon. Even driving a car was more dangerous than riding a roller coaster. On a freeway he knifed his way through traffic at high speed without a second thought. The difference, he knew, was that on a roller coaster, or any thrill ride, you were at the mercy of a machine and utterly powerless. You couldn't change direction, slow down, or stop. When skiing or driving a car, an accident was usually your own fault, and even up to the last split second there often were moves you could make to avoid it.

Jack's aversion for heights and loss of control weren't paralyzing, but they did give him twinges of embarrassment. As an engineer, he believed his life shouldn't be governed by the irrational. His discussion with Carl Ott convinced him that Thrill was going to be among the safest rides in the country and that there was no reason for anybody to fear it. Yet he did. Worse, he was going to tell other people that their fears were groundless. It was an indefensible position, an intolerable position ... which was why he was standing in line with fifty other people at Wildcat Mountain Amusement Park waiting to experience the Loop of Doom.

The Loop of Doom, he had decided after taking a look at all of the park's attractions, was a good place to start in overcoming his phobia. It was one of the milder rides. If he survived it without serious psychological consequences, he could face a ride on Thrill with some measure of equanimity. After all, it wasn't a full-blown phobia he had about heights and helplessness, it was just a distaste. He could overcome it if he put his mind to it.

The Loop of Doom was simple. Passengers boarded a train and were hurled down a track with enough speed to carry them through a vertical loop and up a steep deceleration ramp. The train slowed to a stop at the top, then rolled down the hill backward, through the loop again, through the loading platform, up a second deceleration ramp to another stop, and finally downhill frontward into the station. To stop it for unloading, friction brakes were applied so hard that the riders were thrown forward against their shoulder restraints. What was to fear? The whole ordeal lasted only thirty seconds, which is one reason Jack chose it—he couldn't get sick to his stomach in so short a time.

Jack was going to ride for reasons of research and behavior modification; why the other people were in line he couldn't imagine. They weren't all young people, though most were. There were a few middle-aged parents, and, judging from heads of gray hair, a few grandparents as well. His feeling of discomfort and apprehension contrasted with the air of excited anticipation around him.

There was always the possibility that everybody else in line was crazy. On the other hand, maybe what was crazy was his fear. The Loop of Doom, he lectured himself, is safer than eating egg salad at a church picnic, safer, probably, than driving to the picnic. Statistically, there was nothing to worry about. And yet . . . and yet his skin felt as though it was preparing to crawl off his body.

Every minute or so there was a roar like a Manhattan subway train as another cycle was completed, and the line of fun-seekers advanced. After fifteen minutes, Jack had reached the platform steps; five minutes more and he was on the platform itself, separated from the tracks by a railing.

In front of him were two fidgeting little girls no more than ten or twelve years old. One looked up at him and said, "First time, huh?"

"How did you guess?"

"You look jumpy and your face is all wet." Her friend tugged at her sleeve to make her stop talking to a stranger. They giggled and poked each other.

Jack was in fact sweating. He wiped his forehead and cheeks with a handkerchief. "It's hot today."

The girl grinned through the braces on her teeth. "You're gonna be really scared," she said. "This ride is *baaad*. The first time, I thought I was going to die. I screamed so hard I couldn't talk for a week."

"So why," Jack asked her, "are you riding it again?"

"Because it's fun!" Her playmate nodded enthusiastically.

Because it's fun. That explained nothing. Jack looked at the people behind him. Except for one or two, they didn't look peculiar . . . no more peculiar than, say, people lined up in a post office. They didn't have the doomed expressions you would expect to find on patients about to get shock therapy. They looked, for the most part, happy. All of them were volunteering to subject their bodies to forces that in real life were usually preludes to violent death. *Why* they were volunteering remained a mystery.

A train whooshed into the station from the right and came to a flying stop, jolting the passengers. A uniformed attendant, his face a page torn from a book on acne, moved from car to car releasing the riders, who climbed out on the opposite side of the track. The younger ones were laughing, Jack noticed, or at least smiling. The older ones didn't look quite as pleased, but he had to admit they didn't look miserable—except one pale old gentleman who seemed ready to promise never again to commit the crime for which the Loop of Doom was the punishment.

Most of the people waiting to board were paired and would sit with their companions, but there were a few singles. Jack ended up in a middle car with a grossly overweight, bearded man in a leather jacket and a San Francisco Giants cap. They had to squeeze together to fit. For some odd reason, the feel of the big man's soft leg and arm was comforting, as if he would cushion the fall if there was a derailment.

Jack asked his seatmate if he had taken the ride before.

"Dozens of times," the mountain man said. His voice was as large as his head and his eyes were like two white eggs in a bird's nest.

"Why do you like it?"

"The way it starts." He squared himself in his seat and and took hold of the lap bar with great sausage fingers. "The train gets thrown down the track the same way aircraft carriers throw planes into the ocean. We gotta get up to a hundred miles an hour in a big hurry or we won't make it through the loop. We'll hang upside down like barbecued chickens."

Jack looked down the track. The loop looked impossibly close. "Actually, sixty miles an hour in seven seconds," Jack said more to himself than to the man beside him. "They get the acceleration with a flywheel and a clutch. Some parks use a more primitive method, a fifty-ton block of concrete that drops inside a tower. Cables connect the block with the undercarriage of the train."

"What?"

"Just talking to myself. Don't mind me."

The attendant moved from car to car to make sure everybody's restraints were in place. "Take it easy on us, okay?" Jack said to him, immediately realizing the request was misguided. Full speed had to be reached at once to make sure the train made it through the loop. "Just kidding," he added hastily. "Let 'er rip!"

"Better button your shirt pocket," the fat man said, "or you'll never see your pen again." He took off his cap and tucked it under a massive buttock.

The two girls Jack had talked to while waiting to board were in the car behind his. They let out a few warm-up screams.

Jack seized on the notion that concentrating on the physics of the ride would calm his nerves. "The interesting thing about loops," he said mostly to himself as he buttoned his pocket, "is that a circle isn't the best curve. The g-force you feel depends on the radius and the speed. To keep the g's constant, the curve is gradual at first, then sharper and sharper as the train rises and slows down. That's why the loop is shaped more like a teardrop than a circle."

The man turned his massive head and looked at Jack. "Friend of mine told me there was an accident one time on a ride like this down in Atlanta. A few years back. The train shot off the end of the ramp. People fell on the miniature golf course like a rain of giant frogs."

"Prepare to launch," a voice said over a loudspeaker.

"The loop is called a Klothoide curve," Jack muttered, whitening his knuckles on the bar. "Named after some guy named Klothoide, I guess. Don't know his first name. Maybe Boyd. Maybe Floyd."

At the end of the platform was a girl in a booth with her finger on the launch button. Jack gazed at her. She had a cruel mouth. Her hair was like spaghetti hanging from tongs. "Launch!" she shouted into a microphone. She pressed the button, throwing her back into it.

There was a shriek of protest from machinery under the platform and the train shot forward like a bullet from a gun. The suddenness took Jack's breath away and drove him backward so hard he thought he had been hit by a truck. The platform vanished in a blur and the rising track of the loop rushed toward him like the bottom of an elevator shaft. His mouth dropped open and every hair on his body stood on end; he gripped the bar desperately and tried to resist the profound vibration that threatened to shake him apart. When the train shot into the loop and climbed the wall of track, the force that was flattening him against the back of his chair shifted and crushed his rear end against the seat. Sky and earth changed places. The roar of the wheels, the hurricane in his face, and the screams of passengers made it impossible to tell if he was screaming himself. Any sound he might have been making was drowned out by bellows of joy from the man beside him.

The G force revolved wildly, and almost before he had time to realize it, the loop was behind him and he was right-side-up and pitched onto his back as the train rocketed up the deceleration ramp. The train was slowing down, but to Jack's horror it looked as though it wasn't slowing down fast enough and would fall off the upper end of the track, which jutted into the air like an icepick. The train groaned to a stop a few feet short of disaster, and for an exquisite instant was motionless. Jack knew that somewhere beneath his back was a splendid view of the park. Rather than look down, he stared fixedly at a cloud formation in the sky, which for some reason made him think of a scene in the Bible where graves split open and the dead walk the earth.

"Oh, man," the fat man shouted, "was that a blast or what?"

Jack was unable to respond.

Gravity tightened its grip and the train began to slide backward, faster and faster, down the ramp, the roar of the wheels and screams of the riders growing in unison. Jack tightened his fists on the bar again, clenched his teeth, and shut his eyes. He opened his eyes almost immediately because the wild lurching when the train hit the loop made him think that it had derailed. Once again he watched the sickening sight of the horizon revolving like a pinwheel, slower this time, so slow that the train seemed to be upside down for a delicious extra moment at the top of the loop.

The train sped backward through the launch building and the platform and climbed the second deceleration ramp. This time at the top the passengers were suspended from their shoulder straps, looking down at the buildings below as if they were about to be dropped head first from a plane. There was a pause, then again the train rushed downward, gaining so much speed as it approached the terminal that there seemed to be no way that it could be stopped in time. Suddenly, brakes grabbed the train in a powerful fist. Jack felt his pen fighting to get out of his shirt pocket and his stomach climbing up his windpipe.

A final lurch, a death throe deep in the machinery, and silence.

There were a few after-screams from the girls and a series of metallic clanks as the lap bars and shoulder restraints were released. Jack was alive, but for the moment unable to move.

The fat man hopped lightly from the car and gave Jack a hand. "You okay?"

"I think the tibias and fibulas have been thrown from my legs." He took a tentative step forward, then another.

"You look like you don't know whether to shit or go blind."

"To shit, yes, I thought of that. I was getting messages to that effect from the lizard part of my brain."

"Let's ride it again."

"No, thanks. We should tend to the dead and wounded."

There weren't any. Jack's fellow passengers were generally a happy throng, trooping down the stairs in search of another nightmare. Most were smiling. Some were laughing. There was no figuring it out.

The young girl with the braces bounded up and said, "Wasn't that *awesome?* I told you you'd be scared." She ran off chasing her friend.

"Scared? Me? That will be the day."

A woman with orange hair was waiting on the platform. She took the fat man's arm and they strolled away. Jack heard her say, "You're nuts to ride that thing."

The experience taught Jack something. Bad as the ride was, it wasn't as bad as he expected. It was exciting in its way, and he had lived to tell about it. He walked across the platform feeling a little better about himself and about his ability to endure a ride on Thrill. The coaster couldn't be *that* much worse.

CHAPTER TEN

Jack spent Friday with Carl Ott at the headquarters of Speedtech Corporation in San Jose. Ott showed him every step of the operation, from preliminary sketches to packing and shipping. Engineers used computer-assisted design programs on Tektronix workstations to try out variations and produce working drawings. Everything was done in-house, from the building of the fiberglass cars to the fabrication of steel rails and supports.

When Jeremy Allbright joined them in the middle of the afternoon in the conference room, Jack told him that he was very impressed with what he had seen.

"The new computers are terrific," Allbright said. "Once you have your general layout and know what g-forces you want and so on, the computer makes it easy to quantify your other variables—your lengths, heights, slopes, curvatures, and what have you."

"Another time-saver," Ott added, "is that computers divide up the track into segments and print out working drawings for the fabrication shop."

"But we don't rely completely on what the computers tell us. We set the finished product up and ride it before sending it out. When it's at the park, we ride it again. We send sandbags through first, naturally, with accelerometers to record the forces. We make any necessary adjustments, then people take a ride. Our *own* people. It's important to show the client that you stand behind your product."

Jack, smiling, raised his forearms in defense. "Okay, okay! I believe you! I feel like I'm being attacked by a couple of car salesmen."

"Well, we're proud of the operation. I don't mind telling you that we were glad to hear that an independent investigator was going to

69

check us out, because we knew he'd like what he saw. We've got the best engineering and quality control in the business.''

"Tell me something, Mr. Allbright. Do you ride the coasters yourself?''

Allbright laughed heartily. "I was afraid you'd ask that! The truth is, I don't ride the big wild ones. My stomach won't let me. I'll have to make an exception for Thrill, though, because of all the attention it's getting.''

On the walls of the conference room were a dozen architectural renderings of Speedtech Corporation's best-known coasters, among them The Corkscrew at Frentress Lake, Illinois, The Wicked Witch at Fantasy Garden, Florida, and The Scream Machine at Twelve Flags Over Georgia. The three men made a circuit of the room, stopping at each one in turn.

"Colorful names," Jack said. "They remind me of women I used to date.''

At the end of the row was a discoloration on the wall where a picture had once hung. "Thrill," Allbright explained. "Out with the old, in with the new. The new rendering should be ready in a few days. Always pressure for something different. It's what keeps us going. Every park wants a ride that's the biggest, the fastest, the highest, the scariest, whatever. It gives them something to hang advertising on.''

They took seats at the end of the oval table and spent half an hour on technical details. Jack filled several pages in his notebook.

"I've told Carl," Allbright said, rising and preparing to leave, "and all of our people to give you every possible assistance. A lot is riding on the success of Thrill, both for us and the park. We're double and triple checking everything. If you can find a flaw in what's being done by us or by Van Zant and his people, by golly, we'll all be grateful. And amazed.''

"I'm glad to hear that. I want to take a look at the parts of the structure that aren't being changed. Van Zant told me you might have the original plans and specifications.''

Allbright shook his head sadly. "Afraid not. The man who designed it, Ernie Krevek, kept most things in his head or on the backs of envelopes. He wasn't much for paperwork.''

"We did some checking of the old sections a few months ago, Jack," Ott said. "We set up strain gauges and sent a few trains through. Deflections in the structure were well within the safe range. We strengthened some connections all the same, just to be on the safe side.''

"Could I talk to Krevek?"

Allbright and Ott exchanged glances. "I don't think that would be too helpful," Allbright said. "He's forgotten the details. You'll be better served if you stick with Carl, who works on the project every day."

"Ernie is a little strange," Ott offered.

"He's retiring soon," Allbright said. "Very soon. He's become . . . difficult in recent years. Impossible, really."

"Still, I'd like to talk to him."

Allbright sighed. "Just take whatever he says with a grain of salt. He's no longer in the loop, as they say." He shook Jack's hand. "It was a pleasure to meet you! Call me any time . . ."

When Allbright was gone, Ott told Jack why the company president no longer rode "the big wild ones." Fifteen years earlier, Speedtech had assembled a steel coaster, one of the first of the new tubular steel designs, in the back lot. Usually there was no problem getting volunteers from the company to take the first ride, but not that time.

"We were all afraid of it," Ott recalled, chuckling at the memory. "Jeremy called us a bunch of cowards, and climbed aboard to take the first ride himself. We stood aside and watched him go. When the train came back, he was as white as a sheet, and we had to pry his hands off the bar." Ott laughed out loud and had some trouble containing himself and finishing the story. "There was vomit on his shirt and pants and he was staring straight ahead like a statue. His only words were, 'We've got to slow it down . . .' It's a company joke. If you hear somebody around here use those words, you'll know why."

"I sympathize with him. What about you? Do you ride the things?"

"I do, but not for pleasure. One of my responsibilities is setting up new coasters. I usually ride the first train to show the customer it's safe."

"And Krevek?"

"In the old days, I'm told. He hasn't been in an amusement park in ten years, as far as I know. I never talk to the guy anymore, if

71

you want to know the truth. He's off in his own world. Strange character. You'll see.''

"Where's his office? I've never met a living legend.''

Ott walked with Jack to the door of the conference room and pointed across the drafting tables to the far side of the floor. "That's his office in the corner. Can I give you a tip? Let him think you're against the redesign of Thrill. Do that and he'll talk your arm off.''

"You're not coming with me?''

"Better if I don't. I'm on his shit list, like almost everybody else. Last time I stuck my head through his doorway, he hit me with an eraser. Next time it might be a scissors. Good luck. I'll say a prayer for you.''

After twenty minutes of talking to Ernest Krevek, Jack had a headache. For one thing, he was unsettled by the man's appearance. Krevek's face was so narrow and hawklike it could have been used for chopping wood, and his dark eyes were penetrating and full of restless energy. For another, there was such an air of tension about the man that Jack was afraid a wrong move might set off an explosion. The old engineer was suspicious and tight-lipped at first, but loosened up when he was convinced that Jack was independent both of Speedtech and Wildcat Mountain. Jack told him that he wasn't crazy about the new design, but had to seek all points of view before writing his report.

"Working drawings,'' Krevek responded to one of Jack's questions, "who needed working drawings? In those days I worked with men that knew what they were doing. All the construction crew needed was a sketch of the layout and the elevations. We cut the wood to fit in the field.''

"How did you pick the size of the structural members?''

"Because we had done it fifty times before! We knew what worked.''

"What about connections? A wooden coaster is statically indeterminate, so before you had computers to crunch numbers, what system of analysis did you use to find the loadings at critical points?''

"Where are you from, Mars? Where beams and girders and columns came together we put in a big fat bolt. If it didn't look strong enough, we put in another one. We didn't need to know the stress

72

and strain. After a while you can just look at a connection and tell if it's strong enough.''

"Hmm. Without specific values, I don't see how you could end up with the right factor of safety. Didn't you have to conform to state codes?'' Jack had his notebook and pen in hand, but so far hadn't written anything.

Krevek looked around the room in exasperation, then leaned forward and spoke in a tone that suggested he couldn't stand much more irritation.

"We did what every engineer did. We overdesigned the hell out of it. You can go to Thrill and take out every other structural member and it'll still be safe. As for the state, they didn't have anybody who knew diddley-squat about coasters. We were the experts. They relied on us. Same as now.''

"So you feel Thrill is completely safe.''

"No chance of a major failure at all. I'm talking only about the part I designed and built myself. The new junk they're tacking on doesn't have the redundancy we used to build into everything. Too much reliance on computers. Engineers now can refine the design over and over, taking out a pound of material here, a pound there, until they're down to skin and bones. Maximum efficiency . . . in theory. Trouble is, some workman with a hangover and a negative IQ puts in a bolt that's too small and the whole structure is in trouble.''

Krevek looked through the window of his office at the bullpen, where a dozen men and women worked at drafting tables and computer workstations. He waved his hand in contempt. "Those people don't know what a two-by-four smells like when you saw it in two or how heavy it is or what sound it makes when you drive a nail into it. All they know about coasters comes from numbers in handbooks and blips on screens.''

Jack looked at his blank notebook. Getting facts and figures from Krevek was impossible. He decided to try a more general tack.

"Why are you so against the new Thrill?''

Krevek's eyebrows shot up. "Because,'' he said, spitting out the words, "the changes wreck an almost perfect design. The people who love coasters are going to laugh at it when it opens. It'll flop. It'll ruin this company. We'll look like fools. Put that in your report. Write that I predict that the reopening of Thrill will be a disaster for all concerned.''

To avoid hurting the old engineer's feelings, Jack picked up his notebook and jotted down a few comments: "Hates computer analysis. Predicts flop. Needs counseling."

"What about the girl who was killed last year?"

Krevek crushed a sheet of paper into a ball. "What has she got to do with the design? The problem is that the park relies on an ape-man for maintenance and lets drunks ride. Hamstringing and neutering Thrill is sure as hell not the solution."

"There were other accidents as well. Mr. St. James won't give me the accident file and neither will the insurance carrier, but Thrill has a reputation as a pretty rough ride. Was that part of the concept?"

"Absolutely!"

"It was?"

"Yes! Why do people ride coasters? To be scared. If nobody ever gets hurt, or at least shaken up, what's to fear? My coasters are among the most popular in the world. Why? Because you have to take them seriously. They aren't toys. If you don't keep your wits about you, they'll beat you black and blue. There are plenty of customers who like the element of risk in my rides. They complain that the new steel designs are too smooth, too safe. They like knowing that on a ride like Thrill, there's at least a chance that they'll taste real pain, even if the chance is only one in ten thousand. I'm talking about the old Thrill, not the one they've cut the nuts from."

Jack nodded as if he agreed. "I see what you mean," he said. In his notebook he wrote: "Krevek could go to group therapy all by himself."

"I've got nothing against family rides. I just think there should be something for people who want *real* excitement."

"They could go skiing."

"Just to irritate the fatheads around here, I sometimes argue in favor of coasters for capital punishment instead of electric chairs and lethal injections. Why not? Build a one-car coaster so dangerous that it has, say, a one in two chance of killing the rider. Strap convicted murderers in and let the world watch on TV. You'd have a real deterrent to crime then, I'll betcha."

"That's quite an idea!" In his notebook he wrote: "Get flowers for Ruby; toothpaste; battery for calculator."

Krevek reached for a book on the shelf behind him, flipped through the pages, and opened it to a grainy photograph of a particularly

74

vicious-looking roller coaster. "Look here. This is Cyclone in Crystal Beach, Ontario, designed by Harry Traver. Opened in 1927, torn down in 1946, thanks to the insurance companies. Look at those twists and turns! I rode that baby as a kid, and let me tell you it was one rough son of a bitch! There was a first-aid station and a nurse at the exit, and not just for show, either. Traver had a couple of others, too, that were just as violent, Lightning, in Boston, and another one called Cyclone in Fort Lee, New Jersey, both torn down in the early thirties. Compared to Traver, I'm a pussycat."

"One of the pussycat's rides almost killed me the other night."

Krevek, punctuating his narrative with a jabbing finger, didn't hear the remark. "I'm telling you about this so you can see that I'm part of a tradition. I go back to Traver, back, in point of fact, hundreds of years."

"A train got loose and Van Zant and I had to jump off the tracks."

"Would you believe the fifteenth century? The Russians built ice slides in St. Petersburg and Moscow, and some of them had hills as steep as fifty degrees. The steepest drop I know of today is fifty-three degrees, the Texas Cyclone in Houston."

"It was only a drop of ten feet or so, but it was dark and we were lucky we weren't hurt."

"Come again? You jumped off what?"

Jack told him the story, and as he did, Krevek's eyebrows climbed his forehead again.

"That couldn't happen!"

"It happened. Apparently a flaw in the computer program. I'm insisting that the computer be relieved of any control function."

Krevek whistled and shook his head. "This is amazing! I was wondering a couple of weeks ago if software bugs could—what was your name again? McKenzie? I want to apologize to you, McKenzie, on behalf of Thrill, for giving you a fright you didn't pay for. It goes to prove what I was saying earlier, that there's too much reliance on technology, not enough old-fashioned common sense. At least you know what to put in your report. You're going to recommend that the project be stopped, right? That's what I would do if I were you."

"I'll consider it, Mr. Krevek. Thanks for the discussion."

"Always a pleasure to talk to a man with an open mind. Not many left.'"

"I have one small request before I leave."

"Anything."

"Do you have an aspirin?"

At twenty minutes to eleven on Friday night, a car turned off Highway 121 two miles south of the town of Sonoma onto a narrow dirt road. There was a car parked on the shoulder just before the intersection, but Leon Van Zant didn't notice it. He had had a couple of drinks and was concentrating on making sure he turned down his lane and not the one that led to the county dump.

Leon owned an acre of land, a stucco house in the California bungalow style, a barn, and a silver Airstream mobile home. He was remodeling the house in his spare time, but in three years he had managed only to rip up the floors and tear down the inside walls. The old refrigerator and stove were in the front yard. The barn was large and in fairly good shape, and Leon was considering various ways to put it to use. Cockfights were a definite possibility. Lots of money to be made on events like that ... provided a man didn't get greedy.

Leon parked next to a towering eucalyptus tree and unlocked the Airstream. As usual after a hot day, it was intolerably stuffy inside. He opened all the windows, left the door open, and settled on the couch with a beer. The room would cool off in a few minutes. That was the great thing about northern California. No matter how hot it got, the nights were cool.

A flick of the remote control and the television came to life. He clicked the selector and stopped at a news show. Just in time for the sports report. What a great invention was the remote control! The greatest thing for couch potatoes since the invention of ... well, the couch.

There was a commercial. He let his eyes close, then opened them. No sense falling asleep on the couch again, as he no doubt would if he rested his eyes. As soon as he got the scores he would force himself up and into bed.

The end of his toothpick felt frayed against his tongue. Using his tongue and lips, he rotated the toothpick and pushed the frayed end out of his mouth. Shit, the other end was frayed, too. He spit it toward the door, and what he saw there made him sit up straight.

"Hey, what are you doing here? Put that damned thing down! Is

76

that loaded?'' Leon hoisted himself off the couch and raised a hand. ''Jeez, don't point it at me . . . are you nuts?''

He couldn't believe it at first when he was shot, even though he saw the muzzle flash, saw pieces of his hand disappear, and felt the sledgehammer blow to his chest. He staggered backward a step and managed to keep his balance. He tried to speak and couldn't. His mind struggled to understand what was happening. The second shot knocked him back into a sitting position on the couch. His head lolled and fell still, his eyes fixed on the ceiling. A massive blood-stain spread quickly down the front of his shirt.

''Bad news for the Bay Area's baseball teams,'' the sportscaster said in a happy voice. ''Both the Giants and the A's lost to the weakest teams in their divisions. Even the organists left early!''

Two more shells were casually inserted. The shotgun was raised and pointed at the television screen. When the trigger was squeezed, the sportscaster vanished in an implosion of sparks, smoke, and slivers of glass.

CHAPTER ELEVEN

Washoe House was a red barn of a building outside of Petaluma in a valley of gently rolling pastureland. Flowered wallpaper in the small dining room, dark and dusty woodwork in the bar, and a kind of haphazard rusticity throughout made Jack McKenzie feel as if he had fallen through a time warp into the Old West. Many of the patrons had a weatherbeaten look and mud on their boots, and it was easy to imagine them hitching their horses to posts and checking their six-guns at the door.

According to a historical note on the paper place mats, the establishment was founded in 1858 and served for decades as a stop for stagecoaches. General Ulysses S. Grant once stood at the railing of the outside balcony and addressed a crowd of admirers gathered below. Now it was a tavern and restaurant catering to the dairy ranchers and truck farmers of rural Sonoma County ... or anybody who liked steak and potatoes served by take-charge waitresses with mileage in their faces.

"I can see why you like this place," Jack said to Ruby when they were seated at a table. "You don't have to dress up."

"For that I go south, to Marin County. Trouble is, down there everybody thinks food is dangerous. Cholesterol, fat, calories, sodium, fiber ... you never hear those words in Sonoma County, certainly not in Washoe House. Here you can enjoy your prime rib in peace. One time an old guy at the next table leaned over and told me that he owned the steak I was eating when it was on the hoof. I checked with the cook and it was true."

"May I say that you look terrific? Even though you're not dressed up."

"Oh, but I am. Jeans, lumberjack shirt, turtleneck sweater, all freshly laundered and pressed." She pointed to her hair, eyes, and mouth and said, "Fifty strokes of the comb here, eyeliner here, lipstick here. Beauty like this doesn't just *happen*. It's a form of show business."

"You're a hard person to compliment."

She apologized, reaching across the table to touch his arm. "I'm sorry, I shouldn't make a joke of everything. I should just lower my eyes and say thank you. You think I look terrific? It's a charming lie and I appreciate it. Honest."

Nothing General Grant said when he visited Washoe House could have been as interesting to Jack as Ruby's explanation of her mind-reading abilities.

"You handed me your jacket when you were shooting baskets. Your business card fell out of your breast pocket into my hand."

"Fell right into your hand, did it?"

"I hardly had to fish for it at all."

"That only gave you Chicago and my name and occupation. How did you—"

"I looked at you. The way you were dressed. Shined shoes! I haven't seen shined shoes in years."

"You knew what kind of car I have. How—"

"It's amazing what people don't notice! Before you wrung the water out of your pants in the garage, you emptied your pockets on the table. Your billfold was right there. You told me to open your suitcase and lay out some clothes. I found out a lot in thirty seconds."

"You went through my billfold? That's a federal offense, isn't it?"

"All I did was a little speed reading."

"I feel like a yokel," Jack said as the mystery melted away, "yet I'm the one from the big city."

"Never ask a magician to explain the tricks. The methods are never as lovely as the illusion."

The food arrived. Baked potatoes with sour cream and chives. Canned green beans. A slab of medium rare prime rib as delicious as any Jack ever tasted. The conversation centered on cooking for a while, then drifted to travel, movies, and autobiography. They exchanged details of their lives; Jack had to exaggerate a little to make his life even half as interesting as hers. Her life was peopled with circus roustabouts, traveling swindlers, fire eaters, and cons on the lam; his with neighbors who didn't keep their lawns mowed, an uncle who had a small tattoo on his ankle, and a college professor of differential equations who once stood before his class with his shirt-tail protruding from his fly. Pretty tame stuff by comparison. Ruby seemed fascinated, nevertheless, possibly at the very normality of it. His upbringing, she said, was so conventional it almost brought tears to her eyes.

While Jack was put under irresistible pressure to go college when he graduated from high school, it was just the opposite for Ruby. She had to run away from home to do it. Her mother, who was in failing health, wanted her to continue helping with midway games, her father wanted her to continue helping with fireworks, she wanted to continue going to school. How many kids have ever run away *toward* school? Ruby summarized the attitude of her parents as, "You don't need no stinking college."

Aiming herself toward a degree in English literature at San Francisco State, Ruby supported herself by waitressing, poker playing, telling fortunes, and, on several occasions, running a three-card monte game in the city's financial district. She dropped out in her junior year when her mother died and took over games of chance at Wildcat Mountain. She thought it would be a temporary sidetrack. Four years later, her father disappeared in an explosion at a fireworks warehouse in Vallejo, and Ruby took over his job as well. In response to a direct question, she told Jack she had never been married, despite her "advanced age. I guess I should lower my standards. I lived with a guy once for a while but didn't much like it. Not enough closet space."

Driving home after two hours at Washoe House, the conversation drifted back to fortune telling. "Wait a minute!" Jack said, slapping his hand on the steering wheel. "You knew I kept a first-aid kit in the trunk of my car! There was nothing in my billfold or luggage that could have told you that."

Ruby shrugged. "A lucky stab. I figured a man with such clean hair and fingernails and whose suitcase was so organized was somebody who took good care of himself. I'll bet you have a first-aid kit in your office, too."

"Amazing. I do have one in my office."

"I made some wrong guesses, but you don't remember those. The right ones stick in your mind. My mother was great at making guesses about people, watching for clues, zeroing in when she saw

80

she was on the right track. Cold reading, it's called in the trade. She was exotic looking, which helped. She had wiry hair that stuck straight out and she spoke in a trembling voice, as if she was frightened of her own powers."

"You could do the same. You could make a lot of money cheating people."

"Not me. I feel too sorry for the victims. It used to scare me how much some of them wanted to believe the stuff I was making up. And you know what? Sometimes I was right. I get feelings about things."

"Like what?"

"Like the night the girl was thrown off Thrill. I was trying to decide whether or not to walk underneath it, and I had a feeling that I shouldn't."

"Oh, oh, I think we're going to have our first argument. The feeling you had, the foreboding, did you tell anybody about it or write it down?"

"No."

"That's the problem. It's like you said a minute ago, you remember the hits and forget the misses. Here's what you have to do. Describe on paper every premonition you get. Be as specific as possible. After six months, look at the list and see how many panned out."

"And make charts and graphs?"

"If you want to get at the truth, you have to make sure your mind isn't fooling you."

"I don't want to analyze myself. I might find out I'm completely ordinary and don't have any miraculous powers."

"Ruby, you aren't ordinary. I can't look at you without falling under your spell."

"Really? That might be useful sometime."

They were driving through west Petaluma, through neighborhoods of impressive Victorian homes. Ruby directed him into a driveway that led to the rear of a towering gingerbread mansion that even Queen Victoria might have considered overdone.

"Don't get the wrong idea. I live in what used to be the carriage house."

Jack was glad when she invited him in for coffee. As they walked to her door, she took his arm, which made him wonder if he would still be there for breakfast. That possibility was ruled out in the kitchen, where they embraced and kissed.

"I'm not comfortable with this," she said.

"You feel comfortable to me."

"You know what I mean. I don't want to get involved with somebody who's leaving town in a week. That won't help me any."

"I'm going to stay for a while."

"Why?"

"To look for a job. To get to know you better."

"Men will say anything to get what they want."

"I'm not men. I'm Jack McKenzie of Chicago and I'm thinking of making a career change to get closer to the ski slopes and farther away from dear old dad."

"What about me?"

Jack adopted a dry, professorial tone. "It would be unscientific to include you as a factor in the equation this early in the calculations. You are a variable that requires a good deal more study before its long-range effects can be estimated with any accuracy."

"I love it when you talk dirty."

He moved to kiss her again, but she turned away and busied herself making coffee. Jack looked around the kitchen. It was full of homey touches: framed needlepoint samplers, arrangements of dried flowers and grasses, a collection of copper-bottomed pots and pans hanging from hooks and shined to a fare-thee-well.

"Nice place you have here. Maybe you should change careers, too, and become an interior decorator."

"I'm a nest builder. Probably a reaction against my childhood. We were never in the same place more than two weeks."

"Your answering machine is flashing. It spoils the nineteenth-century atmosphere."

She rewound the tape. "This might be bad news for you," she said. "A better offer may be coming in. Maybe from Whitey the Beer Salesman, my main romantic prospect aside from yourself."

The voice of Wilson St. James crackled over the tiny loudspeaker: "Ruby, this is Wilson, and it's seven o'clock on Saturday night. Have you seen Leon? He didn't come to work today and he knows damned well how much there is to do. He doesn't answer his phone. Do you know where he is? If he's a no-show again tomorrow, he gets the ax, which I'm sure would make you happy. If you know anything, leave a message on my machine. G'bye."

"Hmmm," Ruby mused. "That's odd. I hate Leon, but not be-

82

cause he skips work. Since he quit drinking, he's never missed a day.''

"Are you going to call St. James?"

"Why should I? I don't know where Leon is, and I don't want to know."

They sat at the kitchen table. The coffee was excellent.

"Tell me something, Ruby. Why did Leon tell me you were too much trouble? I asked you before, but I didn't get an answer."

She thought for a moment. "I don't think I should say. As you said, it's a little early in the calculations."

"Can't we be open with each other? Speed up the process a little?"

She sipped her coffee, then put the cup down and said, "Okay, I'll tell you. When my father got killed, Leon was very helpful. He took care of a lot of the details. He looked better in those days—not so gross. His beer belly was still in its first trimester. Against my better judgment, I went to dinner with him once. He propositioned me during the soup course. I said I wouldn't even go to dinner with him again unless he had an AIDS test. He hates doctors and hospitals and homosexuals, so I knew he wouldn't do it."

She looked around the room, stirred her coffee, and drummed her fingers on the table before continuing. "It gets worse. I'm almost positive he put something in my drink when I was in the rest room. Outside the restaurant I got sick and dizzy, as if I'd been drugged, and I was sure Leon did it."

"How did you know it wasn't the food?"

"Because he looked at me with this lecherous smile instead of trying to help me. I wanted to sit down for a minute, he wanted to stuff me in his car. I was passing out, but I fought like a tiger as long as I could. Thank God there were some people around who got me away from him. Over his protests they called an ambulance. I spent the night at the Petaluma Valley Hospital. That's my romantic adventure with Leon Van Zant, and that's why he thinks I'm too much trouble."

Jack shook his head and whistled. "You lead an exciting life."

"He hasn't given up, though, the pig. He's always trying to corner me, always trying to spoil it for me if I show an interest in somebody else. I hope he gets fired. I hate him so much it isn't healthy."

"Did he ever get an AIDS test?"

83

"Are you kidding? A lot of men won't. I don't know why. They get lost when I suggest it. Would you take one?"

"Me? For you I would. Not that I think there's much danger. I'm a white civil engineer from the Midwest who doesn't take drugs. I don't even smoke. I'm not exactly in a high-risk group."

"The human race is a high-risk group."

"Maybe so. You, on the other hand, work in a circus and hang around with snake charmers, Bulgarian acrobats, and Whitey the Beer Salesman. I should be the one insisting on an AIDS test."

"I work at an amusement park, not a circus. Not the same at all."

They eyed each other.

"Tell you what," Jack said. "I'll take an AIDS test if you will."

"Okay, on one condition. If we both test negative, that doesn't give you the right to jump my bones. I don't know you nearly well enough."

"It's a deal."

They shook hands on it.

At the door there was another kiss, more lingering than the first and sweeter, more full of promise.

CHAPTER TWELVE

Monday was a day of surprises for Wilson St. James and Jack McKenzie. It began as Mondays often did for St. James, with a searing hangover and sunlight stabbing into his eyes like pokers. A pillow solved the light problem, but there was nothing he could do about his head. Sometimes after a weekend of excess his head felt like a bowling ball being crushed in a vise, sometimes like a well-struck gong. The feeling was different this time. Someone had filled his skull with boiling oil and was stirring it . . . and not too gently.

Carefully, oh so carefully, St. James snaked his hand across the sheets to the far edge of the bed. No one was there. Thank God for that. Having to be polite to another human being would have been out of the question. By the width of the mattress he could tell he was at home and not on the boat . . . another blessing. With his head in its present condition, the gentle bobbing motion and the soothing sound of wavelets would have been intolerable.

Grimacing, he pulled the pillow a few inches to one side and focused on the clock radio. Ten to nine. Balls. He'd have to get up. How glorious it would be when Wildcat Park was safely in Japanese hands and he could do whatever, whenever, and wherever, and for as long as he wanted, and with anybody money could buy! No more responsibilities and no more payrolls to meet!

He lurched into the bathroom and peed loudly into the toilet with his eyes shut and his forehead pressed against the cold glass of the mirror. He drank a glass of water and downed a row of pills he had brilliantly laid out the night before. In the living room he surveyed a sorry scene. There were bottles and glasses, two plates of half-eaten pizza, a trail of crumpled clothing. The relics of debauchery stood out in the bright morning light like a pop-art collage. Where was the fog when you really needed it?

A note was taped to the front door. He peeled it off and held it in the light: GOT TO RUN. THANX FOR YR GENEROSATY! SEE YA! LOVERKINS. Generosaty? The little whore couldn't even spell.

St. James shuffled into his den and lowered himself into the chair at his desk. He picked up the phone. Memory 5 was Leon's home number. Ten rings without an answer. Memory 6 was Leon's office at the park. Ten rings without an answer. Memory 2 was his own secretary. She answered with bizarre élan and friendliness, lowering her voice when she realized her boss's condition. No, there were no messages from or about Leon. Yes, she had checked the garage, the maintenance yard, the parts warehouse. Julio, Leon's number one assistant, had called a few minutes earlier, looking for him. Nobody knew where he was or had seen him since Friday night.

Wonderful.

An hour later, Wilson St. James steered his silver Lincoln down the lane he thought led to Leon's house, but which in fact ended at the county dump. That didn't help his mood any. He had to jockey the the car back and forth a half dozen times to turn around, much to the amusement of an old man with a Safeway cart full of cans and bottles who gummed him a smile and directed his maneuvers with idiotic gesticulations.

St. James was muttering angrily to himself when he finally found the right road. He cut his speed to a crawl to minimize the dust he was raising. Two years earlier, before Van Zant accepted his ultimatum to knock off the booze and dope and binges or find another job, St. James was driving to the bastard's digs every few months, it seemed, to rouse him from his stupors. Not that he was any model of sobriety himself, but he never let his indulgences interfere with his work. He was always at his desk in the morning even when he felt like the wrath of God. A man had to learn how to tear himself from his bed in the morning when people were depending on him. It was a matter of duty. The military taught him that.

Leon's mobile home and house-in-progress came into view. St. James decided that if the fat slob was simply bombed out of his mind and unable to answer the bell, he'd give him another chance. It was useful to have a low-life like Leon on the payroll, somebody who would bend the rules when necessary without asking questions.

On the other hand, there were limits. If Leon had gone to Vegas and conked out there, then it was all over.

Aha! There was his truck! He was home, all right. In fact, the door of his Airstream was standing open. Had he reeled home Sunday night so sloshed he forgot to close the door?

St. James parked behind the truck and marched toward the house trailer with rising anger. He would drag Van Zant out of bed by the ankles if he had to, right down the stairs to the ground where he could spray him with the garden hose, if that's what it took to wake him. No fooling around. Thrill was opening in five days and needed Leon's loving touch.

"Leon! Leon!" St. James waited in the doorway to let his eyes adjust to the gloom. There was a buzzing of flies and the sound of rodents scurrying for cover. There was a foul smell. St. James made a face and stepped inside. "Leon . . . ?"

The television set was on its side on the floor; the picture tube was gone and there were glass slivers everywhere. Leon was in a sitting position on the sofa looking more bloated than usual. His head was thrown back at an odd angle, and his eyes and mouth were fixed in a mask of amazement. There was a jagged cavity in the center of his chest, and from his collar to his shoes his clothes were dark with blood.

St. James gagged and turned to face the light of the door. He swallowed hard to calm his stomach and his suddenly leaping heart. In Korea he had seen hundreds of dead and wounded men, some of them torn up worse than Leon, and he had become hardened to it . . . but that was in field hospitals and on battlefields where horrors were almost routine, and it was over forty years ago. This was different. This was a man he had known for ten years, this was in the man's home . . .

He stepped unsteadily outside. On the small porch, he tightened his hands around the wooden railing and hung on until the threat of being sick had passed. He turned, half hoping that what he had just seen was a hallucination. Nothing had changed.

St. James returned inside and forced his mind to deal with the facts before him. Breathing through his mouth, he looked at the body again. Leon had been shot at close range, obviously with a shotgun. Once or twice in the chest, and once, it looked like, lower down, in the groin. Who would do that? Who was filled with so much hate?

There was a dried stain of blood that stretched across the linoleum from the sofa to the wall next to the kitchen. The stain was criss-crossed with small footprints—rats, raccoons, maybe even dogs from the surrounding ranches had apparently visited the scene since Leon Van Zant had been murdered. The fingers and arms showed marks of teeth and claws.

Leon's wristwatch was in place, his pockets weren't turned inside out, and the rest of the room—a chest of drawers, a trunk, a cabinet—looked undisturbed. It didn't look as though robbery was the motive, and there were no signs of a struggle.

On the floor to the right of the front door was a group of small metal tubes. St. James recognized them as shotgun shell casings. he dropped to one knee. There were four. Three shots hit Leon and the fourth smashed the television set.

Good God, the casings were made entirely of brass, just like the one Leon said he found on the launching platform after someone had blasted one of the coaster's cars in the middle of the night! That incident was never reported to the police for fear that it would find its way into the newspapers. He picked one up and turned it over in his hand, satisfying himself that it was identical to the earlier one. A clerk in a gun shop had told him that brass casings of that type were collector's items. The way it was made and the markings estab-lished it as fifty years old, at least. Plastic cylinders had been the norm since the 1960s, cardboard before that.

St. James wiped his fingerprints from the casing and put it back on the floor. It looked as though the vandal plaguing the coaster and Leon's murderer were one and the same. If the sheriff thought so, too, and the news got out, there was liable to be no reopening of Thrill on the Fourth of July. Too risky, the state might say . . . better keep it shut until the madman is caught. There was even a chance that sentiment would be rekindled for closing the whole park.

On the other hand, maybe nobody would connect the murder with vandalism at the park. Maybe there was no connection. It could be that the somebody had a grudge against Leon, not Thrill and not the park, and now that Leon was dead the trouble would stop. Yes, that sounded good . . . so good it might be true. Leon had a lot of ene-mies, he'd remind the sheriff. Gamblers. Drug dealers. Maybe prosti-tutes—he had a reputation for being rough with women. Any one of them might have pulled the trigger. This had nothing to do with

Leon's job, St. James would stress, and nothing to do with the park. He rehearsed in his mind the tack he would take: Leon was a hard worker and a model of decorum. He'll be missed. This is a sad day.

St. James took a step toward the telephone, then stopped. The murderer's fingerprints might be on the receiver as well as on the shell casings.

He reeled outside like a drunken man and dialed 911 from his car phone—not an easy task, for when it occurred to him that whoever killed Leon Van Zant might also want to kill Wilson St. James, his hands began to tremble uncontrollably.

At the other end of San Francisco Bay, in San Jose, Jack McKenzie was getting a surprise of a different sort. The administrative offices of Speedtech Corporation were located in a two-story stucco building flanked on three sides by lawn. Jack arrived at ten in the morning, having spent two hours in his hotel room working up his notes. Sunday had been spent most productively with Carl Ott, who at the end of the day had taken him out to dinner and kept him up so late there was barely time to call Ruby before going to bed . . . and no time at all to work on his report.

There was a parking spot at the curb near the front of the building, so Jack parked there rather than driving to the lot in the rear. Walking down the sidewalk swinging his briefcase, his thoughts were occupied with Ruby. They had talked on the phone until midnight, and he was more anxious than ever to see her again. There was something about her voice that got to him. It had a dark, smokey quality and she used it like a lure, like a musician playing the cello.

Jack slowed his stride. On a corner of the lawn near the curb opposite Speedtech's main entrance, somebody was sitting in a swivel chair. It was a gray-haired man in a dark business suit with his arms crossed on his chest. His eyes were closed and his face was lifted toward the sun. Jack drew to within a few feet before recognizing him.

"Mr. Krevek? What are you doing out here? Catching a few rays?"

The sharp eyes popped open. Krevek looked at Jack suspiciously. "And you are . . . ?"

"Jack McKenzie. We talked the other day about Thrill."

"We did? Oh, yes, I remember. You're the so-called independent investigator."

"Not 'so-called.' I really am independent."

"Ha! Don't make me laugh. You're being paid to approve the thing."

"Only if I think it's safe."

"It isn't. I don't have a good feeling about it at all. What are you staring at? Haven't you ever seen a man who's been thrown out of his office? I'm not here getting a tan, I'll tell you that."

"You've been what?"

"Fired and thrown out. Set on the curb like a bag of garbage. Can you believe it?"

Jack couldn't believe it. He glanced around. There was nobody at the Speedtech entrance or at the windows facing the street. There were no pedestrians and no traffic. He was alone in the sun with Ernest Krevek, the legendary Ernest Krevek, the dean and wild man of roller coaster design. In the bright light, away from his desk and the other furniture of his office, he seemed smaller than Jack remembered . . . and older and weaker as well. He was seventy-five years old if he was a day. There was nothing worn out or weak about his eyes, though, which were full of fire.

"Philpott in Personnel told me Friday I was terminated—terminated!—and should clean out my desk and turn in my keys. Allbright didn't have the guts to tell me himself! I told Philpott to crawl back under his rock. Pisspot, I called him." Krevek laughed, enjoying the memory. "I knew what would happen next, but I outfoxed them. I got here this morning when it was still dark, before they had a chance to post guards at the doors. When everybody else arrived, I was at my desk working away as if nothing had happened! You should have seen the whispered conversations, the mini-conferences, the worried looks! All the while I'm busy working on my Capital Crimes Coaster whistling a happy tune! Man, I should have been an actor."

"Can I walk you to your car?"

"I took a cab today. I was afraid they'd be watching for my car. Anyway, here comes Allbright, finally, into my office, to try to talk some sense into my head, whispering, you know, trying to keep me calm. Everything I said I shouted, so everybody in the place could hear, and I had plenty to say."

"Mr. Krevek, isn't there something I could—"

90

"I told him he had a lot of goddamned nerve firing me after all I had done for him and his company. He whispered that I had been well paid for my contributions and that I was way past retirement age, and I shouted that I had made him the pompous piece of poop he was today and wasn't ready to retire. He said that I should stick to the issues and not resort to *ad hominem* tactics, and I said I'd knock his *ad hominem* into a cocked hat. Too bad you missed it. It was priceless! They left me alone for a while, maybe an hour, then four big rent-a-cops converged on my office, picked up my chair with me in it, carried me out the door and dropped me right here. I'm going to sue if I can think of some grounds. If only they had dropped me on my head . . ."

"Why don't you let me give you a ride home? My car's right here."

"I don't want to go home. I want to stay right here as a living monument to the ingratitude and stupidity and cowardice of Jeremy Allbright and the company he is destroying. He told me it was obvious that I wasn't taking my medication, and I told him that when I was through with him he'd need all the medication he could get."

"But you can't just—"

"I'm happy right where I am. I enjoy being an embarrassment to the company. I enjoy the peace and quiet here in the sunshine. I'm planning my future. I'm going to be a full-time disgruntled ex-employee. I'm looking forward to it."

"If you won't let me take you home, I'll call you a cab." Jack headed for the lobby door. Krevek called after him: "Don't do me any favors."

As Jack neared the door, it was pulled open from the inside, and he found himself looking up at a very large security guard.

"May I see your identification, sir?"

"I don't have any. Look, call a cab for Mr. Krevek, will you? You can't leave him sitting out there."

Jack heard a female voice. "It's Mr. McKenzie, Richard. You can let him in."

The guard stepped to one side. Jack saw the receptionist sitting behind her semicircular desk. "For God's sakes," he said to her, "aren't you going to do anything?"

"We called his wife. She'll be here in a minute. Mr. Allbright and Mr. Ott want to see you. They said it was important."

91

"Later."

Jack returned to Krevek and told him that his wife was on her way. The old engineer was stretching his arms and yawning like a man relaxing on a hammock.

"By golly," Krevek said, "maybe I *am* paranoid. I have the feeling that people are trying to help me behind my back."

CHAPTER THIRTEEN

A tall, gaunt woman emerged from the car. Krevek stood up to greet her, shrugging off Jack's attempt to assist him.

"Claudia," Krevek said, "I'd like you to meet McKenzie, an old friend of mine. Theopholus Q. McKenzie, meet my wife."

"The name's Jack," Jack said, briefly clasping the limp hand Mrs. Krevek extended to him. She was at least twenty years younger than her husband and had two of the hardest eyes Jack had ever seen. Her face had an imperious cast to it, and her thin, tight lips turned downward at the corners. She wore no makeup. Her gray-streaked black hair was pulled so severely into a bun it stretched the skin on her temples and cheeks.

"Are you all right, Ernest?"

"I'm fine, hon. I was just telling McKenzie here about my new career. I've always tried to be the best at whatever I attempted, so I intend to be the most *disgruntled* ex-employee the world has ever seen."

Jack couldn't help suggesting that there were better ways to spend free time. "Take a vacation. Don't you think you've earned it?"

'I sure do. I'll tell you what else I've earned. I've earned twilight years filled with happiness, and what makes a man happier than revenge?"

Jack glanced at Mrs. Krevek, but she was busy unlocking the car's passenger door.

"Yes!" Krevek said, warming to the idea. "What could be sweeter? Name something! Taking revenge is one of the most satisfying feelings there is. Nothing compares."

The sparkle in the old engineer's eyes and the half-smile on his lips made Jack wonder if he was kidding. "What have you got in mind?" Jack asked.

"I'll think of something. An April Fool joke. Or should I say a Fourth of July joke? That's when Thrill runs again, or what's left of it."

"Come, Ernest," Mrs. Krevek said. "Let's get away from this place. I can't stand the sight of it." She took his arm and urged him toward the car.

"You shouldn't do anything for a while, Mr. Krevek," Jack said, "except enjoy a vacation. Throw away your alarm clock. Read some books." He was about to suggest spending some extra time with his wife, but her dour expression, which seemed to be permanently imprinted, made the words die in his throat.

"You think I should see a psychiatrist, don't you?" Krevek said with a chuckle. "So does Allbright. He said so right in front of everybody. Well, let me tell you something. I've seen a psychiatrist. More than one. I drove 'em all nuts. You know why? Because I can imitate a normal person to perfection anytime I want to."

Jack watched with discomfort as Krevek gave his impression of "normal" behavior.

"Hello!" he said, waving and bowing. "So nice to see you! I've been thinking about you! You're looking great! How's the family? Come over to dinner sometime! It would be great to get together. Give my love to everybody. Hello! Good-bye!"

With that, Krevek got into the car and slammed the door.

"If there's anything I can do," Jack said to Mrs. Krevek as she walked around the car to the driver's side, "just ask."

She didn't look at him and gave no indication of having heard his words.

"You're a reasonable man, Mr. McKenzie," Jeremy Allbright said, making sure his office door was tightly closed, "and a patient one, too, I would imagine, but even you would have lost patience. You have no idea what we've had to put up with for the last five years."

"Ten years," Carl Ott corrected. "Don't forget the incident at the skeet club."

Jack wasn't persuaded that the old engineer had to be ejected by force and left by himself on the lawn, and said so.

Beads of sweat sparkled on Allbright's ruddy forehead. "He had every chance to retire with dignity. He thumbed his nose at every one."

"Still . . ."

"This morning he was shouting like a crazy person. Security carried him outside and I called his wife. It's over now and we can go on to other things. Like the news we just got from Wilson St. James."

"Is he crazy?" Jack asked. "He talked about revenge. He mentioned you. He mentioned the coaster."

"Just talk," Allbright said with a wave of his hand. "He's been making threats for years. Nothing ever comes of them. He likes to scare people, that's all. He's a coward at heart."

Jack shook his head worriedly. "I don't know, he makes me nervous. I was relieved when his wife drove up."

Ott chuckled. "Cute couple, aren't they? Claudia makes Ernie look almost cuddlesome."

Allbright leaned forward and lowered his voice. "Jack, listen. Something terrible has happened. St. James just called to tell us that Leon Van Zant is dead. Murdered in his house trailer."

"What?"

"With a shotgun. Blood everywhere."

Jack felt his throat tighten in a way that made it hard to speak. "Do they . . . do they know who . . ."

"Not yet."

"It's hard to believe. I saw him Friday morning before I came down here . . ." His voice trailed off as his thoughts turned to Ruby. Was she in any danger? He would phone her and ask that she spend the night with friends until the murderer was caught.

"Wilson wants you to know that no expense will be spared to make sure that testing and maintenance will go on as before . . . better than before." He drew a handkerchief across his brow and gestured to Ott. "I'm loaning Carl to the park as resident maintenance engineer until a replacement can be found."

"Is anybody else in jeopardy? The murder might have something to do with the coaster."

"No, no," Allbright said, shaking his head vigorously, "it has nothing to do with the coaster. There's no evidence for that at all. Van Zant had more enemies than he could count. He had a gift for making enemies. What, you think somebody who doesn't like the

95

coaster is going to kill everybody connected with it? They would have started with St. James or me, not Van Zant. He was just an employee, and not a very good one, at that."

"You're not at all worried?"

"There's no reason to be. A low-life got killed. He probably had it coming. How does that affect me?"

"We'll take precautions," Ott said reassuringly.

"One of the precautions you should take," Jack offered, "is to keep an eye on Krevek." He repeated as accurately as he could what Krevek had said about revenge, about the coaster, about the Fourth of July.

"Look," Allbright said, "we appreciate your concern and all that, but you don't know the old geezer like we do. He's a bag of hot air, believe me. Forget him. He's out of my life now and I can't tell you how happy that makes me. Morale around here is already up. What concerns us is that you might discuss Leon's murder in Sacramento the day after tomorrow. You wouldn't do that, would you? It could scuttle the project." Allbright turned to Ott. "The Assembly-Senate committee on Thrill meets on Wednesday. That's when our Mr. McKenzie here will flash the green light . . . we hope."

"I'll stick to the facts as I know them," Jack said. "I'm an engineer, not a detective."

Ruby laughed into the telephone when Jack called. "Don't be silly," she said. "I'm in no danger. I'm probably safer now than I was when Leon was alive. He was the man I hated most in the world. I'm glad he's gone, if you want to know the truth. Is that a terrible thing to say? I'd be just as glad if he had moved to another country . . . like Iraq."

"Make sure all your doors and windows are locked, at least. Will you do that?"

"I'll do it. I'm touched that you're worried about me!"

"Got any ideas about who might have killed him?"

"No, other than everybody he ever had anything to do with. I'm probably a suspect myself."

"Do you have a friend you could stay with tonight?"

"I have friends, but none I want to spend the night with. With the possible exception of you. Does that make you blush? I can

96

feel you blushing into the phone. Don't fight it. When will I see you again?''

"What's tomorrow, Tuesday? I've got a doctor's appointment at noon. Wednesday I'm in Sacramento. Thursday I'll be able to show you a document proving that I don't have AIDS. Or the AIDS antibody, if you want to get technical.''

"I don't want to get technical. I just want the coast to be clear. I'll have my results on Thursday, too. I'll show you mine when you show me yours, as we used to say in grade school. This is so exciting! It's like ancient times, when people had to wait *ages* before they could know each other in the biblical sense. Not that you and I ever will, but there is always the chance, slim though it is.''

"Stranger things have happened.''

Wilson St. James took lunging steps back and forth behind his desk, raising his arms and letting them drop. "This is terrible! This is terrible!''

"Jeez, Willie, will you sit down and relax? All that pacing makes me nervous.'' Ed Flohr, Sonoma County Sheriff, closed his notebook and pointed at the chair behind the desk. He watched as St. James dropped into it with a thud. "Keep ranting and raving and I'll begin to think *you* did it.'' Ed was a serene, self-composed man whose heavy-lidded eyes gave him an expression of perpetual boredom. As always, a dead cigar was parked at the side of his mouth.

"Oh, God, Ed, don't say that, not even in jest. Lots of people heard the shouting matches I had with Leon. How do you stay so calm? A guy gets killed, blood all over, and you sit there like Buddha.''

"You want me to be hysterical? Every time there's a crime, you want me to run in circles flapping my arms and shouting, 'This is terrible! This is terrible!' The deputies would panic.'' He tapped his cigar on the ashtray as if it were lit and returned it to his mouth. The only way he could stop smoking was to pretend he still was. "Okay, can you think of anybody else who might have wanted to kill Leon?''

"You mean other than his friends? His enemies, I guess. Sonnenvold's a possibility, the father of the girl who was killed. He shook his fists at Leon one time in the parking lot, blaming him for doing a lousy job of maintenance. Interview the street corner whores in

97

San Rafael and his gambling buddies at the card clubs and you'll have enough suspects to last a year."

"We may not have to go to the trouble. There were good prints on the shell casings. If the bad guy has ever been arrested before, we'll have his name and maybe his address before you know it."

"How long is 'before you know it'?"

"Depends. We'll run them through the state system first—that'll take a day or two or three according to how short-handed and backedup they are. We can fax the prints to the FBI center back East, too. They can make an ID in hours if they really want to. Usually takes a week to track prints down. Something else we'll do as time permits is check all the gun clubs and gun stores in the Bay Area. Somebody might know who uses those old-fashioned brass casings."

St. James blew his nose and shook his head in despair. "I hope to God you catch the guy before the Fourth of July."

Flohr looked surprised. "You definitely think, then, that it has something to do with the coaster?"

"No, no, it's just that I'm under enough stress getting the damned thing rolling again without having to worry about a murderer on the loose. My name might be on a list."

"If I were you I'd park my little sailboat in the middle of Richardson Bay and spend the nights there till we make an arrest. Or, you could make a full confession and move into the jail. You'd be safe there, especially in solitary."

"You really do think I killed that rotten bastard."

Flohr shrugged. "All I know for sure, Willie, is that *I* didn't do it."

CHAPTER FOURTEEN

Jack parked in the underground garage at Union Square in downtown San Francisco. He emerged from the concrete depths to the sounds of a street musician playing blues on a saxophone, the rattle and clang of a cable car on its way up Powell Street with a fresh load of tourists, and two fashionably dressed elderly women chattering about a display of jade figurines at Gump's that they were on their way to see. A panhandler with a Van Dyke beard suggested that giving him money would make them all feel better. The women regarded him as invisible and pressed on without missing a syllable; Jack handed over a dollar bill in exchange for directions to the 450 Sutter medical building.

"A block up and a few doors to the right. What's the problem? Teeth? Prostate? Piles?"

Jack thanked him and headed across Post Street.

"With tax," the panhandler called after him, "it comes to $1.08. Oh, well, skip it. Saves us both a lot of paperwork."

There was only one person in the waiting room of the Coast Medical Clinic, a woman seated in the corner hiding her face behind a magazine. Jack went to the counter and caught the eye of an Asian man in glasses and a white smock, who put down a pile of file folders and greeted him pleasantly. A name tag identified him as Al Lee, MD.

Jack spoke as softly as he could, "I called earlier about a . . . a test. The name's McKenzie."

"You don't need a name. I'll give you a number. Have a chair and I'll be with you in a minute."

Jack hesitated. "Do you want me to fill out anything?"

Dr. Lee shook his head. "All we need from you is a vein and seventy dollars."

Jack nodded and took a seat on the opposite side of the room from the woman; she was reading *San Francisco Focus*. Her dress came to just below her knees. Nice legs. Jack picked up a magazine and stared at it unseeingly, too nervous to read. What if he tested positive? The chances were slim, but still ... Somebody he slept with five years ago might have slept with somebody five years before that who ... The more he thought about it, the more depressed he became, and he had an impulse to walk out. No, that's what a coward would do. That's what his father would expect him to do. If he was brave enough to ride The Loop of Doom—and soon, Thrill—he was brave enough to take a blood test and deal with the consequences, whatever they may be. One of the consequences of testing positive would be telling his father. Was he brave enough for that?

It surprised Jack that he was going through such an ordeal for a woman he hardly knew. What was it about her? He compiled two columns in his mind. On the plus side were her sunny disposition, her sharp and quirky sense of humor, her competence and self-sufficiency. He liked her wide smile and her mischievous eyes. She couldn't be called voluptuous, but, as a physics teacher once said in describing a shapely woman, there were intriguing changes in cross-section on the vertical axis from hips to waist to chest. Surrounding the whole package that Ruby presented was an aura of mystery and danger stemming from her unorthodox upbringing. Engineers didn't meet women like that every day.

Let's see, Jack mused, closing his eyes, what could he list in the negative column? There was the way she teased him and her way of implying that just because he was an engineer he was therefore stiff, stuffy, and uncool. She was geographically undesirable, too, unless he moved to the San Francisco area or could convince her to move to Chicago. Then there was her unorthodox upbringing, so unlike his own. Or had he already listed that in the pro column?

To get his mind off Ruby, women, and the HIV antibody, Jack turned his attention to the magazine he was holding. It was a child's coloring book. He threw it aside and stared at a framed print on the wall of dark clouds looming over a stern and rockbound shore. He marveled at the inappropriateness of the scene in a clinic that did AIDS tests. Better would have been a sunrise or a field of spring flowers ... anything but a gathering storm. He was glad that engineers didn't believe in omens.

100

"Come in here often?"

Jack looked at the woman across the room, who had lowered her magazine and was looking at him. It was Ruby, Ruby of the silken hair, snapping brown eyes, and curiously appealing off-center smile. He gaped in amazement, then joined her in laughter . . . remembering that she knew when his appointment was.

"In answer to your question," Jack said after regaining control of himself, "no, I don't come in here often. Only when I have a date."

"Can't be too safe these days," Ruby said. She couldn't stop grinning.

"Better safe than sorry, I always say," Jack added.

"I envy your lady friend. A lot of guys would refuse to have an AIDS test. Too chicken."

"What makes you think my friend is female?"

"Women can tell. Vibes. There's an aura about you, an aura of testosterone. In fact, I think you're coming on to me right now."

"You have delusions of grandeur. And where did you get the idea that I'm here for an AIDS test?"

"I doubt if you came to see if you're pregnant or to have a Pap smear."

"Oh. Well, I did meet an interesting woman recently. I want to equip myself with the right medical documents just in case. A guy never knows when he might get lucky."

"How true. A woman always knows. When she's ready, all she has to say is 'Oh, Jack! Oh, Jack!' "

"How did you know my name was Jack?"

"It's written in your billfold."

Dr. Lee came to the counter and nodded to Ruby. "Please come in. I'll buzz the door open."

Ruby bounced to her feet. "Doctor, this man here, can he come in with me? Can we give blood together?"

The doctor eyed Jack. "A friend of yours, is he?"

"No," Ruby said. "I just met him. But he looks like a good possibility, wouldn't you say? Probably could be taught to be a good lover."

Jack laughed out loud. "Good grief, Ruby!"

Dr. Lee, not a jovial sort, frowned briefly before waving them both through the door. "No names, please. We want to provide our services on a completely anonymous basis. That way your identities

101

can't become public even as a result of a court order or a search warrant.''

He led them to an examining room and shut the door. He asked them to sit down and roll up their sleeves. ''These are your code numbers,'' he said, handing them each a small card. ''Keep the number strictly confidential to protect your privacy. When you come in again or phone for the results, refer to yourselves only by code, not by your names.''

While Dr. Lee took two syringes from a drawer and removed their paper wrappers, Jack and Ruby showed their cards to each other. What was the point of secrecy?

''The test is for the antibody, not the virus itself,'' Dr. Lee said in a flat voice. ''A false positive is rare, but any positive result will require a second test. A false negative is more common, particularly if the infection was contracted in the previous six months. Roll up your sleeves.''

''I don't know about you, GP40,'' Ruby said brightly to Jack, ''but old LN36 here hasn't had a lot of action in the last six months.''

Jack nodded philosophically. ''It's been a slow year for me, too. Maybe the next six months will be better.''

''Or the next six minutes, for that matter,'' Ruby said. ''When we leave here we might be alone on the elevator.''

Dr. Lee ignored the jokes. ''Which means,'' he said, ''that two people who test negative should still practice safe sex with a condom or a vaginal sheath.''

Jack sighed. ''I'll tell you one thing, Doc. Future historians aren't going to refer to the 1990s as The Age of Romance.''

Dr. Lee swabbed Ruby's forearm with a disinfectant and positioned the needle. Ruby closed her eyes and looked away. She reached for Jack's hand and held it tightly.

''Squeeze hard,'' Dr. Lee said. ''It makes the vein stand out.''

''Be gentle,'' Ruby whispered.

The long corridor widened at the elevators. There was a drinking fountain and a couple of thinly-padded chairs. Through the third-story windows, Jack could see the dome of the Capitol, as grand and imposing as the one in Washington, D.C. That was as it should be, for if California were a country—a wall poster proclaimed—it would rank among the top half-dozen in the world.

102

State office buildings lined the south side of Capitol Park like blocks spilled from a toybox, and it had taken Jack half an hour to find the right one, a search that led him through several of Sacramento's older neighborhoods. The streets were shaded with towering maples, oaks, and elms, and the frame houses, many of which had porches and swings and sizable yards, reminded him of his boyhood in the Midwest. There was nothing about Sacramento that suggested San Francisco, Los Angeles, San Diego, or any other California city Jack had ever seen. It was more like Madison, Wisconsin, or Des Moines, Iowa. He could imagine living there, only an hour or two from the Sierra ski slopes, though the Central Valley heat would no doubt get oppressive in the summer. It was 11:00 A.M. on July 2, and already the outside temperature was over ninety degrees.

Opposite the windows was a door marked Conference Room 3A. Jack shifted his briefcase to his left hand and reached for the knob.

"Here for the meeting of the safety committee? You must be McKenzie."

Jack turned and nodded. "Yes, I'm McKenzie." He shook the hand of a ruddy-faced man with thinning blond hair and an oddly fixed smile.

"Thought so. I was watching you. You look like an engineer." The voice was breathy, almost a whisper.

"I do? How does an engineer look?"

"Organized. Like he has everything all figured out and knows all the answers."

Jack might have taken offense at the remark if it weren't for the man's pleasant expression and soft voice. "I've only figured out one thing, and that's that I don't know all the answers. You are . . . ?"

"Arnold Sonnenvold."

"And you are with . . .?"

"You might say I'm with my daughter. She's dead."

Jack frowned, not sure he had heard the words correctly.

"You don't recognize my name, do you, Mr. McKenzie? Sonnenvold?"

"I'm afraid I . . ."

"That's typical."

"I don't mean to be rude, Mr. Sonnenvold, but I'm already late. Could we continue this another time?" Jack reached for the door again, but the man extended a hand and held it shut, the expression on his face never changing from one of friendly interest.

"They can wait a few minutes, since it's all cut and dried anyway. Holly Sonnenvold, that's my dead daughter's name. Still doesn't ring a bell?"

Jack's lips parted as the significance of the name stole over him like a cold caress.

Arnold Sonnenvold nodded in satisfaction. "Yes, now you remember. She was the rag doll that your roller coaster tossed aside. If it weren't for her, we wouldn't be here."

Jack now saw the wooden smile and the earnest eyes as threatening. "Mr. Sonnenvold, it's not my coaster. I'm an independent consultant. I was in Chicago when the accident happened. I'm terribly sorry about your daughter. I sympathize with you, really I do."

The man took his hand from the door and closed it tightly around Jack's forearm. "I'm sure you sympathize deeply. So deeply you want to make sure it never happens again, isn't that right? So deeply that you are going to tell the committee that Thrill should be destroyed, isn't that right?"

Jack tried to peel the fingers off his arm, which were as hard and tight as handcuffs. "It's not up to me. I was hired to assess the safety of the new design, that's all, and today I'm going to present my findings. Now let me open the door . . ." Jack felt the weight of his briefcase in his left hand. If necessary, he could swing it against the side of Sonnenvold's head . . .

The door suddenly opened from inside and two men emerged. One was Wilson St. James, the other was a uniformed state policeman. Sonnenvold released his grip.

"Jack!" St. James said. "There you are! Come on in, the committee is ready for you." Turning to Sonnenvold, he said, "If you'll excuse us, Arnie, we have a meeting to attend. It's closed, sorry to say, so we'll see you later."

"That's what you think," Sonnenvold said, still with his inappropriate half-smile. "The meeting is open. It is illegal to keep the public out." He unfolded a piece of paper and held it in St. James's face. "A letter from my attorney about my rights as a citizen."

St. James looked exasperated.

"He's right," the policeman said, holding the door open. "The public *is* welcome. But any disruption, Mr. Sonnenvold, and I'll escort you out of the building.''

"This is Officer Stoltz, Jack, who's here in case there's trouble.''

Jack followed St. James through the doorway. "You're expecting trouble?''

"You know how it is. Whenever you try to do something for the public good, crackpots try to stop you.''

Conference Room 3A was small, with room for about two dozen chairs, half of which were occupied. Jack and St. James took seats in front facing a long table that was littered with documents, folders, clipboards, microphones, and plastic cups. Behind the table was a row of earnest-looking men and women busy with a discussion among themselves. Jack recognized the man in the center as State Senator Dan Pezzotti, whose mane of gray hair was practically a California landmark. Glancing over his shoulder, Jack saw Officer Stoltz position himself at the left rear of the room, close to Arnold Sonnenvold.

"Sad about Arnie," St. James whispered. "The accident has taken over his life. Settled with us out of court for less than he could have gotten because he needed money to bail out his dairy farm, which was about to go bankrupt. Now he feels guilty about it." St. James turned to answer a question from Pezzotti.

"Did you find your man, Willie?''

"Yes, Senator. This is Jack McKenzie.''

The senator nodded. "All right, let's get on with it. We have a long agenda to cover." He adjusted his glasses and peered at the contents of a folder. An aide made sure the microphone on the table was turned on. "Now, Mr. McKenzie, as you know, this is the joint Assembly-Senate committee charged with overseeing public safety regarding certain matters having to do with commercial activities of a recreational nature. I want to thank you on behalf of the committee for appearing here today in such hot weather, and I hope for your sake that you are being well paid." Pezzotti had a baritone voice and an oratorical style; he rolled the longer words off his tongue as if savoring their flavor. "Would you mind taking a seat at the table? Thank you. Not you, Willie, just Mr. McKenzie. Please state your name, your affiliation, and the nature of your business before the committee. Speak into the microphone. We don't tape anybody secretly; it's all out in the open.''

105

"Jack McKenzie, senior engineer with McKenzie and Son of Chicago, Illinois. I was retained to make an assessment of the safety of Thrill, a roller coaster at the Wildcat Mountain Amusement Park in Sonoma County."

"An *independent* assessment," St. James put in, waving his hand for attention. "That point should be stressed."

Senator Pezzotti looked at St. James sternly. "You are not the testifier, Willie. Mr. McKenzie is a college graduate and can speak for himself."

From the rear of the room, Jack heard Sonnenvold's quiet voice: "Independent? That's a laugh. The whole thing was cooked in advance."

"Quiet, please," said Officer Stoltz in a loud whisper.

The senator looked at Jack over the top of his glasses. "And have you completed your assessment?"

"I have." Jack removed three binders from his briefcase and laid them on the table. "My conclusions are in writing, in triplicate, and I submit them herewith to the committee."

Pezzotti took the reports and handed two copies to the man on his right, keeping one for himself. He riffled quickly through it before laying it aside. "How were your conclusions reached?"

"A number of ways. Visual inspection of critical stress points, measurement of deflection of structural elements under various loadings, checking conformance between the coaster as built and the coaster described in the plans and specifications, discussions with the designers at Speedtech in San Jose and with the field maintenance people at the park."

From the rear of the room came Sonnenvold's voice. "Did you factor into your equations that the original designer has spent time in a nut house? That the ride has a long history of accidents? Did you see my daughter's blood on the ground and did you measure it and photograph it and make charts out of it?"

There were scuffling sounds. Sonnenvold was on his feet and moving toward the front of the room, but he was blocked by Officer Stoltz, who grabbed his arm and tried to force him back into his chair.

Senator Pezzotti raised a hand in a calming gesture. "Mr. Sonnenvold, I'm so glad you could be with us. Another interruption and you'll be removed from the room. Understood?"

106

Sonnenvold jerked his arm free. "I want everybody to know that this so-called expert is giving testimony that was bought and paid for by the people guilty of the cover-up and isn't worth the toilet paper it's written on."

"Mr. Sonnenvold, I must ask you to sit down and be quiet. Sit down *right now* or you will be gone."

The door opened and four uniformed officers came in. They took up positions along the rear wall. Sonnenvold glared at them and slowly sank to his seat.

"Good," the senator said. "May I say again, Arnold, that everybody is very sorry about the loss you suffered. But since it can't be undone, I really must urge you to try to put it behind you and get on with your life and let this committee do its work. Let me remind our other guests that while we are on the subject of the roller coaster, we are not having a public hearing. Everybody concerned has had plenty of opportunities to make their views known."

A young man with several shaving cuts on his cheeks rose and announced himself as Jason Foster of the *Press Democrat* of Santa Rosa. "I was told that Mr. McKenzie would take questions . . ."

"What you were or were not told is of no interest to the committee. If Mr. McKenzie wants to answer questions he is free to do so, but not on the time of this committee, which has other things to consider besides Thrill, the controversy over which has strained the patience of the taxpayers, to say nothing of this committee and its chairman, who wants to be fair to all sides. May I remind all here present that the rendering of Mr. McKenzie's report was the compromise worked out by the contending parties. Wildcat Mountain already has a conditional use permit to reopen the ride the day after tomorrow, the condition being that Mr. McKenzie doesn't raise a serious objection. At this time and in this place, we are merely taking official possession of his report and hearing him express his conclusions in person. Any questions will be put to him by me or by staff and by nobody else. Mr. McKenzie, you may proceed."

Before Jack could speak, there was another interruption, this time from an elderly woman with a piercing voice. "If this is not a hearing, Senator," she said in a manner every bit as theatrical as Pezzotti's, "then how can new evidence be considered?"

"Vera Harker!" Pezzotti said in mock delight, "how nice to see you! What new evidence would that be?"

107

Jack turned and saw St. James, seated close behind him, lower his eyes into his palm and mutter, "Not her again . . ."

"New wetlands evidence," the woman said, brandishing a sheaf of papers. "If the park is not torn down and the land allowed to revert to the wetlands it was at the turn of the century, then we have lost forever two and possibly three species of California swamp grass."

The eyebrows rose on the senator's forehead. "Swamp grass? Are you sure you don't mean swamp gas?"

"Oh, sure, joke about it, but that doesn't diminish the tragedy. My group has completed a study that shows—"

"Look, Vera, I'll make you a promise. Give me your study and I'll personally consider it."

"When?"

"Tonight at home."

The woman came forward and slapped the papers on the table. "Okay, Dan, but you better not be lying."

The senator watched her return to her seat and managed a benign smile. He nodded to Jack.

Jack cleared his throat. "Many of the design assumptions, thanks to modems and fax machines, were recalculated using computer equipment at our Chicago headquarters. Both the design and construction of the old parts of the ride as well as the new were compared with industry practice. In the last few days, a dozen test trains have been sent over the course carrying accelerometers."

"For the benefit of our friends and neighbors here gathered," the senator said with an expansive gesture, "suppose you tell us what an accelerometer is."

'It's an instrument that measures forces caused by changes in speed or direction. If the g-forces stay within certain well-known limits—the details are in my report—then a passenger will not experience undue discomfort, or at least will not be subjected to stresses or strains that would be likely to cause physical injury."

Someone in the audience made a scoffing sound.

The senator picked up Jack's report and riffled through it again. "So, in brief, what are your conclusions?"

"They're listed in the first two pages. In general, I found no reason to delay the opening. The old supports have been strengthened to meet and in most cases exceed current structural codes. The new sections were designed and built with a factor of safety larger than comparable rides at other parks."

Vera raised and dropped her arms in disgust. "Why am I not surprised?" she said. She called across the room to Arnold Sonnenvold: "You're right, this was a done deal before we even got here."

Jack felt a flash of anger and resisted the urge to whirl in his chair and confront the woman. "I resent that," he said quietly, not turning his head.

The woman laughed. "He resents that! That's really funny . . ."

She was interrupted by Senator Pezzotti's booming voice. "Enough, Vera! I'll not warn you again. Now, Mr. McKenzie, I ask you to ignore the guerilla tactics from certain members of the audience and direct your comments to me. Certain members of the audience have had ample opportunity, believe me, to air their views."

Jack waited a moment for his temper to subside. "I want to state for the record that my opinions are my own, that they are based on facts, and that I was not pressured in any way by anybody."

"Yes, well, the record will show that. Your expertise and your independence are not under question. They are, in fact, the reason you were hired in the first place. Moving along, our friend Mr. Sonnenvold mentioned the history of accidents this particular roller coaster has. Did you look into that?"

"Not in detail, because Thrill in its present form is essentially a new ride, shorter, slower, and safer. As proof of that, let me mention that two days ago I put balloons on the seat of one of the cars at the start of a test run. The train returned to the platform with all three still in the car. Two were on the floor, the other was still on the seat. The ride now is so mild, Senator, you might consider riding it yourself."

"I might do that. If I did, I'd win five dollars from my grandson."

"Go ahead," somebody in the audience said in a barely audible voice, "commit suicide if you want to."

Senator Pezzotti chose to ignore the comment. "Let me put in the record of these proceedings a word about the safety of roller coasters as opposed to risks the public faces every day." He sifted through a sheaf of papers until he found the one he wanted. "Staff has provided me with the hazard list compiled every year by the federal government's Consumer Product Safety Commission. According to their figures, roller coasters rank one hundred and thirty-fourth, be-

109

tween aquariums and dollhouses. I think it can be fairly said that you are more likely to get injured at home than you are at an amusement park." He peered around the room. "So let's keep this matter in perspective. Now, Mr. McKenzie, have you finished your investigations?"

"I'll stay on the job until the coaster has reopened, and I plan to be aboard for the ceremonial first run. If I notice anything of significance between now and then, I will of course contact the committee."

"What about vandalism? We've received reports that it's a problem."

"That's a matter for park management and not in my area of expertise."

Wilson St. James raised his hand. "May I answer that, Senator? Vandalism was a problem a while back, but not since we've installed an electrified perimeter fence and hired extra security. When Thrill reopens and for as long afterward that we think there is any threat to the park, we will have levels of security far beyond any amusement park in the country."

Sonnenvold was on his feet again. "Are you going to believe him? He's the worst liar of them all—"

Senator Pezzotti slapped his hand on the table. "That's it! Remove Mr. Sonnenvold from the room . . ."

"You can't do that," Vera Harker said. "He lost a daughter and deserves to be heard."

"Remove Mrs. Harker from the room as well. Sorry, Vera, but we have other matters to discuss and we have to get on with it."

Two policemen flanked Mrs. Harker and tried to escort her toward the door; she resisted and had to be pushed. On the other side of the room, Officer Stoltz tried to take hold of Sonnenvold's arm without knocking down a woman who was trying to protect him.

"No!" Sonnenvold shouted. "You can't let them reopen that killing machine! How will you feel when you have the blood of a whole trainload of people on your hands?"

The senator ignored the growing commotion. "I want to thank you for your time," he said pleasantly to Jack. Lowering his voice, he added, "Willie, why don't you and Mr. McKenzie come around the table and go down the back way? You'll avoid a confrontation with some of our more emotional constituents."

A minute later, Jack and St. James were hurrying down an interior

110

stairwell, Jack complaining that he should have been warned there were going to be protestors, St. James swearing unconvincingly that he was surprised himself and apologizing for the melee.

"I never wanted to be an engineer in the first place," Jack said, laughing. "My father had to talk me into it. Know what I was afraid of? I thought it was going to be dull."

CHAPTER FIFTEEN

Thursday, July 3

In the morning, Jack dressed quickly and skipped down the stairs to the lobby, planning the coming day. First he would have a substantial breakfast, something with lots of fat and sugar in it so he could skip lunch; French toast with syrup and links of juicy sausage ought to do it. Next, he would call the clinic to get the results of his blood test, then head for the park and a nine-thirty meeting with Ruby and a tour of the family fireworks factory, a side trip she promised wouldn't take more than an hour. He could hardly spare the time; there were a lot of last-minute checks he wanted to make before Thrill was ready to resume its career of scaring people half to death. Two days more. Thirty-seven hours, to be exact. He strode toward the restaurant, wondering if he should add orange juice and strawberries to his order.

"Mr. McKenzie? Mr. McKenzie?"

Jack was so lost in thought that the clerk at the front desk had to call him twice.

"Yes?"

The clerk gestured toward the front entrance. "There's a woman waiting to see you."

"Oh?" Jack's first thought was that it might be Ruby, but the woman in black he saw sitting erectly in one of the lobby's upholstered chairs was as unlike Ruby as could be imagined: thin, severe, rigid. She rose as he approached. She was tall and thin, only an inch or two shorter than he was, and appeared to be about fifty or sixty years old. Her hair was gray and pulled tightly into a bun under a small black hat with a half veil, a style he hadn't seen since he was child going to church in Chicago with his mother.

112

"I'm Jack McKenzie. You're waiting for me?" There was something familiar about her. He hoped she wasn't one of the protestors from the previous day's melee in Sacramento who wanted to continue the shouting and fist-shaking.

"Hello, Mr. McKenzie. Don't you remember me? I'm Claudia Krevek."

Ernie Krevek's wife! "Of course, of course! Excuse me for not recognizing you right away." When he saw her in front of the Speedtech building she was in casual clothes; now she was dressed like a grieving widow. Her powdered skin was marked with two penciled arcs for eyebrows and her lips were a thin red line. "What brings you here this morning?" Jack asked, taking the chair facing hers. "How's your husband? I'm sorry about the scene the other day. I hope you've both gotten over it."

His cheerful manner wasn't reciprocated. Mrs. Krevek dropped her eyes to her hands, which were folded in her lap. They were large, rough hands, Jack noticed, at odds with her generally regal bearing; maybe she did a lot of gardening. The haughty cast of her eyes and mouth and her prominent cheekbones made her face look like an image graven on an old coin.

Mrs. Krevek had some difficulty in beginning, and when she finally did speak she avoided looking directly into Jack's eyes. "It's about my husband," she said. "He worries me. He's full of anger."

"Maybe when a little more time passes—"

"He's making threats."

"Against Speedtech?"

She nodded. "And against the park. If the ride opens tomorrow, I just don't know what he'll do." She raised her eyes. "Have you turned in your report?"

"Yes. There are probably stories about it in the morning papers. The hearing was . . . boisterous."

"Did you tell them that the ride shouldn't open?"

"Afraid not. I had no reason to."

She sighed and turned away. "Can't you change your mind? Say the opening should be delayed?"

"No, Mrs. Krevek. I can't change my conclusions just because somebody, your husband, is unhappy."

"It's more than unhappy. Those things you heard him say about revenge? He wasn't kidding."

113

"Maybe you should go to the police."

She made a contemptuous sound. "They won't do anything. Ernest has complained to them about a lot of things over the years—noise, neighbors, kids—even made threats that he didn't carry out. They'll just laugh. They don't have time for the fears of an old lady."

"Then go to Jeremy Allbright. Or Wilson St. James."

She shook her head. "My husband would kill me if he ever found out I went to them. He hates them and they hate him. They aren't fond of me, either, for that matter."

"Mrs. Krevek, what do want? Why did you come to me?"

"You seemed different. You offered to help." Her fingers straightened and relaxed nervously.

"I can't do the impossible. I don't run the park and I'm not the police. I'll tell you one thing I'm going to do, though. I'm going to pass on what you've told me to Mr. St. James. If he thinks some action should be taken, then he'll take it."

"Yes, tell him. It's something I can't do myself. Tell him I think Ernest should be watched for a few days."

"You mean put under surveillance?"

"Yes. To make sure he doesn't leave the house. Or followed if he does."

"Can't you watch him yourself? Phone somebody if he leaves?"

She stared down at her hands a long time before answering. In a voice so soft Jack could hardly understand the words, she said, "What if he locks me in a room?"

"Now really, Mrs. Krevek, how likely is that?"

No answer.

"Has he ever locked you in a room before?"

She kept her eyes down.

"Jesus," Jack breathed. "Okay, I'll see what I can do."

Jack phoned the park, and by the time he arrived there Wilson St. James was waiting him in his office. Someone was with him, a big, unfriendly-looking man with the shoulders of a fullback.

"This is Max Costello, Jack, my chief of security. Sit down, gentlemen. Now, what's this all about? You talked to Krevek's wife?"

"She was waiting for me when I came down for breakfast. Strange woman."

"I've met her. She used to work here, did you know that? In the

114

machine shop, ten, fifteen years ago. Good with engines, as I recall. From what I hear, her personality hasn't improved any."

"She's worried about her husband. She thinks he's going to do something, maybe disrupt the opening, she doesn't know what."

"He's always been a blowhard," St. James said, "shooting off his mouth. What you call your harmless crank."

"She's afraid it's going to be different this time."

"Jack, bring Max here up to speed. Tell him what you told me when Ernie got kicked out of his office."

Jack recounted the incident in as much detail as he could, trying to remember everything Ernie Krevek had said that was even vaguely threatening. Costello listened intently without changing his expression. Jack then told them both about his meeting with Claudia Krenek at his hotel an hour earlier.

"What do you think, Max?" St. James asked when Jack was finished.

Costello replied in a hard, even voice. "I wouldn't trust the old buzzard as far as I could drop-kick him."

"He's full of bluster," St. James insisted. "He never actually does anything."

Costello was unmoved. "In my experience," Costello said, "people who makes threats eventually carry them out."

"Maybe we could get a restraining order," Jack suggested. "Get a judge to order him to stay away from the park."

"That wouldn't stop him," Costello said.

"Nothing public like that," St. James said. "It would be all over the papers."

"How about I send a man into his garage to screw up his car? Sugar in the gas tank or something. That would slow him down for a few days."

"No, no," St. James broke in, waving his hand in alarm. "Somebody might get hurt. The old fool might have a shotgun and not be afraid to use it." The word "shotgun" made St. James think of a possibility he hadn't considered before, that Ernest Krevek might have murdered Leon Van Zant. He'd tell the sheriff to add Krevek's name to the list of suspects. Maybe there was a way to find out quietly if Krenek owned a shotgun.

"Understand one thing," St. James added. "I'd close the park if the threat was specific, like if somebody phoned and said a bomb

115

had been planted. But over something as vague as this? Because some old guy in Los Gallinas is unhappy? No. We'd be closing the park all the time and never know when to reopen it."

"Then do what the lady suggested," Jack said. "Keep an eye on him."

"What do you think, Max? Can you put a tail on Krevek?"

"Sure. I'll give the job to Ike Melloy. He has a surveillance van."

Jack had another suggestion: give Krevek's photo to the park's employees and tell them to be on the lookout for him.

Costello made some notes on a small pad. "Everybody already has shots of Arnie Sonnenvold and Vera Harker. I'll make sure they have photos of Krevek, too. We've got security people posted at every key spot. If he gets by Melloy and shows up here, he'll face a real welcoming committee."

"Vera won't be a problem," St. James said. "I happen to know that she's on her way to a family reunion in Salt Lake City. Satisfied, Jack? No need to amend your report?"

"I'm satisfied."

Ruby was feeling happier than she had in a long time. The weather was perfect, she had the rest of the day off, and she had Jack McKenzie on the seat beside her. She turned her red 300ZX east on Highway 37 and stepped on the gas. Jack must be feeling happy, too, she thought. She had never seen him so talkative and animated. With great verve and many humorous asides, he recounted his meeting with Claudia Krevek and the melee at the Sacramento hearing. She looked at him appreciatively. The more time they spent together the better she liked him.

"Claudia Krevek is one strange human being," Ruby said. "When she worked here I tried to befriend her, as a challenge, but it was impossible. She had so many chips on her shoulder I don't see how she got dressed in the morning. Now Ernie, I sort of liked him. He spent a lot of time here years ago when Speedtech was installing some rides. Those crazy ideas of his, like using killer coasters on criminals, were just to get everybody stirred up. I still think of him as mainly an entertainer, not a threat to society."

"He's gotten worse, according to Allbright and St. James."

"Could be. He never was what you would call *normal*."

The air was so clear that once they crossed the Solano County line she could see all the way to Vallejo and to the hills beyond. Without a trace of summer's usual cooling fog anywhere in sight, the air rushing through the open windows was warm and getting warmer.

"Wilson told me you did a great job in Sacramento," she told him. "He said you spoke with such conviction and authority that even old Senator Foghorn was afraid to say boo." She raised the windows to cut down the noise of the wind.

Jack admitted that he sometimes put on an act to discourage argument. "I learned it from my father, who hardly ever gets contradicted by anybody. He has a voice like James Earl Jones, and when he's with clients or on a witness stand, he acts as if his calculations and opinions come directly from God."

"And do they?"

"No, usually from handbooks."

"Don't imitate him. I like you best when you're awkward and unsure of yourself, which is most of the time."

"Only when I'm around you. I never know what you're going to say or do next."

She looked at him and smiled. She liked his square shoulders, the strong line of his chin, his wavy hair, his old-fashioned good manners. Were all the good men in the Midwest? Maybe that's why she hadn't been able to find one. "You know what, Jack McKenzie? I like your looks. You're cute. I like your eyes and your mouth."

He laughed in embarrassment. "Well, I like your eyes and mouth, too."

"Is it enough to build a relationship on?"

"I intend to find out."

"Then let's get down to brass tacks, big boy. Did you call the clinic?"

"Yes I did. Did you?"

"Of course. And?"

"You tell me first."

"No, you first."

Jack shrugged. "Okay. I'm negative. No trace of HIV. I was relieved, if you want to know the truth. And you?"

"Negative."

"All right!"

"Way to go!"

"We're clean!"

They exchanged high fives.

Ruby looked at Jack coquettishly. "What are you going to do about it?"

"I'll think of something."

Ruby turned her attention back to the highway and slowed down. After a few minutes, she turned onto an unmarked dirt road and stopped at a chain-link gate.

EXTREME DANGER
Authorized personnel only
NO EXCEPTIONS!
Trespassers will be prosecuted

Jack frowned. "I usually obey signs like that. I'm not authorized personnel."

"But I am. I'm licensed by the State of California as a pyrotechnic operator." At the touch of a transmitter button on the dashboard, the gate rolled to one side, closing automatically behind them ten seconds later. Ruby parked the Z a few hundred yards farther on, alongside a half-dozen other cars. There was another sign, even larger and sterner than the first.

NO SMOKING BEYOND THIS POINT
No engines or motors
No cameras or power tools
No matches or lighters
THINK SAFETY
Welcome to Skyfire Productions
Fireworks for every occasion

Jack got out of the car and nodded toward the sign. "So many warnings! Reminds me of the singles scene. Makes me envy married people."

Ruby took his arm and led him down a path toward a one-story building with bars on its windows. "Just when I think you might be too square for me, you make me laugh. Hey, do you lift weights? Your arm feels like a tree."

"It's nervous tension."

Dotting the surrounding grassy slopes were concrete blockhouses protected by earthen berms. "Storage bunkers," Ruby explained. "We keep the stuff separated. If one batch blows up, we don't lose everything. Most of them are empty now, though. We've supplied half a dozen towns in the Bay Area for tomorrow's celebrations."

She pushed a button beside a steel door and looked down at Jack's shoes. "Take off your shoes. Leather can build up static electricity. We don't want a spark to end our affair, do we?"

"Is that what we're having?"

"I haven't decided yet."

The door was opened by a short, round-faced man wearing blue coveralls and white latex gloves. He frowned at Jack, but brightened when he saw Ruby.

"Ruby!"

"Hi, Uncle Frank. Jack, this is my father's brother, Frank Tetracelli. Frank, meet Jack McKenzie."

"What?"

"This is Jack McKenzie," she repeated louder. "He wants to get into the fireworks business."

Tetracelli snapped off a glove for a handshake, revealing a hand with two missing fingers. "Your name's what? McKenzie? No good. You want to get ahead in the fireworks game in California, you better be Italian or Portuguese. We more or less got a lock on it. Ha ha! Come on in . . ."

"Glouster," Jack whispered to Ruby as they stepped through the doorway, "you said your name was Glouster."

"Didn't like Tetracelli, so I named myself after a town in Massachusetts, but without the weird spelling. It's where I was conceived, according to my father."

"Where you were *conceived?*"

"It has a more musical sound than where I was born. Bullhead City, Arizona."

"This is it," Frank said with a wave of his arm. 'This is where Fourth of July begins."

Half a dozen women working at a long table called greetings to Ruby.

"What the gang is doing today," Frank said, "is some last-minute shells for the city of Berkeley, which only just decided that it wanted to be patriotic this year. We do mainly aerial stuff at this location, for a hundred and twenty-five feet and higher. Why do you want to get into fireworks?"

"I don't," Jack said. "Ruby made that up, for some reason."

"You must be crazy to want to get into this."

"You've got a cute butt," Ruby said to Jack, who looked at her

119

in alarm. She watched with amusement as he gradually realized that her uncle was hard of hearing. She knew just how loud to talk to make herself heard by Jack but not by her uncle.

"The pile of pellets at the end of the table," Frank went on, "those are the stars, what we call the 'effects.' A little fuel and oxidizer to make 'em burn mixed in a filler with a salt for color. Barium chlorate for your greens, strontium carbonate for your reds, and so on. Phyllis and Hilda are mixing them with a filler and a bursting charge and molding them into cylinders and spheres, what we call your shells. Looks like cookie dough, doesn't it? Want to try it yourself?"

"I'm afraid I don't have time. I've got to get back to the park."

"Don't be bashful. Know what we used to use as a filler? Bay mud. That's why the factory is where it is. Of course now we use your shellacs and your red gums."

"Of course." Speaking softly, Jack said to Ruby, "If we are having an affair, I'd like it to be romantic. Suppose I make a reservation at an inn up the coast?"

"That's sweet of you. I'll think about it." He really was a nice guy, she thought, but she didn't want him planning a seduction scene. Just like a man, to want to be in control. She had other ideas.

"The charges are just black powder," Frank said, "same as the Chinese used five hundred years ago. Potassium nitrate, charcoal, and sulfur. Probably find them in your kitchen."

"Not my kitchen," Jack said. "This is very interesting, but we really have to be getting back to the park."

"What Peggy and Mrs. Calvelli are doing is sticking on the lifting charges." Frank picked up a completed shell and showed it to Jack. "See this string here? That's your quickmatch fuse. Runs around from the top down to the lifting charge. Inside of that there is another fuse, timed to cat's ass so the star bursts at the top of the flight. I could put one of these together in my sleep."

A plan formed in Ruby's mind. "I don't want you to make reservations anywhere," she said to Jack. "Too much like a honeymoon. When the park closes tonight, meet me at the Ferris wheel, okay? There's something I want to show you." Jack looked puzzled. She squeezed his hand.

"If you're afraid of sparks, you shouldn't touch me."

"Oh, sorry."

120

Frank led his visitors to a wall lined with bins full of cardboard tubes of various diameters and lengths. "These are your mortar tubes." He pulled one out, peered through it, and replaced it. "You stick a wooden plug in one end and nail it in place, see, maybe use some glue, too, to contain the gases, drop in a shell—with the lift charge down, of course—light the fuse, and BANG! ZOOM! POW!" He raised his arms over his head and spread them slowly out with his fingers fluttering to imitate a star exploding into a thousand points of cascading light. He looked at Jack with shining eyes. He was a man who enjoyed his work.

Ruby tapped Jack on the shoulder. "You know what my dad and I used to do? Go down to the water's edge with mortar tubes and shoot at balloons a hundred feet in the air." She rested a mortar on her shoulder and aimed it upward like a duck hunter.

Jack was amazed. "You can hold it in your hands without getting killed? Wouldn't the kick knock you flat?"

"Good thinking, Doctor Science! We used rockets, which hardly have any kick at all. It's fun. It would make a great concession if you could get insurance. You'd have to charge at least twenty bucks a pop, though."

Frank Tetracelli couldn't catch what Ruby was saying. "What? What?"

"I was telling him," she said in a strong voice, "how Dad and I used to shoot rockets at balloons."

"Your father," Frank said gravely, shaking his head, "was a crazy person who would try anything. A little like you, Ruby."

CHAPTER SIXTEEN

"You should spend more time with him, just the two of you," the mother said, so the father took their five-year-old son to the playground in the park. The lad was excited by the attention from his father, bouncing up and down in the car to the extent the seat belt would allow, and talking nonstop about a drawing he had made the day before in kindergarten, about a water pistol he wanted, and about how much he hated the sweater his grandmother had given him, which he said made him look like "this incredible dork."

The father made a few brief cautionary comments but no attempt to be an equal partner in the conversation. He had little interest in kindergarten affairs, and, if pressed, would have found it difficult to supply a precise definition for the term "dork." He didn't know how to talk to a child, even his own. Most of what he had to say to his son—on weekends when he wasn't at the office or out of town—had to do with noise reduction, grammar, and table manners. When the boy was older, he assured his wife, and could carry on a semiintelligent conversation, then he would spend more time with him. That was a promise. At the present, the pressures and distractions of his business were just too great.

At the park, the boy made a beeline for the swings, while his father, still dressed in the suit and shined shoes he wore to work that Saturday morning, hurried after him. The swings were all taken. The teeter-totters were full. There was no room left on the small merry-go-round, which, in any case, was being made to go much too fast by several boisterous teenagers.

"The sliding board," the father said. "Go down the sliding board." It was a big one with a platform ten feet above the ground and a chute that ended in a square of soft dirt. Kids, some younger than his boy, were clambering up the ladder and hurling themselves downward with obvious glee.

"No."

"No? What do you mean, 'no'?"

"I don't want to."

"Why not?"

"Because."

He tried to nudge his son onto the bottom rung of the ladder. The boy planted his feet and refused to be nudged. "Go ahead," the father urged. "Don't be a sissy."

"I'm not a sissy."

A redheaded girl with freckles looked down from the platform and said, "What's the matter, is he a sissy?" She went down the slide head first and landed on her stomach in the dirt.

The father had played varsity baseball and basketball in college and was embarrassed by a son who was afraid of a sliding board. A brief, one-sided argument ensued. Still the boy would not move. The father, losing patience and feeling that the boy's cowardice was a reflection on himself, picked him up and placed him halfway up the ladder. Speaking sternly—but softly enough not to be overheard by a group of mothers standing nearby—he ordered his son to climb the rest of the way and go down the slide.

"Are you a scaredy-cat? Are you a big baby?" The boy shook his head vigorously. "Then go ahead. Even the girls aren't afraid." The boy sniffled and raised himself one rung. His eyes filled with tears. "Go on," the father urged. "If you don't, no television for a week. I'm warning you."

The boy climbed slowly, agonizingly slowly, ignoring the complaints of the impatient children behind him. He began to sob. At the top he froze completely, embracing the handrail as if his life depended on it and crying helplessly. No amount of coaxing had any effect.

Exasperated, the father had to climb the ladder, peel the boy's hands loose, and carry him to the ground. One of the watching mothers shook her finger. "Bullying him is not the way to do it," she said.

"Go fly a kite," the father mumbled as he marched the boy back to the car.

The sliding board confrontation was one of Jack MacKenzie's earliest and most vivid childhood memories. He had no doubt that it colored his relationship with his father for years afterward, probably right up to the present. As Jack remembered it, his refusal to use the sliding board had less to do with his fear of heights—though that was a factor—than with simple defiance. After all, it was only days later that he found the courage to climb the ladder by himself and go down the slide. He was in the park with his mother. "You can do it," she said, patting him on the back. "But if you don't want to, fine. We'll try some other time." Two minutes later he was picking himself up off the dirt with a proud smile on his face.

The memories came flooding back when Jack was standing on Thrill's launching platform with Carl Ott. It was late in the afternoon and they had just watched a train loaded with sandbags make another successful run.

"Let's take a ride," Carl said. "Enough tests. The sandbags are having all the fun." He grinned at the look that came over Jack's face. "What's the matter, are you a sissy?"

"I was when I was five years old." He added with a chuckle: "Now, of course, I fear nothing."

"Time to give this monster a taste of human flesh, right? Let's take the lead car so we can see where we're going."

Maybe this was the best way, Jack told himself. Acting on the spur of the moment gave anxiety no chance to build. A practice run might clear the fear away and prepare him for the grand opening the following night, when a crowd would be watching, and Ruby, if he could change her mind, would be seated beside him.

Carl called to nearby workmen. "Hey, Julio! Jackson! Bert! We're going to take a ride. Anybody want to come? We need guinea pigs!"

Jack was surprised at the response. In a blink of an eye, the sandbags were removed and every one of the train's ten cars had at least one rider. More would have climbed aboard if Carl hadn't stopped them with a shout: "Enough! A half load is good for starters. If we come back alive, we'll try a full house."

Tim, the husky teenager who would be posted in the crow's nest on Friday night, went from car to car checking seat belts and lowering the shoulder restraints, which were padded U-shaped bars hinged at the top of each seat. When Jack felt the bars close over his shoulders and chest and snap into place, he knew he was trapped; he was squeezed between the side of the car on his left and the ample figure of Carl Ott on his right. The U-bar couldn't be unlocked from inside, and there wasn't enough room between his knees and the front of the car to slide out in that direction. Jack twisted slightly and sat up straighter in an effort to get comfortable. "This is like a straightjacket," Jack said to Carl. "There's no escape."

"That's the idea."

"Have a nice ride, Mr. MacKenzie," Tim said cheerfully. "I hope your affairs are in order."

Jack knew that Tim was a "surfer dude" in his spare time and used to risking his neck. "Want to trade places with—"

Jack's mouth snapped shut when the train lurched forward. As part of the redesign, a series of cogwheels under the platform gave the train an assisted start, which saved ten seconds over letting it slowly roll away by gravity. Ten seconds saved in a three-minute cycle meant twenty extra loads of paying customers every day. The extra income, if all went well, would pay for the reconstruction in three years.

There was another jolt at the bottom of the first hill when the train's undercarriage engaged the chain lift. Jack and Carl were tilted against the backs of their seats as the train turned upward and began its slow climb to the top. The safety dogs under the cars that prevented the train from rolling backward bumped over the ratchets. The clunk-clunk sound made coaster lovers squirm in delicious anticipation; Jack was reminded of Edgar Allen Poe's story about a telltale heart.

The slowness of the climb to the top was by design, Jack knew, to give the passengers time to notice how small everything on the ground was getting and how sickeningly high they were. Then there was the level section at the top, the slow, trembling roll of the train toward the edge of the precipice.

"Nice view from up here," Carl said blandly. Jack ignored him, concentrating instead on getting a good grip on the handrail in front of him.

The train edged forward, making noises and motions that made it seem that the wheels were having trouble staying on the tracks. A derailment was almost impossible, Jack knew, because the wheels were in vertical pairs, one on top and one on the bottom, pinching the track between them. Jack also knew that the evil geniuses who designed roller coasters made the first downward curve of track sharp enough so that it seemed as if the train was falling off the edge of the world, an illusion that was stronger in the rear cars. The slope

125

of the first hill was only fifty-four degrees, although it would seem like straight down. Jack knew all these things, and he tried to wrap the facts around himself in a protective shield, but still he wasn't prepared for the effects of that first breathtaking drop.

The train almost stopped—but not quite!—giving the riders the feeling of being dangled over the edge of a canyon. Jack couldn't lean forward to see how close they were to the downslope, but he could no longer see any tracks beyond the front rim of his car. There was only empty space. Krevek had deliberately aimed the train away from any nearby structure or hill. Psychologically and emotionally, there was nothing to hang on to, no anchor or reference point. All that could be seen was a distant horizon of rolling hills . . . which rose sickeningly as the train nosed downward.

Down, down, and down dropped the train, faster and faster, so fast that Jack had the feeling his stomach had been left behind. The train and its load of passengers, each one pressed to his seat like an insect on a slide, hurtled toward the ground in what seemed to be a free fall, surrounded by a roar of wheels that grew with the speed. In only four and a half seconds the ground was rushing toward Jack's face at fifty miles an hour. The wind reached fifty miles an hour, too, making it hard to breathe or speak.

"God save me!" Jack forced the words through clenched teeth, while beside him the usually reserved Carl Ott yelled, "Yoo hee! Man alive!"

At the bottom, just before his life was snuffed out like a skydiver's whose chute hadn't opened, the train leveled off and Jack's seat rose to meet him with a vengeance. The blackness of a tunnel, a blinding blaze of afternoon sun, a hard right turn, a hard left, jolting rises and drops: they came at him so furiously he couldn't catch his breath or organize his thoughts or lecture himself about the art of illusion in roller coaster design and their statistical safety.

There was a momentary lessening of tension when the train glided with spooky smoothness up a straight section of track; it was almost as if it was relaxing while planning its next assault. The assault came quickly in the form of a sharp and sustained left turn. So severe were the angled g-forces and vibrations that Jack feared the cars were about to disassemble themselves into their component parts.

"This is sup— This is supposed to—" He was trying to say with a touch of sarcasm that this was supposed to be a family ride, but a vicious sequence of twists and turns kept him from getting the words out. He had to focus his full attention on squeezing the handrail and bracing himself.

Carl Ott, on the other hand, had no trouble talking. "Relax and enjoy it," he shouted, grinning into the wind. "Resisting makes it worse ..."

Just before the so-called "Banshee Curve," Jack's chest was forced hard against the U-bars and the roar of the wheels dropped several decibels.

"Feel that?" Ott shouted. "The brakes."

Magnetic brakes had been installed under the tracks to slow the train as it headed into a series of particularly sharp curves. It was eerie to feel the braking effect without hearing the noise of one abrasive surface rubbing on another. The silent resistance of one magnetic field being forced to pass through another was sufficient to cut the speed by twenty percent.

"No moving parts," Ott said. "Low maintenance."

Jack's face was distorted from the effort of staying alive, but he felt better now that the worst was over. His stomach caught up to him from behind and settled into its accustomed place in his midsection. He realized he had slid down in his seat so that his knees were touching the front of the car. He straightened up in time to get the full effect of an illusion that Jeremy Allbright had dreamed up. The track ahead was blocked by a brick wall, and to riders who had their eyes open and their wits about them, it looked as if the joy ride was going to come to sudden stop. At the last possible second, the train dipped and passed under the wall.

"That looked good," Jack said.

"A nice effect," Ott agreed. "Having fun yet? Your color is coming back."

"The beginning was hell, but I like this part. Now its like the Toonerville Trolley."

The train climbed the last upslope, which was just long enough to slow it to a crawl. The kinetic energy of the train was transformed back into potential energy. Jack liked potential energy better.

Under the tight control of another set of magnetic brakes, the cars slipped slowly into the "Crash Landing" tunnel. Images of the coaster's wooden supports were projected on the walls, and as the train bumped to a stop, a recorded voice came over a loudspeaker: "Please watch your step when exiting ... the cars ..." At that moment, as planned, the track dropped downward two feet in four-inch increments, pivoting from hinges at the tunnel entrance, coordinated with jumps in the projected pictures. Beams and columns were shown breaking apart, accompanied by sounds of splitting wood and women screaming. "Oh!" said the voice in mock alarm, "Oh, my! This is awful!"

The combination of sounds and movements was designed to make the riders think that the structure was falling apart, but Jack didn't find it very convincing. He turned to Carl and made a face. "This won't fool anybody."

"The timing is a little off. We'll tinker with the audio. Tomorrow night you'll hear some screams, I guarantee it."

"The beginning, the old section, is a killer. I almost lost my lunch."

As soon as the lower end of the track was aligned with the track leading back to the loading platform, doors swung open at the end of the tunnel and the train rolled by gravity into the sunlight. The recorded voice was bright: "Just kidding, ladies and gentlemen, boys and girls. When the train stops at the platform, exit to your right. See you again soon on ... *Thrill!*"

Jack was smiling. The ride wasn't as terrifying as he was afraid it would be. Not once did he really think that he was going to die. A feeling of euphoria came over him when he realized that a nameless dread that had lurked in his unconscious all his life no longer seemed to be there.

The trained rolled smoothly onto the platform and stopped within an inch of the target line. Workmen on the platform cheered and applauded along with the passengers.

"How'd you like it?" Carl asked.

"I almost fell asleep."

"Want to go again? This time we'll fill every seat."

"Sure, why not?" Speaking like a blasé roller coaster veteran, Jack pointed at Carl's shirt and added, "Better button that pocket if you don't want to lose your pen."

At ten o'clock a rapid-fire series of rockets, aerial bombs, and whistling stars decorated the black sky and signaled the end of another day at Wildcat Mountain Amusement Park. Ruby was waiting

128

for Jack at the Ferris wheel. Instead of the jeans she was usually in at the end of her shift, she was wearing a skirt and a white silk blouse that glowed with a blue sheen in the reflected fluorescent light. Her wide smile and her shining eyes were as he remembered them. She looked good enough to kiss, so he did.

"Wow!" she said. "A public display of affection! I thought you said you were a *civil* engineer . . ."

"You look so delectable I couldn't help myself."

"You look pretty foxy yourself."

"What do you want to do? Go out for a late supper? Go hot tubbing in Marin? I don't want to stay out too late because tomorrow's the big day."

She gave him a mischievous smile. "And tonight's the big night. Have you been on the Ferris wheel? No? Then follow me, said the spider to the fly."

She took him by the hand and led him through the entrance gate. They watched while the gondolas stopped at the bottom one after another to discharge passengers. When the wheel was empty, the operator, an old gentlemen with a BUFFALO BILLIARDS cap, turned away from his control station and greeted Ruby.

"Jack," Ruby said, "I want you to meet a friend of mine, Barney Laffoon. Barney has agreed to give us a special VIP ride, just the two of us. He'll stop us at the top so we can enjoy the panorama."

Laffoon was a man with long silky hair and soulful eyes. For some reason, he winked at Jack as if they shared some delicious secret.

The wicker cars were unexpectedly roomy, wide enough for four people side by side on a padded bench. As Ruby and Jack took their seats, he told her about riding the coaster earlier that day. "The amazing thing," he said, "was that I almost enjoyed it. I stayed on for a second run, can you believe it?"

"My hero!"

"I really think I've gotten over my fear of heights. Thrill has made me a new man. You're going to ride with me tomorrow night, aren't you? You're on the list. It's a hot ticket."

"Count me out, Jack. I loathe that coaster. I'll watch you risk your neck, then I'll go help Uncle Frank. He's got a couple of hundred pieces to fire."

Barney gave them a wave and pulled back on the clutch lever. The wheel was so big that the first movement of the gondola was

129

almost horizontal. Grandly, they were swept outward and upward, and the surrounding lights and buildings dropped away.

"Wheee!" Jack said, uncharacteristically. He embraced her and kissed her again.

"You're out of control," she laughed, pushing him away so she could look at him. "Good! I like it!"

"Ever since conquering Thrill, I've been higher than a kite. I have the feeling I could step out of here and fly like a bird. I need a sedative. Got one?"

"I might have something in my purse."

When they reached the top, the wheel stopped, setting the gondola swaying. Jack grabbed the lap bar to steady himself. A touch of vertigo came over him, but quickly ebbed away. "The view from up here is great," he said, looking around. He pointed and added, "You can look right down into the crow's nest . . . and I thought *that* was high. Is this what you wanted to show me . . . the view?"

"Yes, and my new blouse. Bought it just for you. Thought you might want to see my new attitude, too." She surprised him by throwing her arms around him and pressing her lips to his, pushing him against the side of the gondola. It was a different kind of kiss than any they had exchanged before, more intense, more serious, more exciting.

"We have fifteen minutes," Ruby whispered in his ear when their lips parted. "That's what I told Barney to give us."

Jack smiled and closed his eyes. "Being assaulted by a beautiful woman . . . it's what every man dreams of."

"The dreams have only just begun. The night is young."

Ruby pressed a small packet into his hand. He turned his palm toward the light. "What's this?"

"The sedative I mentioned. Acts a bit like booze. Stimulates you at first, calms you down later."

Jack's eyes narrowed, then widened. "A condom!"

"Stops babies in their tracks."

"You . . . you mean now? Here?" He spread his arms. "Is there room enough? Is it even possible?"

"Let's see if love will find a way."

Love did.

There were more rockets and bombs and whistling stars that night, but only Ruby and Jack could see them.

CHAPTER SEVENTEEN

Friday, July 4, 3:30 P.M.

Elizabeth Holmes: Wherever you are in radioland on this holiday afternoon, in your car, at home, at a family picnic in one of Sonoma County's beautiful parks, welcome back to "Let's Talk," on KPET Petaluma. I'm your hostess, Elizabeth Holmes, and I'll be with you till the top of the hour. I have two interesting guests with me in the studio who have been waiting patiently, and I for one am anxious to hear what they have to say. They are Professor Robert Cannafax of Sonoma State College, whose specialty is the psychology of fear, and Eldon Carver, who comes to us all the way from Muskegon, Michigan, and who is called the Coaster King. How did you get that title, Eldon?

Eldon Carver: Thank you, Liz, it's a pleasure to be here. Being the Coaster King sure has gotten me on a lot of shows. This isn't the only one by any stretch of the imagination.

Elizabeth: How did you get the title?

Eldon: I rode more coasters more times than anybody else. It's awarded by *Coaster World* magazine, put out by the National Union of Thrill Seekers. This is the trophy that comes with it, which I lugged down here thinking it was a television show. I've been invited to be on the first ride tonight, too.

Elizabeth: Impressive! The National Union of ... It stands for NUTS! Some say you have to be nuts to ride roller coasters.

Eldon: I say you're nuts if you don't. I've met some great people, some really great people, seen a lot of the country, and had my picture taken with the governors of three states. Not just the two of us alone, there were other people. I have a wall at home covered with pictures. I should have brought a picture of it.

131

Elizabeth: Let's get the professor in on this. Dr. Cannafax, why do people ride roller coasters?

Robert Cannafax: For the same reason they sky dive, hang glide, bungee jump, ski too fast, or whatever. The common denominator is fear. It may be that there is a craving for thrills hard-wired into the human brain at a primitive level.

Elizabeth: Not my brain, I can tell you that, and it has a lot of primitive levels.

Professor Cannafax: People differ. Conquering peril and escaping unharmed from great danger can cause a sense of self-affirmation and self-esteem.

Elizabeth: Interesting . . .

Eldon: Self-esteem! You're big on that in California. In two days I've heard "self-esteem" three or four times. Nobody mentions it in Muskegon.

Professor Cannafax: Research suggests a neurological need for the biochemical state that results from excitement. Fear activates the reticular activating system at the base of the brain, which "wakes up," so to speak, the rest of the brain.

Eldon: It's fun, is another reason.

Professor Cannafax: An imbalance of a brain chemical, monosmine oxidase, may be a factor, which has also been implicated in some forms of depression. Fear, the theory holds, changes the level of the chemical and lifts some people from torpor to aliveness.

Eldon: Can I stick my oar in? Do any of the theories and the research say that people like coasters because they're fun? Do I look like alive enough to you? Am I torpish?

Elizabeth: Torpid.

Eldon: Torpid. I'm *too* full of pep all the time, if you ask my wife. You wanna know why I like coasters? I'll give you a reason. I like being a cannonball. Yes! Shooting through space like a cannonball or a meteor at blinding speeds. There's nothing like it. It gets your attention, lemme tell you!

Professor: Attention, that's another part of it. The speed demands your full attention and engages all your senses. If you have any other problems in life, they disappear, at least temporarily. Fear erases them.

Eldon: What's to fear?

Professor Cannafax: Violent death, for starters.

Eldon: Oh, puh-leez . . ."

Elizabeth: I want to remind my guests that this is "Let's Talk," not "Crossfire."

Eldon: Skydiving and bungee jumping, yeah, I can see a reason to be scared there, because you can turn yourself into a grease spot awful fast. But roller coasters, for god's sakes? They're safer than a bar stool.

Professor: As the Coaster King, you probably know the statistics on safety, but the average rider doesn't. If coasters aren't particularly dangerous, they present the *illusion* of danger, and the parks try to enhance it. T-shirts and buttons are on sale saying things like "I rode the Circle of Death . . . and Lived!" Signs warn you against riding if you are on medication, are under five feet two, have a heart condition or a pacemaker, or are pregnant.

Elizabeth: I rode Thrill once years ago and it was like giving birth. Lots of waiting and then all hell broke loose.

Eldon: That's good! That's good!

Professor Cannafax: Besides, fear rising from the subconscious levels is often impervious to facts. Many intelligent and educated people, for example, are afraid to fly even though they know planes are relatively safe.

Elizabeth: Maybe you two experts can clear something up for me. A story is going around that there once was a terrible tragedy with a new coaster. Don't know when, don't know where. A train full of dignitaries left on a ceremonial first ride, the story goes, and when it returned to the platform, all the passengers were dead of broken necks. Is that true?

Eldon: Hell, no! That's so old it has carbuncles growing all over it. Or monocles. I mean barnacles. What did I say, carbuncles?

Professor Cannafax: I agree with the Coaster King. The story is what is called an urban myth, something that never happened but that people want to believe. It resonates. I've heard versions where the riders are staring straight ahead, wide-eyed, all dead of shock or heart attacks.

Elizabeth: So the reopening of Thrill tonight—just hours from now—is nothing to worry about?

Eldon: It's gonna be a slow news night for you media types, Liz. Thrill is a pussycat. Even my wife is going to ride, and she gets most of her excitement from knitting.

Professor Cannafax: That's exactly my point. People differ in this regard. Some avoid stress, some seek it. Some people are serene, others get bored easily and want action. Maybe it's a difference in the way they were treated as children, maybe it's neurological, maybe it has to do with chemical trace elements.

Eldon: Some people enjoy having fun and some don't. Professor, are you going to ride Thrill?

Professor Cannafax: I wasn't planning to, no.

Eldon: Hah! Thought so! I woulda bet on it!

At 6:30 P.M., a gray van was parked on a quiet residential street in Los Gallinas, California, ten miles west of San Jose at the south end of San Francisco Bay. On the sides of the van were the words CRYSTAL WATER TESTING CO., INC. and a phone number. Anyone dialing the number was told that it was "not in service at this time." Set back about fifty feet from the curb was a two-story house of white brick flanked by heavy-limbed oak trees. A shake roof extending beyond the exterior walls provided a shaded walkway on three sides. Smoke rose from one of two fireplaces.

Inside the dark interior of the van sat Ike Melloy, private investigator, holding a cellular phone and looking through a pane of one-way glass. He was describing the peaceful scene to his client at Wildcat Park and recording the conversation at the same time. "Nice place, nice neighborhood," he droned in a monotone. "Houses in the four- to five-hundred-thousand class, I'd guess. I have a clear view of the rooms in the front and the attached garage. Husband is in the living room watching television. I saw the wife in an upstairs room a minute ago. So far nobody's closed the drapes. The husband did some yard work a little while ago. Shouted quite a bit at a neighbor's dog."

Max Costello asked if the house had a rear exit.

"Not for a car. On the far side of the house is a creek and a wooded slope leading up to the next street. Couple hundred yards up. He could sneak out that way on foot, after it gets dark, but why would he? He doesn't know he's being watched. If he leaves in his car, he'll have to come up the driveway toward me."

"Call if he does, or if he walks away from the house."

"Will do, Max. Been here four hours now. How much longer? This looks like a waste of time."

"Stay till nine-thirty. If he's still at home then, he can't get to the park before closing time. Call me if there is any change in the situation.''

"Right. Good-bye."

The situation changed immediately.

Melloy saw Krevek's wife cross the living room and disappear into what he assumed was the kitchen. A minute later she was in front of the garage and climbing into what Melloy assumed was the couple's second car, a ten-year-old Buick. She backed the car in a U-turn, then headed up the driveway.

Melloy swiveled toward the rear windows of the van to see which way she turned and to try to get a license number. He was surprised to see her car pull up behind him and stop with the bumpers almost touching. She got out, a tall, spidery woman in black slacks, and walked to the street side of the van. He turned in his chair to keep her in sight. What the hell was she doing? She tried to peer through the one-way glass and tapped on it with her car keys.

For the love of God, Melloy thought to himself, has some idiot tipped her off?

"Yoo hoo! You in there! I have to talk to you . . ."

Melloy held his breath. Her face was so close that if it weren't for the glass he could reach out and twist her nose.

"I know you're in there," the woman said. "I'm the one who asked for somebody to come and watch my husband. Would you show yourself, please?"

Who the hell else has Max told about the stakeout? Melloy wondered. There was no time to phone him and find out, nor to ask his advice on what to do next. The woman rapped on the glass more insistently. Thank God there was nobody on the street to see or hear her.

Melloy grumbled, pushed aside the curtain at the front of the van, and crawled into the driver's seat. He rolled down the window and stuck out his head. "What do you want, lady? I've got work to do in here."

"Oh, there you are . . ."

She came to the door and brought her face close to his. It was not a face he would have chosen to be close to. She had the same frowning, pinched expression as his late mother, who was never known to smile. When she spoke she opened her mouth as little as possible, as if trying not to show her teeth.

"I'm not going to stay inside that house another minute with him in such a foul mood. Can you see him in the living room? I cut the cord on the drapes so he can't close them and block your view. There's a Giants game on tonight that he's going to watch. Maybe he'll forget about . . . the other things."

Melloy wanted to draw away from her, but that would have been a sign of weakness. He matched her stare defiantly and said, "You got me mixed up with somebody else."

"If he gets up, it will be to go to the bathroom. He'll come back because he likes the downstairs TV better than the one in the bedroom. He might fall asleep on the sofa. If he starts pacing back and forth, watch out, because it means he's getting worked up."

Melloy thought it best not to tip his hand. "What's the matter," he said slowly, "you don't like baseball?"

"I'm going over to the church to play bingo, which I usually do on Friday night. Having you here is a great relief, a load off my shoulders. You are going to watch him for a few more hours, aren't you? Until the danger's passed?"

"Lady, I'm a technician with a testing company. The drift I get from you is that you're worried about your husband for some reason. Why don't you stay home and watch him yourself?"

"Because I'm afraid for my . . . I'm afraid that he . . . You know very well, and stop playing this ridiculous game with me when I'm the reason you're here. Just watch him, okay? Call the police if he tries to leave." She turned on her heel and walked with mannish strides back to her car.

Melloy watched her drive south. He crawled back into the van and picked up the binoculars. The old man was still parked in front of the TV. By adjusting the focus slightly, he could see what was on the television screen; yes, it was baseball. Melloy turned on a small radio and tuned it to 680. If the game was close, the old coot might get caught up in it and be less likely to leave the house.

CHAPTER EIGHTEEN

Friday, July 4, 8:30 PM.

Cars streamed into the parking lot at Wildcat Mountain as darkness approached. The late arrivals were joining a record crowd. There were lines at every ride, every concession, and every bathroom. Along the shoulders of the access road and on nearby hillsides, families were spreading blankets and unfolding chairs. Why pay for parking and admission when the fireworks display could be watched absolutely free? Besides, fathers were telling their wives and children, fireworks are better seen from a distance. You don't get a stiff neck from looking up.

Laughing Sal, a six-foot-tall papier-mâché head, cackled insanely at the entrance of the Fun House as if amused by the merry-go-round's recorded, calliope music, which hadn't been changed in fifteen years. Competing against both Sal and the calliope was a brass band hired for the night to play patriotic music in honor of the holiday. Several hundred people in a bleachers facing the bandstand were enjoying the cacophony, fanning themselves with programs, resting their feet, and trying to pacify children with sugar drinks and Cracker Jacks.

The line leading to Thrill was longer than Wilson St. James had ever seen it, stretching past the Fun House and doubling back to the bandstand. A lot of people were going to be disappointed; there was no way they all were going to get a ride this night, even though the park would stay open an extra hour. St. James instructed an aide to hand out admission tickets to anyone still in line at closing time. Maybe that would head off a riot or a wave of petty vandalism.

Wilson St. James was behind a velvet rope on Thrill's loading platform. Never had he seen such a large and happy throng. The walkways and grassy areas were filled with customers of all ages and types, and a high percentage of them were carrying food or souvenirs from the park concessions. Nothing like publicity—even the bad publicity that Thrill had generated for a year—to bring out the crowds.

The park owner was standing with Jeremy Allbright, Carl Ott, Jack McKenzie, and a group of journalists and local officials who would be aboard for the first two rides. More were arriving all the time, and the introductions were almost nonstop, as were congratulations for finally getting the coaster back in action. To reassure the riders, empty trains trailing balloons and streamers were leaving the platform and returning every few minutes. Everything was running like finely tuned clockwork. St. James was sure that after he made a few remarks over the public address system and after a ceremonial ribbon-cutting, the VIPs would climb aboard and Thrill would begin decades of profitable operation. He was also sure that the implications of the long lines and the festive atmosphere were not lost on Fujima and Onoda, who represented the Japanese consortium negotiating to buy the park. Onoda he liked, Fujima got under his skin like a splinter.

"Big crowd," he said to Fujima with an expansive wave.

"Big crowd," Fujima agreed. Even when repeating English words, his heavy accent made him hard to understand.

"It's a good omen. Future success. You guys will make a pot full of money."

"Pot full?"

"The more people, the more money you will make. I think the income estimates I gave you will have to be revised upward. You know what I mean?"

Fujima considered the words carefully, then waved his arms. "A whole pot full of people. All crowded together."

"Forget it . . . I'll talk to you tomorrow when there's less noise."

"I know what you mean. It is a great victory for both sides."

The hulking figure of Max Costello came up the stairs and stepped over the rope. St. James detached himself from the Japanese to have a word with him.

"Everything's under control," the chief of security reported. "I just got a call from the van. Melloy says Krevek is watching a Giants game and the wife is playing bingo at a church."

138

"One less thing to worry about." Bingo?

"There's more good news. Arnie Sonnenvold. A potential problem. He and his wife were on the way to the park and got stopped for speeding on the Gravenstein Highway. The sheriff tells me they were both drunk as skunks, had picket signs and stink bombs with them and were going to cause as much trouble around here as they could."

St. James felt a stab of sympathy for the Sonnenvolds, and it showed on his face. "Those poor people. I'd like to tell them how sorry I am for the accident, but my lawyer says absolutely not. Where are they now?"

"In the pokey drying out. Ed Flohr says he'll keep 'em overnight as a personal favor to you."

"Good old Ed. It looks like we're in the clear, eh?"

"We've got the fence electrified, we've got men patroling the perimeter, we've got men checking arrivals at the parking lot and turnstiles. There's even a guy under the coaster on the walkways."

"Nice job, Max." He slapped the big man on the shoulder and laughed. "I'll remember you in my will."

"I'll settle for ten cents on the dollar if you pay now."

St. James waved him off and turned to shake hands with three members of the Petaluma Planning Commission. They wanted to know if the park would contribute to the cost of widening Lakeville Highway. They knew he would say no, they admitted, but they thought they'd ask anyway. As they talked, St. James could hear Jeremy Allbright telling Jack McKenzie and several other men a story about somebody with an antique shotgun. He tried to eavesdrop without being rude to the Petalumans.

Allbright was talking about somebody—St. James didn't quite catch the name—who twenty years ago had joined a South Bay skeet club. He had paid a thousand dollars for an old handmade shotgun and was convinced it was so much superior to modern guns that he could outshoot anybody. "The shotgun was so old," Allbright recalled, chuckling heartily, "it wouldn't even take regular shells. He had to buy brass shells at great expense from some specialty gun store in Texas."

"Because eleven percent of the traffic on weekends," one of the commissioners explained to St. James, "is headed for the park, we think it would be fair if—"

139

"Call my office," St. James said. He cut them off abruptly and added himself to Allbright's audience.

"By golly, it turned out that Ernie was the worst marksman ever heard of. Nobody was safe! It got to be quite a joke in the club. When he got ready to pull the trigger, everybody dove for cover, hid behind trees, every damned thing, making fun of him . . ." Allbright dabbed at the corners of his eyes with a handkerchief and blew his nose before continuing. "There was this one guy, a doctor, who used to razz him unmercifully. Once when Ernie blasted away for ten minutes without a score, the doctor asked him if maybe he was holding the gun backward. He told Ernie he couldn't hit a barn even if he was *inside* of it. Couldn't hit the ocean standing on the bottom! Well! Ernie was not amused! He pointed the gun at the doc and said something about sending him to the graveyard to join his patients. The gun wasn't loaded, but they kicked him out of the club anyway, and the doc wanted to sue him for reckless endangerment or emotional distress, lock him up as a clear and present danger, or some damned thing. Finally settled out of court."

St. James touched Allbright's arm. "You talking about Ernie Krevek?"

Allbright nodded, still chuckling.

"He owns a shotgun? An antique shotgun with brass shells?"

"I don't know if he still has it. It's one of the many things you can't talk to him about without boxing gloves."

The men laughed appreciatively.

St. James walked away slowly with his fingers to his lips. Ernie Krevek has an antique shotgun that shoots brass shells! That's enough for a search warrant, no doubt about it, maybe even an arrest for suspicion of murder. He'd have Max pass the information along to Ed Flohr. Ernie Krevek! A harmless blowhard, that's what he'd always thought. Maybe everybody was wrong about him. But what did Krevek have against Leon?

"Excuse me, aren't you Wilson St. James?"

St. James shook hands with a small, neat, perfectly composed woman in a tailored suit and a breast-pocket handkerchief.

"My name is Kali L. Delareaux. K-A-L-I. I'm with California Commercial Bank." Her grip was firm and her eyes steady. There was a certain strength about the woman, despite her small stature.

"Kali Delareaux," he repeated aloud to make sure he was pronouncing her name correctly. "Don't tell me the park is in arrears on a loan."

"Nothing like that. We may do some business with Speedtech, so I thought I'd drive up and watch the opening of Thrill."

Much to his astonishment, St. James found this doll-like creature enormously appealing, and he released her hand reluctantly. "Watch? Would you rather ride? There is still a seat or two on the first train."

Delareaux's laugh was controlled and self-confident. "No, thank you. I get my excitement . . . in other ways."

Their eyes remained locked. "Cal Com Bank is headquartered in San Jose, isn't it?" St. James asked. "Did you drive all the way?"

"Afraid so. Traffic was heavy. Took me a half hour to go the last five miles. I hope it isn't as bad on the way back."

St. James had the mad notion of asking Delareaux if she wanted to spend the night in his guest suite, or maybe on the yacht, to avoid a long drive at night, but he saw no way to do it without sounding predatory. "You should have let my office know you were coming," he said instead. "I'm sure we could have found you a suitable place to stay."

"That's a nice thought, thank you. Next time I will. You better rejoin your colleagues."

St. James heard Allbright call his name. "Come on, Willie, it's nine o'clock. Let's get this railroad rolling!"

"I have a ceremony to conduct," St. James said to the banker, "and a little ride to take."

"I quite understand."

They shook hands again, and their hands stayed in contact a second or two longer than business etiquette required.

Ruby came to the side of the platform and raised her hand. Jack leaned down and touched her fingers. "Do you want to ride?" he asked her. "I'm still saving your seat."

"No thanks, you go ahead, I'll watch. I've got a box full of rockets in my truck I'm taking to Uncle Frank. Tonight's the biggest display he's shot in years. It'll take half an hour to send everything up."

"I'll see you afterward?"

"Of course. Do you mind waiting until eleven? I have to shoot the display at closing time." She glanced over Jack's shoulder, then unhooked the two-way radio from her belt and brought it to her lips.

"Frank, can you hear me? Just got the high sign from the boss man. Send up some shells."

Fifteen seconds later, three aerial bombs detonated in the darkening sky with stunning impact. Even though Jack and Ruby knew the explosions were coming, they both winced at the loudness.

"Yikes!" Jack said. "That was some wake-up call!"

"I hate the bombs. My favorites are the rockets and stars."

"Well, I better take my seat . . ."

Ruby raised the radio again. "That was good, Uncle Frank. Okay, stay by the radio. When Willie is through talking, I'll let you know and you can start the big show. I'll be there a few minutes later." To Jack she said, "He doesn't need me. Everything's wired up to fire by itself. All Frank has to do is stand there with his fingers in his ears." She pursed her lips and frowned. "I wish you wouldn't go. That damned coaster . . ."

"Will you stop worrying? Nothing's going to happen. Everything's been tested a hundred times and there are guards everywhere. We've been running the coaster all day with no problem. St. James told me that Ernie Krevek is watching a baseball game tonight. So relax, please. I'll see you later."

He squeezed her hand and walked across the platform toward the train. She watched him go with an unhappy look on her face.

Wilson St. James stepped to the lectern, turned on the microphone, adjusted his glasses, and smoothed the sheet of paper with the names of the people he wanted to introduce. "Testing," he said. His voice boomed around the park. He scanned the sea of faces for the trim, compact figure of loan officer Delareaux but couldn't spot her. He wished now he had asked her to have a drink later. Sometimes there's just no substitute for a woman when you just want to relax and talk. With another man there was often a competitive tension that could get awfully tiring.

The crowd was still buzzing after the flash and shock of the aerial bombs. "Ladies and gentlemen, can I have your attention?" For some reason, the game of bingo came into his mind. Why would anyone want to play bingo on the Fourth of July instead of watching fireworks? "There are a few people up here on the platform I want you to meet, people who have contributed a lot over the last twelve months to get us to this happy moment." He leaned close to the microphone and said, "I'd like you to meet Jeremy Allbright of

Speedtech, whose company designed and built the original Thrill as well as the improved version I know you are going to love. Give him a big Wildcat Mountain welcome!''

Why, he couldn't help wondering as he yielded the microphone to Jeremy, would a church even *schedule* a bingo game on the Fourth of July?

CHAPTER NINETEEN

After leaving the house, Claudia Krevek drove south, keeping the surveillance van in her rearview mirror. When it was out of sight, she turned left and made her way through wooded hillside streets to Highway 85.

She shook her head at the shallowness of men. With the exception of her husband, men were so easily manipulated it was laughable. Usually, all it took was to exploit one of their two main weaknesses, their lust or their assumption that women were helpless. Somebody was vandalizing the park? Somebody was a threat to the roller coaster? Naturally it had to be a man. Keep your eyes open for a man, watch out for a man, that's what they were saying to themselves, Allbright and Ott and St. James and the rest. Watch Krevek, he had a grievance, he was dangerous. Forget the wife; she's just a woman. Because the men who were trying to destroy Ernest Krevek thought like that they were easy pickings and would themselves be destroyed.

She reached the interchange with Interstate 280 and took the northbound on-ramp. The trip to Wildcat Park via 280 to San Francisco, Highway 1 to the Golden Gate Bridge, and 101 to the Highway 37 turnoff, would take no more than an hour and a half, even with traffic congestion near the park. It was twenty minutes to seven; she would get there in plenty of time.

No doubt remained in her mind that she had the nerve and the will to carry out the plan. Confronting Leon Van Zant was a test she had set herself, and she passed it without a problem. It was so easy, in fact, she felt like tracking down her father and getting even with him, too. Her whore of a mother wasn't worth trying to find, but her father—she would enjoy putting the same look of terror on his face that she had put on Leon's.

Claudia was proud of how unwavering she had been when she faced down Leon the previous Friday. She leveled the shotgun and pulled the trigger without hesitation. Far from feeling regrets or guilt, watching him slump into a pool of his own blood gave her a shiver of icy pleasure. One less cockroach in the world, she remembered thinking. True, she was motivated by a special hatred for the man, but she was sure she could take out anyone her husband hated with the same sense of accomplishment. If Ernest was against them so was she.

Ernest Krevek was a great man, a genius, and a man with more honesty and honor than she ever thought possible in a human being. She owed everything she was, everything she had, her very life, to him. Ridding the world of whatever gave him pain amounted to little compared with what he had done for her.

She should have killed Leon years earlier, she scolded herself, instead of letting the rape fester in her mind like an infected wound. She grimaced at the memory of waking up in a daze in the back of his panel truck, spread-eagled on her back on a tattered mattress with him on top of her and thrusting into her and grunting like a pig. If she could have cleared her mind and made her muscles obey, she would have killed him that night, but she kept drifting in and out of consciousness. In the morning she was on the floor of her room without knowing how she got there. For several days she was sick to her stomach and disoriented and unable to go to work. She couldn't even walk to the bathroom from the bed without keeping one hand on the wall for balance. The bastard had drugged her, put something in her bottle of beer when she wasn't looking. What a pleasure it was, even after so many years, to blow Leon Van Zant off the face of the earth.

It was a clear, cloudless evening. To the east and south, the brown hills that enclosed the bay seemed closer than they really were. Near Palo Alto, traffic began to thin out; Claudia moved to the fast lane and increased her speed, alert for any signs of the Highway Patrol. A wave of well-being came over her. She had a difficult and dangerous mission to carry out, but she was thoroughly prepared and knew she would perform well. No more waiting, no more worrying! The world was a lousy place, all things considered; in a few hours it would be a little bit better.

She was exhilarated by a sense of power and control, and she tightened her grip on the wheel until the cords stood out in her wrists and forearms. Barring the unexpected—and she had tried to anticipate every possible problem—she would be back home well before midnight. Ernest would be asleep on the sofa, unaware that Thrill existed only as a perfect memory and that the people he hated most were gone. She pictured herself turning off the television and leading her half-awake husband to bed. He probably wouldn't even realize that she had been out of the house. Her reward would come in the morning, watching him with secret pleasure at breakfast. How astonished he would be when he saw the black headlines in the Mercury News!

Still vivid in her memory was the first time she met him. She was Claudia Katalsky then, thirty-five years old, tall and sinewy, and with a chip on her shoulder a mile wide. She had been out of work for a month, having lost two jobs—one as a mechanic, the other as a welder—for the same reason: refusing to use her mouth on her foremen, knocking them out, in fact, with pop bottles to the side of the head when they tried to force her to her knees. What was it with men, anyway? What made them think just because a woman was homely and talked dirty and wanted a raise she would be willing to haul their ashes? Ernest didn't think she was homely. He told her she had beautiful skin and eyes. She wasn't skinny, she was elegant and statuesque. There were women who were starving themselves, he told her that first night, and making themselves throw up trying to be as skinny as she was. He was skinny himself, he said, and proud of it.

It was at the Veteran's Memorial Hall in Petaluma during the annual arm-wrestling tournament. Claudia was competing in the women's "unlimited" division, which meant most of her opponents outweighed her by fifty pounds and more. She made it to the finals without much trouble, but to win the hundred-dollar first prize she would have to defeat a huge, baby-faced woman from Texas called Big Bertha, whose arms were as thick as fireplugs. She looked flabby, though, Claudia thought as she paced back and forth and dusted rosin on her hands. Her own arms, thanks to years of work on weights and squeezing rubber balls, didn't look like arms at all, but rather like bundles of cables. She could beat any man she ever met, so she ought to be able to beat a tub of lard who got winded climbing the steps to the stage.

"Good luck, honey," Big Bertha said with a dimpled grin as the referee positioned their elbows and made sure their hand grips were fair. One of her hustles was pretending to be a nice person to arouse sympathy in her opponents. Claudia had watched her with contempt in the preliminary rounds encouraging the other women, laughing at their stupid jokes at the bar, flirting with their lame-brained boyfriends. No nice person was going to beat Claudia Katalsky.

"Good luck, honey," Bertha said again.

Claudia glared at her. "Don't pull that shit on me," she hissed. "I know what you're doing."

A hurt look came over Bertha's face. "What?"

"Besides, you're too fat to win."

Claudia anticipated the referee's start signal perfectly and got an initial advantage, pushing her hand forward an inch or two off vertical. Bertha struggled hard to turn the tide, wrapping one massive leg around the corner of the table and throwing her shoulders and back into the effort. The twisted look on her face began to show panic when she realized that Claudia's forearm was anchored in place like a steel post and could not be moved.

There were several hundred people in the auditorium who loved the contrast between the two women: one ramrod straight and motionless, the other as round as a bean-bag chair. Bertha lunged and twisted, and, near the end, bared her teeth and made cries like some sort of tropical bird. Her face got so red it looked as though she were going to burst a blood vessel.

As the two hands and forearms, locked together and trembling, began to bend toward the tabletop, the crowd was on its feet and roaring. Claudia managed to move her hand on top of Bertha's, increasing the advantage in leverage she already enjoyed because of her greater height. With a final hunching of her shoulder, she pressed home the victory. When Bertha's knuckles touched the table, the referee shot his hands to the side signaling the end of the match and shouted, "Katalsky!"

Bertha burst into tears and ran for consolation to her friends, a group of overweight Texans in cowboy boots and idiotic ten-gallon hats.

Claudia had no personal cheering section. She circled the stage and thrust her fists defiantly in the air, then headed for the bar. Her intention was to have a drink, win some money from any drunks

147

who were dumb enough to challenge her, pick up her winner's check, and go home to bed. She was exhausted.

That's when Ernest entered her life and changed her forever. She chug-a-lugged a bottle of Coors, and when she slammed the bottle down on the bar, she found herself looking at the narrow, craggy face of a gray-haired man with the most penetrating eyes she had ever seen. He congratulated her and told her he had won four hundred dollars on her final match, which he wanted to split. He told her to hold out her hand. While she watched unbelievingly, he counted out ten twenty-dollar bills. Her first reaction was to dismiss him as a jerk for giving up half his winnings for no reason, but she needed the money . . . and besides, there was such an air of intelligence and superiority about him that she knew it would be useless to argue. She looked at him and couldn't speak. His eyes were so intense that she felt he could read her every thought. She had the feeling that he could hypnotize her even if she resisted.

Claudia folded the bills and tucked them into the pocket of her sweat pants, glad to have an excuse to look away.

"It's not the money," the man said. "Money is only symbolic. The pleasure comes from proving the other person wrong and making him feel bad. Whoever said 'Money won is twice as sweet as money earned' knew something about human nature. May I shake your hand and introduce myself? Take it easy now . . . you're a lot younger than I am, and in better shape."

He was working for a few days at Wildcat Mountain, Ernest Krevek told her, helping to install and test several new rides made by his company. He had come to the arm-wrestling competition as a lark with several other engineers. Arrogant young puppies, he called them. "I enjoyed humiliating them."

They sat in a booth and talked for hours. Claudia recalled very little of her side of the conversation, but his words stayed in her mind as if they had been recorded on tape. She was particularly struck by his reasons for betting on her to win despite Big Bertha's size and bulk. "It was the hate that showed in your eyes," he said as she stared at him agape. "You were a blue flame of hate, and your opponent was two scoops of vanilla. I don't know what you said to her when you took your positions, but your lip was curled and there was contempt on your face. It was wonderful to see; it

148

made the hair stand up on my neck. Confidence leaked out of Bertha like gas out of a blimp. That's when I put my money down."

He went on to tell her that whether she knew it or not, she was making use of one of life's great forces, the power of hate. Hate was the key factor in most great historical movements, he said, and when a person learned to control and focus the hate within, seemingly impossible feats could be accomplished. In competitions of all kinds, from war to arm wrestling, the side with the most hate had a big advantage, provided, of course, that it was kept aimed at the opposition and channeled into training and discipline and iron will. Every winner has the killer instinct, which is based on hate. Nice guys finish last.

The words hit Claudia Katalsky like thunderbolts. She hated most people, she admitted to him, or at least disliked and mistrusted them, but she let it get her into trouble. She didn't know how to check her emotions. She was always getting kicked out of rooming houses and losing jobs. The secret, Ernest told her, was in learning how to *act* nice, how to act normal when it suited your purpose. Some people hid their hatred and their anger without conscious effort; others, like himself and probably Claudia Katalsky, had to learn how to do it the way they might learn how to tap dance or ride a bicycle.

They met for drinks the next night, and the next, and the next, and by the end of the week, when it was time for Ernest to leave for Pennsylvania and another installation job, they knew that they were soul mates. He was an educated man and an intellectual while she was a high-school dropout who had run away from home at age fifteen, who had twice been hooked on drugs and twice tried to commit suicide, and yet they had the same view of the world.

On the last night, when they were parked in his car in front of her rooming house, Claudia touched him in a way that showed she was willing to do anything he wanted. He pushed her hand away gently and said it was too soon for sex. He laughed and said, "Maybe we should never sleep together. With our sharp elbows and knees? We'd have to get tetanus shots the next morning because of the puncture wounds."

Ernest used his influence to get her a job in Wildcat Mountain's mechanical repair shop. Claudia worked hard at the job, put in extra hours without pay, and tried her best to get along with her fellow machinists and mechanics, which wasn't easy because some of them were incredibly stupid. The foreman liked her, though. He admired her shop skills and he got a kick out of her acid tongue and hard-boiled personality.

When Ernest was back from his travels, he called her every night at ten o'clock from his home in Los Gallinas, in the hills west of San Jose. They began to refer to themselves as "two against the world." For the first time in her life, she enjoyed waking up in the morning. Then Leon Van Zant came along and offered to give her a ride home when her car wouldn't start.

The days following her rape were the worst of her life. She was disgusted with herself for assuming that Leon was just a harmless dope who would be good for a few free drinks. She was disgusted with herself for lacking the nerve to kill him at the first opportunity. What rape? he asked when she first confronted him. He said she should thank him for taking her home after she drank too much and passed out. As for the sex, he had the gall to say with a smirk on his face and a cigar in his mouth that she had led him on and had enjoyed every minute.

Finally, she was disgusted with herself for thinking that complaining to her boss would do any good. She told him that Leon spiked her drink and raped her and was a danger to every woman at the · park and should be fired. Claudia was the one who got fired.

She was a hateful person, all right, only then the hatred was directed at herself. For two days she stayed in her room smoking and drinking beer and wondering if she should put herself out of her misery. Without a job she would run out of money and be evicted and end up where she started at age fifteen, on the streets. She couldn't tell Ernest what happened because it made her look stupid and weak. The truth might make him so mad he would kill Leon himself and end up in the state pen, where he would be no good to her or anybody else. It would have to be her secret, and when the time was right it would be her revenge.

At ten o'clock on a rainy night in January, Claudia Katalsky, without a clear idea of what she was going to do, walked away from a room littered with cigarette butts, food cartons, and overflowing wastebaskets. She drove to Los Gallinas as if drawn by a magnet and rang Ernest Krevek's doorbell. When he answered, she announced that she wanted to be with him, and for some reason started

150

to cry. She hadn't cried since childhood. She turned away in embarrassment and kicked a flowerpot into the yard.

Ernest took her by the arm and drew her inside the house. They made love in the entryway.

CHAPTER TWENTY

It started as a game, the sabotaging of Thrill. In the evenings, when many families let their minds rot while watching sitcoms on television, Ernest and Claudia Krevek exercised their imaginations by thinking up ways to rid the world of people they didn't like.

Punks who play their ghetto-blasters too loud? Force them to listen to Lawrence Welk until they take their own lives. Liberals who want to give money to welfare loafers? Put lethal doses of laxatives in white wine and bean sprouts. Religious fanatics? Print Bibles in toxic ink. The more outrageous the suggestions the more fun they had, and sometimes they laughed so hard they could hardly speak.

They also enjoyed thinking up appropriate punishments for individuals. When a serial rapist in San Jose was finally caught, the Kreveks decided that he should be hung, not by his neck but by his testicles. A drunk driver who killed three people in a car smash-up should be split apart by the Jaws of Life. Jeremy Allbright, architect of the new Thrill, deserved something special. Ernest agreed that Claudia's suggestion was better than any of his own: put the Speedtech owner on a roller coaster so slow that by the time it completed its run he would be dead of starvation. The idea sent Ernest into gales of all-consuming laughter; he rocked back and forth in his chair, clapping and nodding his head, finally managing to say that Allbright would look better anyway if he lost some weight.

"Hoo, boy," he said, calming down. "You know, sweetheart, most people wouldn't find this game funny."

"Screw most people," Claudia said, and they both laughed again.

When the reconstruction of Thrill began and Ernest's position at Speedtech worsened, the game became more and more serious. They didn't laugh as much when they dreamed up ways of getting even with Allbright and St. James and the companies they owned. Claudia wasn't sure whether or not her husband was kidding or giving her instructions.

"You know what would drive them crazy?" he asked one night. "Petty vandalism. Graffiti. Thievery. Something new every week. It would show that the coaster is vulnerable and that they can't protect it."

Claudia looked at him closely. "You mean somebody should hide in the park when it closes and then do stuff in the middle of the night?"

"Nobody would have to hide. There's very little security. There are holes in the fence on the bay side that kids use. Somebody could park on the highway and hike across the field. Sneak in, mess things up, and sneak out again. Easy."

"Mess things up? Like what?"

"Cross wires, throw switches, splash paint, that sort of thing."

The following night he got more specific. He spread a map of the park on the dining-room table and pointed at the places where there were breaches in the fence. On engineering drawings of the coaster, he showed her the walkways that snaked through the substructure. "Once inside," he said, "a person could go all over without being seen and create a lot of mischief."

He wants me to do it, Claudia began to understand, do it and not tell him about it. He must feel he's too old himself, not strong enough, not fast enough on his feet. He hated to drive at night because of his poor eyesight. It was typical of him, she thought, not to order her to do anything, certainly not anything risky. It was his style to lay out the facts and let her make her own decision.

One night after he was asleep, she drove to the park. She walked across the field as he had suggested and crossed the parking lot to the south end of the park. At a spot he had indicated on the map, the rise and fall of the tide had eroded so much earth that a section of the fence stretched across a shallow ditch, a post and its concrete base dangling in midair. It was easy to squeeze underneath. She found her way to the launching platform and spray-painted the floor with profanity, upended a trash can, and stole some tools.

A few days later, Claudia fished for better information. "Ernest," she said, "what if somebody did get into the park after hours and wanted to really foul up the controls. What switches or buttons should be pushed?"

He led her into his den, opened a file drawer, and took out a drawing of the computer-guided electrical system Speedtech was installing for the new Thrill. He explained it to her and showed her what a well-trained industrial saboteur would do.

One night he came home with a smile on his face and told her that the talk of the office was that a vandal had screwed up the coaster's control panel. He acted as if it was merely an amazing coincidence. Didn't he realize she was the culprit? She couldn't tell for sure. As the weeks went by, he never tipped his hand. He seemed to prefer the illusion that all he had to do was mention possibilities, then learn a few days later that they had become realities. In a small way, it was like being God.

"Guess what the fools have done now," Ernest said one night after dinner. "You know the vandalism that's been going on up at Wildcat? They've put up a new fence to try and stop it! Must have cost them ten thousand dollars, at least. They're even going to add electricity!" He scoffed and made a spitting sound. "They think the coaster's safe now."

Claudia looked at him for a moment. "Is it?"

"Hells bells, no! If somebody was serious and didn't mind doing a little work, he could get in by crossing over from the billboards." Into his den they went for another look at the park plans. "See the way the billboards are oriented? The walkway between them is aimed right at what they call the crow's nest. The railing and the walkway are at the same elevation and the gap is only twelve feet."

"So?"

"So a rolling gangplank could be built. Nothing fancy, two-by-fours on skateboard wheels with a couple dozen bricks as a counterweight. It would be duck soup to cantilever that baby across the gap until the far end was on the railing." He went on to tell her about the electric winches between the signs that painters used to haul supplies and about the ladder that was surrounded by a locked cage at the bottom. "Cut off the padlock and put on your own, that's all you'd have to do. Not that anybody would go to the trouble. I'm just saying it could be done." He clapped his hands and said, "It's warm tonight. Let's go downtown for ice cream."

It was the same with his idea for the runaway train. He said it could be done, she asked how, he showed her on the computer in his den. "The way the program is written," he said, tapping a fin-

154

gernail on the screen, "it would be easy to make it launch a train every hundred trips, whatever number you wanted, or every so many days. Take three days, for example. Here's how the code would have to be changed . . ." She watched his fingers fly across the keyboard.

Two weeks later, Ernest burst through the front door with a look of amazement on his face. "You'll never believe what happened," he said, throwing his hat and his briefcase on a chair. "A young engineer from Chicago has been brought in to rubber stamp the plans. He was in my office today picking my brains and you know what he told me? I almost fainted. He and Leon were walking the line the other night when a train got loose! They had to jump! This McKenzie, the engineer, landed in the duck pond! My God, you could have knocked me over with a fender! It was just like we were talking about the other night, remember? About how to make the computer launch trains on its own?"

Claudia smiled and nodded. "I remember." Ernest gave no indication that he suspected her of making it happen. He went on about wonders never ceasing and about how his prayers were being answered. It's okay, Claudia thought. He doesn't want the responsibility for my actions. He wants to play it as a game. Okay. She would answer his prayers. He didn't believe in God, certainly not in a benevolent God who answered prayers, but when she was through he would have to wonder.

She met the engineer from Chicago the day Ernest was ejected from his office. A polite do-gooder with a superior air who wanted to help, the kind of slippery piss-ant who smiled pleasantly while planning to stick a knife in your back. It was because of the threats Ernest made in front of him that forced her to have her husband watched. Otherwise, he'd be the first person suspected when the coaster was destroyed and a trainload of bigshots killed. She didn't want Ernest subjected to questioning and harassment by the cops, and she didn't want cops snooping around the house and garage where they might find something to incriminate her. With Ernest under surveillance and nobody suspecting her of anything, they were both safe. The forces of law and order would have to look elsewhere for their "madman." How could anyone do such a thing? the newspapers would ask. Everybody was so stupid.

Driving to the park, Claudia thought about McKenzie and how easy he was to manipulate when she visited him at his hotel the

155

previous morning. She hated people like him, with their nice manners and politeness and their mouths full of straight, even teeth that they obviously had spent thousands and thousands of dollars on. You can't trust people like that. You can't tell where they stand on anything or what they really think. She knew by the way he looked at her that he thought he was superior to her and thought she was strange. That's why he was so easy to fool. Ernest hated him, too, because he pretended that he had an open mind and said he would see what he could do to block the reopening when all along he intended to support Allbright and St. James. McKenzie was like a snake in the grass, a well-fed snake that seemed harmless but that would strike the second you lowered your guard. If he survived the crash of the coaster, Claudia hoped she would get a clear shot at him with the rifle.

"Hey, lady, what the hell are you doing?"

It was a beefy security guard with a red face and a big gut and tufts of hair sticking out from under his rent-a-cop cap. Claudia was standing beneath the billboards at the corner of the parking lot unlocking the cage at the bottom of the ladder.

She looked at him. No doubt he was one of the extra guards Ernest said the park had hired. His fly was open. He was probably taking a piss between two cars, which is why she hadn't noticed him. All the parking places in that corner of the lot had been taken hours earlier. She glanced around over the tops of the cars. Nobody was within a hundred yards.

"I said, what the hell are you doing?"

He came closer. There was a plastic name tag on his shirt pocket: B. Slatton.

"I'm plain clothes." Claudia said.

"You're what?"

"Plain clothes. Max sent me to check the billboards."

"Max?"

"Max Costello. Are you Slatton? I think Max gave me the wrong key. I'll try the other one." She shrugged off her backpack, dropped to one knee, and unzipped the top pocket. Her hand slipped inside and her fingers closed around the revolver.

"Max never mentioned anything to me. What's your name?" He took the radio from his belt.

156

She stood up and faced him. "Claudia Krevek. Pleased to meet you." She fired twice at the center of his chest. When he was down, she straddled him, aimed, and put an insurance bullet in his head.

She gathered B. Slatton's collar into her hands, dragged him off the asphalt, and rolled him into the reeds at the water's edge.

A band was playing in the distance. Three aerial bombs went off high in the sky. She had to hurry. The festivities were about to begin.

CHAPTER TWENTY-ONE

Jack took a seat in the third car from the front. He scanned the rows of people watching from the sidewalk and spotted Ruby. Pointing to the empty seat beside him, he shouted to her that there was still time to change her mind. "Come on, Ruby, don't be chicken!"

She couldn't hear him over the buzz of the crowd and the whirr and rush of nearby rides. Adding to the din was Wilson St. James, who was still orating over the public address system, and the band, which seemed intent on drowning him out. Ruby waved and mouthed the words "No thanks."

Jack shrugged and turned to watch people boarding behind him. Two cars back was the crazy guy whose hobby was riding roller coasters—Eldon Carver—and whose jacket was covered with souvenir patches from amusement parks all over the country. The nervous-looking woman he was helping to her seat was probably his wife. Carver waved to nonexistent fans and cameramen as if his every move was being recorded for posterity.

In the car behind Jack was Carl Ott and a woman who wrote for one of the local papers. Jack called to Carl, "Take that mike away from Wilson, will you? Let's get this contraption rolling."

"You're a changed man, McKenzie," Ott laughed. "A week ago you would have been back at the hotel hiding under the bed."

It was true, Jack admitted to himself, he had changed. He was on a roller coaster and looking forward to the ride! It seemed like only yesterday that he had marched into St. James's office and told him that he would not ride the coaster under any conditions. Jack felt no nervousness or fear at all. He leaned back in his seat and relaxed. In two or three minutes, the train would be back at the platform and he would be helping passengers to their feet the way the fat man had helped him after his ride on the Loop of Doom.

A searchlight mounted on the back of a truck came on and sent a column of light upward. There was no cloud cover, so the beam seemed to disappear into space.

In the car in front of Jack was Jeremy Allbright and a man named Ora C. Morningstar, who earlier had given Jack a business card that identified him as "Poet Laureate of Marin County." Morningstar had a gray ponytail and a ring in his ear and was telling Allbright how he avoided nausea. "It's the wrist band," he said, holding up his left arm. "The elastic presses a plastic button against an acupressure point called the Nei-kuan. Ever notice that you never see a carsick Chinese person?"

"I use Demoral myself," Allbright said.

A couple wearing "Independent Television Productions" jackets made a last-minute check of a minicam affixed to the front of the lead car. With luck, they'd have some good footage for the eleven-o'clock news. They climbed in and sat down and began interviewing each other with tape recorders.

Jack heard the woman behind him tell Carl Ott what the band was playing. According to her, they just finished "Ride the Train" by Alabama and were now doing "What a Feeling," the theme music from *Flashdance*.

Ruby, barely visible now in the growing crowd of onlookers, was talking into her radio. A few seconds later, three rockets climbed into the sky on tails of red sparks and exploded with soft pops; glittering points of yellow and blue cascaded downward. The operator of the searchlight played his beam on the distant clouds of smoke.

St. James hurried by. Jack called to him to take the seat he was saving but couldn't make himself heard. The park owner climbed into one of the last cars on the train.

Uniformed attendants moved down both sides of the train lowering the shoulder restraints, making sure seat belts were fastened and telling everybody to keep their arms inside the cars. One of them, Clara Silva, took her place in the control booth. Jack could hear her check with Tim, the lad who was posted in the crow's nest.

"Okay, Tim? We're ready to go."

Clara turned on the platform loudspeaker. "Prepare for launch," she said. "Check your seat belts. Hang on to your glasses and toupees. Say your prayers." She counted backward from ten.

The train creaked and began to roll.

Ruby climbed into her truck and drove slowly toward the south end of the ride. The service road was full of spectators, who parted to let her by. She replayed in her mind what Jack had said about a man keeping an eye on old man Krevek. He was as harmless as a scarecrow, in her opinion. Not only was he too old to be a serious threat, he had sense of humor, as black and as negative as it was. She always saw a twinkle in his eye when he spouted his outrageous opinions. In Ruby's experience, you didn't have to worry too much about people with senses of humor. It was the humorless ones who were scary, people like Krevek's wife—now there was a person who should be watched. Ruby could easily imagine the narrow-eyed, tight-lipped Mrs. Krevek mailing bombs to everybody she didn't like.

Ruby's own sense of humor, she often felt, had to be held in check. She had a hard time taking anything seriously, which turned some people off . . . like the psychiatrist she dated for a while. Whenever he tried to say something profound or display his erudition, she cut him down with a wisecrack. Not an attractive trait. On their last evening together, he made the observation that she was a classic example of a person who used humor as "a defense against reality." "Good," she remembered replying, "everybody needs *some* defense."

Ruby had advanced about a hundred yards when she stopped the truck. There was no room to turn around and there were too many people milling about to shift into reverse, so she got out and jogged back to the platform. The train was already climbing the first hill. She saw Mike Sand, one of the security guards, standing near the tracks holding a phone.

"Mike, is Max around?"

"He's in his office. Want to talk to him?" He pushed a button and handed her the phone.

"Max, this is Ruby. McKenzie told me you had a man watching Ernie Krevek at his home."

"Yeah, so?"

"Is he watching the wife, too?"

"Should he be?"

"In my opinion, yes. If anybody is going to try something, it's the wife, not old Ernie."

"I'll check when I get a chance. Pretty busy right now, if you don't mind."

"Just a thought. Sorry to bother you."

Claudia Krevek opened the door at the end of the billboard passageway and watched the young man on the observation platform. He was at the railing at the far side, leaning on his elbows and facing away from her, looking down. She had nothing against him, so she let him live for a few more minutes.

She checked the rifle and the shotgun to make sure they were loaded and ready to fire. Extra ammunition was in her backpack along with the two hand grenades, the transmitter, and twenty feet of clothesline rope. She pulled on a ski mask and squared it on her face. Dropping to one knee, she pushed the gangplank until the far end was protruding a few feet through the doorway.

The crosshairs of the rifle's scope came to rest between the man's shoulders. Claudia hesitated. She didn't particularly want to shoot him in the back, but if she called to him and he turned around, the sight of a rifle aimed at him might make him do something stupid, like throw himself over the railing before she could get off a good shot. Because they were only twenty feet apart, she didn't want to see his face. Better to shoot him in the back while he was unsuspecting.

A woman's voice crackled over an intercom and the man moved to his right. Claudia had to aim again. "Okay, Tim?" the voice said. "We're ready to go. Don't forget to release the second train when the first one is clear."

"All clear," he answered. "Ready for action!"

No time left. The intruder squeezed off two quick shots. One bullet must have split the spinal cord, judging from the way the body folded and dropped.

Claudia shoved the gangplank across the gap and crossed over holding the rifle in one hand and the shotgun in the other to keep her balance. Once safely across, she bent down and grabbed a handful of blond hair and twisted the face to the front; the glassy eyes told her that he was dead.

She took the transmitter from the backpack and extended the telescoping aerial. She set it first to one frequency, then to another,

161

sending signals to the battery-powered servo-mechanisms she had implanted on previous trips, disabling the coaster's magnetic brakes as well as the "fail-safe" backups.

Quickly, she tied one end of the rope to the gangplank and one end to the railing. She gave the gangplank a sharp shove and watched it roll almost completely out of sight between the signs. Now there was less chance that anybody would see it and sound an alarm. When she was ready to make her escape, a tug on the rope would bring it back. It was a precaution she hadn't bothered taking when security was lax.

Everything was working so smoothly it seemed preordained. She could imagine it all in her mind. The coaster would hurtle into the tunnel just below her at ten times its planned speed, and instead of stopping for a movie it would burst through the far end. Ernest had made some rough calculations but wasn't sure if the train would leave the tracks completely and fall to the ground, or simply become a mass of dangling wreckage half in and half out of the tunnel. "It's the kind of question," he told her, "that can only be answered by a field test."

The wreck would shatter forever Speedtech's reputation for engineering competence. And if Allbright and St. James and Ott and all the others who had ruined a great design and ended her husband's career in disgrace somehow survived the crashes, Claudia would finish them off with the rifle. A sniper in the crow's nest! How was that possible! How did a sniper penetrate the security shield? Wildcat Mountain Amusement Park would never again be able to claim that it knew how to protect the safety of its customers and would be finished as a business. If the state didn't shut it down, the insurance companies would.

Three skyrockets rose from the water's edge. She watched them climb and explode several hundred feet overhead. Probably a signal to start the train. One preliminary task remained before the main event—arranging for the escape. Hers was not, after all, a suicide mission. She intended to be with her husband to enjoy the aftermath of what was sure to be called one of the most horrifying disasters in American history. Her lips tightened in a thin smile. It couldn't happen to a more deserving bunch of people.

Claudia set the transmitter for a third frequency and set it on the floor next to her backpack. When the time came, a flick of the on-off switch would ignite the incendiary caps she had taped to wooden columns at ground level. The fresh paint and the gasoline-soaked rags she had hidden on cross-beams would feed the flames and send up plenty of smoke. When the smoke was thick enough, she'd pull the gangplank back into position and disappear into the night.

Everyone would assume that the "madman" had perished in the flames. There would be no reason for cops to come calling at the Krevek residence.

She sat down on a bench. The rifle was cradled in her lap and the shotgun was leaning against the rail. She looked down the track and waited. It was almost too easy! She was so far ahead of her adversaries it was pathetic!

A high-altitude fireworks display began in earnest, illuminating the hills and valleys of Thrill as if by lightning flashes.

The crowd cheered and waved. The band struck up the Air Force Hymn and several people on the train sang the words:

" 'Off we go, into the wild blue yonder . . .' "

The Anvil Chorus would be more appropriate, Jack thought, synchronized with the clank-clank of the lifting dogs as the train climbed the hill. Tilted onto his back, Jack's field of vision consisted of the car in front of him and a dark sky punctuated with bombs, rocket trails, and star bursts. Ruby's Uncle Frank knew how to put on a show.

Higher, higher, higher, until it seemed as though the train was the highest thing in the world. The train leveled off and rumbled toward the brink so slowly that the passengers had plenty of time to watch their lives pass before their eyes. Good old Earnest Krevek, Jack thought: he knew how to put on a show, too. The anticipation he felt as the train crept toward the precipice was almost palpable and was a tribute to the old designer's sense of timing and understanding of the psychology of fear. Already, women were screaming and men were groaning and nothing had happened yet except the approach of the inevitable.

" 'Our Father,' " somebody intoned to nervous laughter, " 'which art in Heaven . . .' "

"Hang on," Jack shouted, "the first step is a big one!"

The lead car tilted sharply downward and almost out of sight, then the second one, then Jack's. One after the other the cars hit the

163

downslope and the speed quickly increased. The first time Jack had ridden Thrill, he closed his eyes and hugged the shoulder restraints as hard as he could; this time he kept his eyes open and absorbed the full visual and visceral effects of falling off a building. He was surrounded by sustained screaming and yelling and a rush of wind that grew in seconds to hurricane force.

Downward g-forces pressed him to his chair when the train hit the bottom, then came the turns and rises and falls that made him feel like a rag doll being shaken by an angry child. In front of him, the Poet Laureate of Marin County was retching violently; Jack could see Allbright's arm raised in defense. So much for acupressure.

Knowing in advance which way the train was going to twist was a big help. It was almost like skiing, Jack thought, the way he leaned and crouched and stiffened and relaxed a split-second in advance of every change in direction. Just before the train hurtled into the magnetic brakes, Jack straightened his legs to resist the force that would throw him forward. The first time, he suffered a small bruise from the way a calculator in his shirt pocket had been driven against his chest. He tensed his muscles and waited for the magnetic fields to grip the train ... but nothing happened. If anything, the train speeded up.

Jack's muscles stiffened. Had he misjudged the location? Before he could orient himself, the train hit Banshee Curve at such a tremendous speed that the centrifugal force almost made him black out. Jack wrapped his arms around the shoulder restraints and hoped the train would fail in its efforts to wrench itself free of the track ... it was leaping and turning and kicking like a rodeo bull trying to throw its rider. Something was horribly wrong, and a quick glance at Ott's face behind him confirmed it. Ott's eyes were round with fear, and he was shaking his head from side to side in disbelief.

The screams of the passengers became shriller and higher and so did the screams of the wheels.

Jack tried to think, but it was like trying to think inside a car that was rolling down a mountainside. He could feel his cheeks bulging one way and another from the horizontal g-forces as the coaster hit one vicious curve after another, and he could see specks of spittle being thrown from his mouth. There were more brakes just before the final tunnel, but even if they were working the train would hit the end with devastating force ... and if they *weren't* working, Jesus, the speed would ... His mind resisted trying to imagine what would happen, but he knew it would be a miracle if anybody survived. The tracks weren't even aligned at that point: the tracks at the end of the tunnel were elevated two feet so they could be dropped as part of the "riskless" feature.

Riskless? He was headed for certain death and so was everybody else. The train could run right off the tracks at the end of the tunnel ... if it didn't wreck itself before then. Jack fought off the impulse to give in to blind terror and tried to clear his mind.

How could the brakes fail and the backup systems, too? Was there some way to stop the train or at least slow it down? He unbuckled his seat belt and tried to slide sideways into the empty seat beside him, then hesitated. Without the shoulder restraints he might be thrown to his death like Sonnevold's daughter. No, that had happened on Lurch, and they were already past that; there were no more changes of direction as severe.

Jack's mind raced. He had no more than thirty seconds to do something? But what? An idea came to him born of desperation, and he resumed the struggle to free himself. He extended his right arm and leg into the space beside him and pushed against the opposite side of the car with his left arm and leg; slowly he managed to squeeze his torso free, a maneuver that would have been impossible without an empty seat to work toward.

He hooked his left arm around the shoulder restraint to keep himself from being thrown from the car and slipped his right arm out of the sleeve of his suit coat. By changing his grip, he got his other arm out of his coat as well. He straightened his legs to wedge himself securely in position and waited for his chance. In ten seconds the train would hit a straight section of track, drop into a trough, then climb a final hill below the crow's nest. At the trough, he decided, that's when he would act. The g-force there would be downward, holding him inside the car.

Carl Ott's face was contorted and deathly white. Either he had fainted or was about to faint. When he saw Jack getting a grip on the collar of his coat, he nodded vigorously, as if to say "Yes! Yes! It's worth a try ..."

CHAPTER TWENTY-TWO

Nicholas "Shorty" Stevens was in no position to enjoy the fireworks. Among the dozen security guards hired for the night, he drew the worst assignment: patrolling under the roller coaster. He stayed on the plank walkway and tried not to step on the muddy ground, which was littered with fast-food debris, newspapers, the remains of a dead fish, and a rusted bicycle. He cast his flashlight beam here and there, watching out for he wasn't sure what. The explosions and starbursts overhead sent eerie flashes of light through the rows of white columns, and with each flash shadows seemed to spring at him. It was creepy down there! The park should charge admission, he thought, and call it The Forest of Horrors or some such.

A particularly loud aerial bomb made him flinch and reminded him of the Korean war and the nights he spent looking upward through trees while fighter planes were blown out of the sky. Well, he never actually saw a plane blown out of the sky, but that's what he told people. He saw plenty of tracer bullets and antiaircraft fire, though.

He stopped and sniffed, then sniffed again. He raised his radio. "Max, can you hear me? Come in Max Costello. Stevens calling. Over."

"I hear you, Shorty."

"I smell gasoline. Are roller coasters powered by gasoline engines? Over."

"Coasters don't have engines, Shorty. You haul 'em to the top and they coast to the bottom. That's why they're called coasters. Over."

"I smell gasoline just the same."

"What's your location?"

"South end. The fireworks are like artillery. It's Korea all over again."

"The south end is all fresh paint. That's what you smell. Paint and paint thinner."

"Maybe. Over."

"Shorty, walk over to the fence under the billboards. Look for Bob Slatton. I can't raise him. Either the radio's busted or he's asleep in his car. Over."

"On my way."

"The first train is coming. Don't stand under it. People drop stuff."

"Yeah, I can see that. Over and out."

The train shot over the top of a crest so fast that Jack's legs rose into the air, then fell back. Next was a sequence of sharp bumps and jolts called The Potholes, which were designed to make the riders think they were losing the fillings in their teeth. Jack kept his left arm hooked around the shoulder restraint, locking it there by clamping his right hand onto his left wrist. He braced his body by pressing his shoes against the right side of the car. He closed his eyes and gritted his teeth as the train hit The Potholes at three times the safe speed.

The violent shaking was a hundred times worse than Jack imagined it would be, and when it was suddenly over, he was surprised that the train was still in one piece. Thank God for factors of safety . . . which his father always called factors of ignorance.

There was no time to think: in four seconds the train would plunge into the final valley and he would have to be ready. He took a breath and opened his eyes. Behind him, Carl Ott flashed the thumbs up sign, then crossed his fingers. When the train fell into the abyss, Ott screamed "Now!"

Jack brought his arm in an arc to the left, swinging his coat against the outside of the car, trying to catch it in the wheels. The coat bounced away harmlessly. He released his handhold and thrust his head and shoulders over the side of the car. He swung the coat again just as the train hit the bottom of the valley. Jack was slammed down on his seat and felt the coat snatched out of his grasp. Immediately there was high-pitched whine from under the train and a thumping sound; Jack was thrown against the front of the car as the train was hit by a powerful deceleration force on its way up the final hill.

167

The coat was caught up in the wheels, yes, and the train was slowing down, but it wasn't going to stop in time. Over the top of the crest it rushed, screaming in protest, across a short level stretch under the crow's nest, and into the tunnel. Jack had to fight against the force of deceleration to reach the back of his chair and wedge his body half behind the shoulder restraints.

As he expected, the magnetic brakes that were supposed to grip the train and feed it slowly into the tunnel at a speed of two miles an hour weren't working. The barriers at the end were designed to stop a train traveling at five times the design speed, or ten miles an hour. At twenty miles an hour it was no contest: the lead car smashed through the cross bars and hit a row of water-filled plastic energy absorbers so hard they exploded like depth charges. Jack saw the arms of the two passengers in the first car flailing helplessly as it jumped oddly upward, then dropped out of sight while the television camera attached to it flew forward like a missile; the car was wrenched loose from the train, and Jack could hear it crashing through the beams and braces on its way to the ground. The car with Allbright and Morningstar also jumped upward before dropping, but the linkage held and it didn't break free.

The train stopped with cruel suddenness and fell silent. The new lead car was tilted downward and angled toward the right, half off the end of the track and poised over a drop of fifty feet to the ground.

Jack climbed out of his car and checked Allbright and Morningstar, who were bloodied and unconscious. He released Ott and helped him to his feet. "You stay here," Jack said, "I'll get help . . ."

Eldon Carver was consoling his wife. "I'm sorry, honey, I didn't know it was going to be so rough." He looked up at Jack and said, "That was awesome! Super! I think I broke a rib!"

At that moment, images of the coaster's underpinnings appeared on the walls of the tunnel, and a recorded voice Jack had heard before came over the loudspeaker. "Please watch your step when exiting . . . Oh! Oh, my! This is awful!"

Jack ran to the end of the tunnel, found the electrical junction box, and cut the current to the audio-visual effect. It made the tunnel darker, but anything was better than watching films of a coaster falling apart.

There was a twenty-foot ladder leading up to the crow's nest, where there was an intercom line to the launch platform. "Tim!" he shouted. "Tim! What's going on? Are you all right?"

He started climbing. The people back at the loading platform would be wondering what happened, wondering why the train didn't come back. Hand over hand Jack climbed toward a sky full of fireworks.

"Tim!" he called as loudly as he could. "Get on the intercom and call for help! Tim! Are you up there?"

Five feet from the top, Jack saw a limp hand and arm emerge over the barrier. He stopped and stared. Timothy Lawlor's face came into view, followed by his other arm. The eyes were half closed and the mouth was slack. Was he on drugs, or what? Jack saw then that Tim was being lifted by someone in a ski mask, pushed all the way over and out. To avoid getting hit, Jack swung himself to one side; his shirt was raked by fingernails as the body fell past him to the track below.

Now the masked figure was aiming a rifle at him; Jack scrambled around to the opposite side of the ladder, under the platform and out of view, just as a bullet hit the rung next to his hands. He edged away from the ladder along a beam, bracing himself by hanging on to floor joists above his head. He didn't have to look down to know that he was seventy feet above the ground. If the gunman came down the ladder to get a better shot at him, he was a goner.

The next shots he heard were aimed at the train riders who were emerging unsteadily from the mouth of the tunnel.

"Look out!" Jack shouted at them. "Sniper! Sniper! Get back in the tunnel!"

A bullet came blasting through the floorboards in Jack's direction. He stopped shouting and changed his position. As long as he stayed away from the perimeter of the platform he was relatively safe, but if he tried to reach the ladder or one of the columns at the corners of the platform in an attempt to climb or slide to the ground, he would be an easy target.

For the moment he was stuck. All he could do was hope that he could maintain his balance and his strength. When he heard footsteps cross the floorboards above him, he scooted along the beam in the opposite direction.

He was too scared and too busy to remember that he was afraid of heights. Questions about the brakes, the crash, the so-called fail-safe systems, the gunman, tried to crowd into his mind, but he pushed them aside. He had all he could do to stay alive. Don't panic, he told himself, and don't look down. He looked up instead, at the blank bottom of the crow's nest's floor, and wondered if getting shot or falling to his death were his only options.

CHAPTER TWENTY-THREE

Shorty Stevens looked through the fence at the rows of cars in the parking lot. Max Costello had warned him that the fence was electrified, so he stayed well back from it. There was nothing to be seen but rows of cars and dimly lit lanes between them. No sign of any living thing. It was as quiet as a graveyard.

"Bob!" he hollered. "Bob Slatton!"

No answer. Where was the old son of a gun?

"Hey, Bob, Max wants to talk to you!"

Silence.

Well, I tried, Shorty thought as he turned away. He picked a path through the litter toward the innards of the substructure. No sense radioing to Max at the moment because the first train was approaching and making a hell of a racket. Man, that thing was *moving* . . .

Shorty looked up and watched the train swoop and swerve and rise and dip and listened to the screams and yells of passengers. It didn't sound to him like the crazy fools were having a good time. He shook his head. There was no explaining some tastes. Funny, though, that the train was going a lot faster than the practice runs he saw when he first came on duty. Didn't make sense that they'd run the loaded trains faster than the empty ones.

He stopped and directed his flashlight upward at the tunnel, which from his vantage point on the ground looked like two milk cartons laid end to end. Earlier he had seen how the train eased into it and stopped, how the whole enclosed section shuddered and pivoted downward until the far end was aligned with a lower set of tracks, after which the train rolled into view again and headed back to the north end. No engine, eh? You learn something every day . . . or night, as the case may be.

171

Here it comes! Jeez, it's one noisy bugger when it's full. Too fast! Way too fast! It'll never stop in time!

The train raced into the tunnel, followed by a tremendous crashing sound. The far end of the tunnel seemed to explode, and a large dark object fell fifty feet to the ground, taking out beams and braces as it went. Shorty found it with his flashlight beam—it was about the size of a roller coaster car and was painted yellow and green, the same as ... It *was* a roller coaster car! He ran toward it, stumbling, trying to keep his flashlight steady with one hand as he fumbled for his radio with the other.

Max Costello and Jose Gonzalez were at a table in the park security office facing a bank of closed-circuit television screens. Costello held a McLean burger in one hand and a cup of coffee in the other. He was frowning at monitor number three, which provided a view of the launching platform. The second train was loaded and waiting for clearance. The uniformed platform attendants were looking toward the south as if something had happened at the far end of the ride. Clara Silva in the control booth was scowling at the microphone that connected her to the crow's nest and shaking it as if it was dead.

"Something's funny, Jose," Max said, gesturing toward the monitor with the pizza. "Look at the way people are acting."

Gonzalez glanced at the screen and then at the wall clock above the monitors. "Ninety seconds since the first one left," he said. "They should be able to see it coming back by now."

Before they could react, a rush of words came over the loudspeaker: "A crash ... a crash ... a car is down, Oh God, two people ... they look bad ..."

It was Shorty Stevens speaking in a disjointed, high-pitched voice they had never heard before. Costello and Gonzalez jumped to their feet and stared at each other.

"Another car is dangling ... God Almighty ... need doctors, ambulances, ladders, oh Jesus, ladders at least fifty feet long ... need lights ... can't see ..."

Costello pointed at a telephone. "Red emergency ... get every agency in here. Tell the fire department we need ladders ..."

A string of incomprehensible sounds came over the loudspeaker, then cacophony and static as several people tried to talk at once.

It took Costello almost a minute to get control of the airwaves in

172

the face of incoming calls. "Will everybody please shut up? Shorty, keep talking . . . What's happening? What do you see? Over . . ."

Costello breathed a curse at the absence of a surveillance camera at the south end . . . but Tim Lawlor was in the crow's nest, so it was decided that a camera wasn't—

"Somebody just fell off the tower! Wait! I see . . . I see a guy in a ski mask! Up on top . . . he's got a rifle. My God, he's using it! God in heaven . . . I'm taking fire! He's shooting at my flashlight . . . Over and out!"

Costello grabbed the microphone that fed the park's public address system. Before ordering an evacuation of the park, he said to Gonzalez: "We need a chopper with a light, and we need sharpshooters . . ."

After relaying her suspicions about Claudia Krevek to Max, Ruby stood on the edge of the platform and watched the train rise and fall and twist and turn until it was out of sight. She decided to wait for the train to return, welcome Jack back to solid ground, compliment him on his bravery, and then be on her way to help Uncle Frank.

She waited . . . and she waited. With growing apprehension she noticed the puzzled looks on the faces of the ride operators. Was something wrong? Clara Silva shouted into her microphone, then shook it as if trying to make it work. Ruby thought she heard a crash in the distance, and faint but unusual shouts, but she couldn't be sure. The operators on the platform were looking toward the south, standing on their tiptoes and craning their necks. The return track remained ominously empty.

Ruby edged through the crowd toward her truck. A ride on Thrill took two minutes with another minute for unloading and loading, isn't that what Jack said? Should be back by now. The train should be back, that's why Clara and Steve and Cindy and Mark were looking so worried. She opened the door of her truck and stepped up, standing on the door sill and peering toward the billboards at Thrill's south end. It was too far away; she couldn't see anything. Nothing was moving inside the structure; there were no signs of a moving train, either coming or going. Three minutes at least had passed since Jack left. She felt her heart beating faster and the skin crawling on her forearms.

"Emergency! Please leave the park at once!" It was Max Costello's booming voice on the public address system. "Ride captains,

173

discharge all passengers immediately ... Employees and visitors, everybody please move away from the roller coaster. Evacuate the south end of the park. Extreme danger! Move quickly and use the north and west exits, please! Don't interfere with emergency vehicles ..."

Ruby started the truck and accelerated down the sidewalk toward the south end of Thrill, leaning on the horn and waving people out of the way. She skidded to a stop and jumped out at the Ferris wheel, where a crowd was gathering despite a guard's efforts to make them disperse.

"Get out of here, lady!" the guard shouted at her, waving her back.

"What happened? Tell me!"

"Sniper on the tower! Back, everybody! Back!"

A bullet smacked against the sidewalk and ricocheted away with a whining noise. That convinced the gawkers, who took off running. Ruby and the guard took cover behind the truck.

"A psycho in ski mask," the guard explained as they crouched down together, "on the tower, shooting in all directions."

Ruby felt the world coming to an end. "What happened to the train?"

"Wrecked in the tunnel. I think there are fatalities." The guard sat down and leaned his back against the side of the truck. "God sakes," he breathed, rolling his eyes upward, "I'm not ready for this. I wasn't even supposed to work tonight."

Fireworks were exploding in the sky as if there were still something to celebrate. Ruby reached inside the truck for her radio and in a flat voice told her uncle to stop the show.

Peering cautiously over the hood, she saw Barney Laffoon and his two-man crew discharging passengers from the Ferris wheel as fast as they could. Barney's control station and loading platform were shielded by the wheel itself as well as by a storage shed. As each group of two, three, and four passengers were helped out of the gondolas, the attendants told them to run as fast as they could to the westside exit, keeping the wheel between themselves and the crow's nest until they were out of the sniper's range.

Max Costello arrived in his truck and parked behind Ruby's. She motioned him to slide across to the passenger seat and get out on that side. A few seconds later the flatbed truck with the searchlight on it pulled up; now there were three vehicles in a row forming a protective wall.

Ruby told Max what she knew. The guard added a further detail: A man was trapped under the platform at the top of the tower. The searchlight was turned on and aimed where the guard was pointing. A man in a white shirt was plainly visible crouched on a beam. Ruby squinted and caught her breath ... The man looked like Jack.

"Is that McKenzie? Is that Jack McKenzie?"

"Whoever it is, he's in a hell of spot," Costello said. "I hope he can hang on until we can get some marksmen in here with rifles."

Two blasts from the top of the tower sent a rain of birdshot against the side of the flatbed truck and put the searchlight out of commission.

Ruby sprinted to the Ferris wheel, keeping to shadows as much as she could, and joined Laffoon, who was crouched behind a corner of the storage shed peering up at the crow's nest.

"Barney, is that Jack up there?"

"Your friend Jack? Afraid so." He told her of watching him climbing the ladder and almost getting shot.

"Every time he makes a move the sniper sends a shot in his direction. You know what the maniac on top did a minute ago? Threw a hand grenade down here! It fell short, or a lot of people would have got hurt."

Ruby brought her hands to the sides of her head to keep it from bursting. She inhaled raggedly. "My God, Barney, what are we going to do?"

"I know what I'd do if I had the right weapon. I'd go up on the wheel and blast him to hell. It'd be point blank from up there."

Ruby looked at him with round eyes. "I have the right weapon! Wait here ..."

When she returned from a dash to her truck, she was carrying an armload of cardboard tubes. "Rockets," she explained to Barney. "Send me to the top. I'm going to drop World War III on the bastard's head. It'll give Jack a chance to climb down."

"Are you nuts? He's got a rifle—you'll be a sitting duck!"

"It's hard to aim a rifle when your pants are on fire."

Ruby peeked around the edge of the shed. All the rides had stopped. Nothing was moving. The night had grown strangely silent. "Hang on, Jack!" she shouted in her shrillest voice. "I'm going to

175

give you chance to get out of there . . ." To Barney she said: "When you see the third rocket, start the wheel and bring me down."

"Let me do it. I'll go up."

"You don't know how to fire these things." Ruby climbed into a gondola and pointed at the sky. "Up!"

"Ruby, nobody's worth the risk."

"Wrong. Good men are hard to find . . . and they're usually either married or gay. Up!"

Barney pushed the start button and the ponderous wheel began to turn.

Max Costello came out of the shadows. "What the hell are you doing?" he hissed at Barney. "Get her off that wheel!"

"She's going to the top. She's going to fire rockets at the sniper."

"She's going to *what?* Fire *rockets?* What if she misses? The guy will blow her away!"

"She won't miss. It's a slam dunk for her. Like throwing a wad of paper into a wastebasket. I've seen her and her father shoot balloons out of the air at ten times the distance."

"Goddammit, Laffoon, bring her down! That's an order!"

Barney's face was turned upward as he followed the course of Ruby's gondola. When it neared the top he touched a button marked "slow crawl."

"In a minute," he said to Costello, "I'll bring her down in a minute."

He stopped the wheel. The gondolas rocked gently, then came to rest.

Staying as motionless as she could, Ruby fished a lighter from her shirt pocket. Clamping a mortar tube between her legs, she dropped a rocket in—nozzle at the bottom, bursting charge at the top—and located the fuse with her forefinger. Slowly she raised her head and peeked over the back of the gondola. What she saw made her gasp. For some reason, Jack had edged his way toward the ladder and was crouched directly behind it. The sniper—clad in black, including a black ski mask—had apparently heard his movements and was standing directly over his head, aiming his rifle at the floor, waiting for another sound to guide his aim. There was something familiar about that black figure—the narrow shoulders, the thin frame, the long neck. Could it possibly be Claudia Krevek? The more she stared, the surer she became.

Ruby snapped the lighter without result. She snapped it again, and again there was no flame. She cursed under her breath, unable to take her eyes from the scene that was unfolding not fifty feet away. The sniper was leaning over the railing now and getting into position to take a shot at Jack's white shirt.

"Claudia!" Ruby shouted in desperation. "Give up!" The way the sniper raised the rifle and looked around for the source of the voice made Ruby sure her wild guess was right. "We know who you are, Claudia! Put the rifle down . . ."

But Claudia, if that's who it was, didn't put the rifle down. She turned it toward the Ferris wheel and fired several shots. Ruby ducked out of sight. After a long minute, she risked another look.

Smoke was coming from somewhere and rising in billows between the Ferris wheel and the crow's nest and obscuring visibility. Claudia was occupied for the moment trying to get a shot at Jack, who had moved away from the ladder and deeper into the shadows. Ruby shook the lighter to bring fluid to the wick. Another snap and a flame appeared. "Thank you, God," she breathed as she touched the flame to the fuse and brought the mortar tube into position braced against her shoulder. She took aim at a point several feet above Claudia's head, estimating as best she could the effect gravity would have on the trajectory. If the rocket didn't hit her in the face or chest, it would at least land inside the platform and be trapped there by the enclosing fence until the bursting charge detonated.

Ruby winced when she felt the push against her shoulder, heard the whoosh, and felt the sting of sparks on her face as the expanding gasses sent the rocket exploding from the tube.

CHAPTER TWENTY-FOUR

Jack saw Ruby arrive in her pickup truck and saw her take cover behind it. He saw Costello arrive, too, and the searchlight, and was momentarily blinded when the light went on. He was almost glad when the lunatic above him shot it out; he preferred what little protection the darkness under the platform provided. In the distance he could see the flashing lights of approaching emergency vehicles and could hear the faint wail of sirens. There was an odor of gasoline drifting up from somewhere down below. The parking lot was a sea of headlights and taillights as cars maneuvered toward the exits. There were plenty of people who weren't leaving, too: Jack could see them everywhere, some of them with children, clusters of them standing what they probably thought was a safe distance away. Occasionally a rifle shot from overhead sent them scampering.

Jack's legs were killing him. He was sitting on his heels atop the narrow edge of a six-by-twelve with his legs doubled. He was afraid to straddle the beam and let his legs hang down for fear that he wouldn't be able to move fast enough if he had to.

He heard Ruby shouting at him from somewhere near the bottom of the Ferris wheel. He heard the words "Hang on, Jack," and "I'm going to give you a chance . . ." What was she going to do, distract the sniper in some way? He wanted to shout back at her and tell her not to risk her neck, but he knew that if he made a sound he'd give away his position and bring a bullet down on his head. Thank God, he thought, the gunman wasn't using automatic weapons. With an automatic, the sniper could simply spray the floor with bullets and take Jack out wherever he was hiding.

He gazed at the ladder at the end of the beam. Maybe it would be better if he left the center of the platform and got closer to the edge . . . then, if the gunman came down to get a clear shot at him,

178

he might be able to grab his legs and throw him off or grab the barrel of the rifle. He edged carefully along the beam, trying not to make a noise, until he was directly behind the ladder. He stretched his legs one at a time and went back into a crouch. In his mind he rehearsed the exact moves he would make—the leap and grab—if he saw a pair of legs come into view.

For some reason, the Ferris wheel started moving, but stopped after making half a revolution.

Jack smelled smoke. He hated to look down and remind himself of how high up he was, but he risked a glance and saw plumes of smoke rising from fires at ground level. The tower supporting the crow's nest had eight columns, one at each corner and one at the midpoint of each side, and every one was in flames. What idiot set those? Had somebody decided to smoke the sniper off his perch or bring the tower down without realizing that Jack McKenzie was trapped on top as well? He braced himself. When the sniper saw the smoke, he'd have to climb down. There was no other way out.

He heard Ruby's shouting again. It sounded like "Claudia, give up!" and "We know who you are, Claudia! Put the rifle down . . ."

Claudia Krevek? *She* was the sniper? *She* was the saboteur?

WHOOSH! There was an eruption of orange sparks from the top of the Ferris wheel; a fountain of fire sailed through the air and angled downward into the crow's nest as if it were following a wire. Jack ducked involuntarily and almost lost his balance, grabbing the ladder to keep from falling. He heard the rocket hit the deck over his head and heard it whiz angrily back and forth between the barriers with tremendous energy until the burst charge detonated with a red flash. When a star went off hundreds of feet in the air, the explosion seemed almost delicate, but at a distance of five feet it sounded like a half-stick of dynamite.

Jack heard something else: screams and curses from the sniper . . . in a woman's voice. Maybe it *was* Claudia Krevek . . .

A second rocket came in on a brilliant trail of sparks and slammed into the crow's nest with deadly accuracy, then another. When the third star exploded, Jack swung himself to the outside of the ladder and found himself engulfed by billows of black smoke welling upward from the ground. Across the way the lights of the Ferris wheel were turning again—apparently Ruby had finished her barrage and was on her way down. Overhead, a cloud of white smoke rose from the crow's nest, reflecting red from still-burning star pellets.

Jack climbed the ladder until he could see over the railing. The ski-masked figure was down on one knee moaning in pain, massaging an ankle with one hand and rummaging in a canvas sack with the other. She brought a small steel ball out of the bag and raised it to her teeth. There was enough light coming from the Statue of Liberty billboard to enable him to see that the rifle and the shotgun were on the floor. This is a woman, Jack reminded himself; I can overpower any woman. He climbed another three steps and jumped over the railing.

As he threw himself at her, she spun around and raised both hands defensively. He knocked her over backward, but not before she hit him hard on the side of the head with whatever it was she had in her hand. He landed on top of her and with furious effort managed to grab both of her wrists. She struggled mightily and writhed like a wildcat, but by scissoring his legs around hers and using his greater weight he was able to pin her down. She was a woman, and a thin one at that, but she was extremely strong.

"It's over," Jack managed to say. "Give up. Don't make me hurt you . . ."

She lunged and squirmed in response.

Jack let go of her with his right hand and tried to hit her in the face with his fist, but she rolled her head out of the way and he managed only a glancing blow. Before he could cock his arm again she clamped her fingers around his wrist and kept it from moving. She struggled to get out from under him; he had to use every ounce of strength he had to keep her down. He tried to tear his hand free to grab the rifle, which was an arm's length away, thinking he could hit her in the head with the stock, but her grip was like a ring of steel.

"Goddamn you," he said in a guttural voice he didn't recognize, "Don't make it worse than it already is . . ."

The ski mask had holes cut only for the eyes; where the mouth was Jack could see the outline of her lips closed around a steel ring with a small pin at the end. His eyes went to her right hand and he saw that her bony fingers were closed around . . . a hand grenade! Jack stared in disbelief as she opened her hand. The grenade rolled lazily away and came to rest in a crack between two floorboards.

Jack lunged for it, but she managed to catch hold of his arm. He

180

strained toward the grenade, she held him back. In a last desperate attempt to save himself, he jerked his hands *away* from the grenade, dropped them on the front of her jacket, lifted her head and shoulders off the floor, and threw her to the left on top of the grenade. The explosion was deafening and lifted them both off the floor as shrapnel tore upward through her torso. Her head snapped back and air escaped from her mouth and holes in her chest. She went limp and he released her; he was hit as well.

He moved away and flexed his arms and fingers. There was blood, but he couldn't tell how much of it was his and how much hers. She was a mess and obviously dead, with blood rapidly pooling beside her. He crawled forward and pulled off the mask. The eyes were staring and the mouth was agape and blood was welling from a wound in her neck. He recognized Krevek's wife even though her face was contorted in fear and pain.

Jack struggled to his feet and backed away. A sharp stab in his knee almost made him buckle. Smoke was curling around all sides of the tower, acrid black smoke that smelled like burning rubber. He leaned over the railing and saw tongues of flame climbing toward him on both sides of the ladder. He limped to the opposite side of the platform and gauged the distance to the walkway at the bottom of the billboards. It was ten or twelve feet . . . Maybe if he backed up and made a run for it he could jump across, or at least get close enough to catch onto something with his hands. Adrenaline sometimes gave people strength they didn't know they had. He'd never make it, he realized with a sinking heart, not with a knee that felt as if it had been hit with a hammer.

He saw a rope. It spanned the gap as if somebody was going to hang clothes out to dry. He grabbed it—it was in fact clothesline, probably not strong enough to support his weight if he tried to cross it hand over hand. Maybe he could untie it and swing across like Tarzan. He yanked on it to see how strong it was and how securely it was tied on the other end . . . and he felt it yield. Through a rising scrim of smoke he saw that the rope was tied to something that was emerging from the doorway between the signs, a plank of some sort that seemed to be on wheels. The harder he pulled, the closer it got, until finally he was able to lean forward and catch hold of it. He pulled it the rest of the way and rested it on the railing, and as he did so he felt the floor beneath his feet shift slightly and tremble.

The flames were eating through the wooden columns somewhere down below and they were sagging under the tower's weight.

He climbed onto the railing and stepped onto the end of the bridge; he stood there like a pirate who refused to walk the plank unless he was prodded by swords. He told himself that this was no time to think about how far it was to the ground. The bridge was at least two feet wide; if it were lying on a sidewalk he could stroll across it with no problem at all; why should it be any different a hundred feet in the air? He took three small steps, favoring his injured knee. He stopped and felt terror closing in on him like a flood of cold water. He fixed his eyes on the doorway. It wasn't so far, he told himself. You can make it. *Crawl* across if you have to ... but he couldn't make himself move.

The tower shuddered again. Jack gritted his teeth and took several more steps forward onto the bridge, then lurched the rest of the way like a drunk and fell in a heap at the other end with his arms wrapped around the end of a billboard as if it were an old friend. Behind him the smoke that was curling around the edges of the crow's nest was suddenly engulfed by flames.

He would have liked to lie still for a minute and catch his breath, but the heat of the booming fire drove him to his feet. He pulled himself through the doorway into the blackness between the signs. Looking down through the grillework that formed the walkway, he could see the roofs of the few cars that were still left in the south corner of the parking lot. He remembered the evening he first arrived at Wildcat Mountain and how he noticed the billboards and the towers that supported them. There was a ladder, if he recalled correctly. He moved cautiously forward, groping, waiting for his eyes to adjust to the gloom and hoping that he could find the ladder before the billboards burst into flames.

CHAPTER TWENTY-FIVE

R uby, kneeling on the seat and aiming her mortar tube over the back of the gondola, smiled grimly. Her first shot had plunged Claudia, if that's who it was, into hell—she was chased around the crow's nest by a fire-spewing devil, stunned by a powerful explosion, then attacked by a swarm of fast-burning pellets of potassium nitrate, charcoal, and sulphur. Before she could orient herself and counter-attack with bullets, Ruby struck again. The second rocket rushed through the air on its downward trajectory and embedded itself in the fence at the far side of the enclosure where the burning propellant ejected a fountain of sparks that completely filled the platform. After the green-and-red starburst, which sent colored points of light erupt-ing in every direction, Ruby could see that the sniper had dropped the rifle and was turning around in a panic, patting her clothes where she had been hit and screaming an oddly high-pitched scream. Jack's head and shoulders came into view under the platform; his arm was reaching around to the outside of the ladder and he was looking up to see if the coast was clear. The smoke was getting heavier, and Ruby saw flames rising from the ground under the tower.

Ruby lit her final fuse, rested the tube on her shoulder, and trained it on the sniper, who now was looking up at her and reaching for the rifle. The rocket left the tube and streaked through the air like a comet chased by a brilliant tail of light. Claudia threw herself to one side to avoid getting hit, then once again disappeared under a boiling lake of sparks.

"Now!" Ruby yelled to Jack as the starburst detonated over his head, "get out of there!"

The instant the third rocket was fired, the wheel began to turn. Ruby's gondola sank and others rose, blocking her view.

She jumped out at the bottom, full of elation at the accuracy of her strikes, and ran toward Barney and the protection of the shed. "Did he get away? Did he climb down?"

Barney was gazing at the top of the tower. He shook his head in amazement. "The damned fool climbed *up* . . ."

"What? *What?*"

"He climbed up the ladder and over the railing."

Ruby stared at the tower in disbelief. Black smoke, rising in columns and blocking the view, made her cough and her eyes water. "Where's the smoke coming from? Did the rockets . . ."

"The fire was first. Must be arson. Only gas or kerosene would send up so much smoke."

Ruby cupped her hands beside her mouth and called Jack's name over and over. Flames appeared at the track level of the tower, climbing quickly up the corners. She dropped her hands and her voice trailed off in despair as the top of the tower disappeared behind a wall of smoke. "God, no," she breathed, "please, God, no . . ."

She felt Barney's hand tighten on her shoulder.

What happened next would always be a blur in Ruby's memory. She remembers the flashing lights of police cars, fire trucks, and ambulances, men running, shouts. She remembers standing like a zombie watching the tower slowly sink and topple in a mass of fire, backing away to avoid getting hit by the upwelling flood of sparks and ashes; she remembers helping survivors into ambulances, streams of water arching through the air and shining under the glare of floodlights. Allbright was dead, she remembers hearing someone say, dead of a broken neck. What about Jack? Nobody knew. Nobody had seen him.

She remembers finding herself sitting in her truck with no idea how she got there, her forehead resting on the wheel. She felt drained of life and too dry and hollow and powerless to cry. The sound of firefighting, of trucks coming and going, of strained voices, gradually lost its meaning and seemed no more relevant than a television set droning in an empty room.

She lifted her head. Rescue workers were hurrying back and forth and shouting to one another as if something still mattered. Her eyes were drawn to two men talking in the shadows a short distance away; one was a policeman, the other made her think of Jack. The man turned and walked toward her, the policeman jogged away in the opposite direction talking on his radio. She squinted . . . no, the man wasn't Jack. Jack had a forceful stride, this man was limping. Jack had an erect posture, this man's shoulders were slumped.

The closer he got the more Ruby began to think it really was Jack, risen somehow from the inferno. Was she hallucinating in her despair, projecting what she wished were true on a random survivor of the fire who only vaguely resembled Jack?

When he emerged from the shadows, Ruby could see blood glistening on his left ear and cheek from a wound on his temple. His white shirt was torn and blackened by soot. He came to the side of the truck and rested his forearms on the open window. He had Jack's face and Jack's shy smile, and when he spoke it was with Jack's voice:

"Thanks," he said, "for saving my life."

"It's you!"

"Sort of. Would you mind taking me to the nearest doctor? I don't think I can drive with this knee." His eyes closed halfway and his legs sagged. Ruby had to wait until he was on the ground before she could open the door to help him. His last words before passing out completely, she later insisted, were: "Let's stop on the way for fries and a sponge bath."

As soon as Carl Ott released Wilson St. James from his shoulder restraints, the one-time military officer took charge, making sure everybody stayed inside the tunnel when the sniper was in control and guiding those able to walk to safety the moment the bullets stopped flying. When the fire broke out, he and Ott became a two-man rescue squad, helping to carry and guide the survivors to the ground despite the smoke and heat and falling embers and the imminent collapse of the tower.

Twice he was told to get into an ambulance. "I'm all right, dammit," he responded angrily, "help somebody who needs it."

He positioned arriving emergency vehicles, he consulted with the sheriff and the fire commanders, and he ordered trucks to batter down the park's new perimeter fence to provide direct access to the highway. But after forty-five minutes of hectic activity, fatigue hit him like a load of sand. He staggered to a bench and sat down, not knowing whether to throw up or burst into tears.

He was approached by Mr. Fujima, one of the members of the

group negotiating to buy the park. Fujima had not been aboard the train and has stayed away from the rescue operation, and as a consequence his tailored business suit was neat and clean. His colleague, Mr. Onoda, on the other hand, who survived the crash, probably saved more than one life with his cool head and knowledge of first aid. St. James eyed Fujima suspiciously. He was ninety-nine percent sure of what the Japanese was going to say. Fine, he didn't want to sell out to him anyway.

"Bad omen," Fujima said with an apologetic shrug. "Calls for new thought. We are not so sure now."

St. James dismissed him with a toss of his head. "Good-bye, then. Give my regards to the emperor."

While Fujima was retreating, somebody sat down on the bench. It was the banker, Delareaux, who was even smaller than Fujima and just as neat and clean, if not more so.

"Are you all right, Wilson?"

"Couldn't be better, aside from total exhaustion and suicidal tendencies. Pooped, in a word."

"I watched the way you took over. You were magnificent."

St. James looked at his new friend and smiled weakly. "I've always been pretty good in emergencies. Take the Korean war . . . if I hadn't been there we would have lost for sure. It's day-to-day life that defeats me. Shit! I better go to the hospital with the rest of them and get checked over. I think I'm going into shock or something."

"I'll take you in my car." Delareaux helped St. James to his feet.

"Kali . . . Kali is okay, isn't it? . . . this is a little presumptuous, but will you stay with me tonight? I don't want to be alone, not after this."

Delareaux hesitated, then took his arm reassuringly. "Why not? I'll play nurse for a night. Maybe some of your heroic qualities will rub off on me."

They walked slowly toward the exit, the big man leaning on the small woman for support.

Three men were on night duty at Los Gallinas police headquarters: Sergeant Cochran was at the front counter, officers Phelan and Schaefer at desks behind him. Through the panes of bullet-resistant glass that separated the office area from the lobby, Cochran saw a man dressed in pajamas and a bathrobe making his way up the walk toward the front entrance. He was tall and thin and his thatch of gray hair needed combing.

"Here comes a guy who's locked himself out of his house, I'll bet," said Cochran. When he got a closer look at the wild hair and the intense eyes, he changed his mind. "Possible EDP." EDP was police shorthand for "emotionally disturbed person."

The man crossed the lobby and slapped his hands on the counter. "I want to report a missing person. Are you in charge?"

"Who is missing, sir?"

"My wife."

"How long has she been gone?"

"Somewhere between thirty minutes and four hours."

"Thirty minutes?"

"I fell asleep on the couch, see, so I'm not sure when she left. When I woke up half an hour ago, I got ready for bed, then I noticed she wasn't in the house. Her car's gone, too."

"Maybe she just went down to 7-Eleven and is a little late getting back."

"When she's late, she calls me. No, this has got to more than a flat tire or whatever the hell you think it is."

"I don't think anything, sir. It's just that in our experience people who are only an hour or so late almost always show up with a story about car trouble or making a wrong turn, things of that nature."

"Your experience has nothing to do with my wife. She's hardly ever even five minutes late, much less missing entirely."

"May I have your name?"

"Ernest Krevek. Wife Claudia. Krevek is with a 'k' fore and aft."

Cochran fitted a form onto a clipboard and began writing. "Did you have an argument tonight? Were either of you drinking? Have you recently been discussing divorce or separation?"

"Absolutely not!"

"Routine questions. Do you have any specific reason to believe that she is in danger?"

"Anybody who is out in the middle of the night in the United States in in danger."

"But no specific threat?"

"Are you really in charge? You seem too young. Let me talk to your father."

187

"My father is a retired appraiser in Denver. Do you want his number?"

"I want you to look for my wife. I want you to check the hospitals, the highway patrol, whatever you do when somebody is missing."

"She might not be. She might be waiting for you at home right now. If she's only been gone for thirty minutes, we can hardly divert scarce police resources—"

"Stuff the 'scarce police resources.' You don't look too busy."

"As for calling the CHP and the area emergency rooms, you can do that yourself. They're listed in the phone book. First, though, you should call every friend and relative who she might be staying with or who might know where she is. She might have some grievance against you that she hasn't communicated."

"My tax dollars at work! By the time you guys do anything she'll be chopped up in pieces and mailed to nine different countries."

"Mr. Krevek, if we hear anything about your wife, anything at all, we'll call you. If your wife isn't back by morning, and you've made all the necessary phone calls, we'll issue an APB."

"An APB?"

"An all-points bulletin. I have your wife's name, Claudia Krevek, K-R-E-V-E-K. Your address and phone number?"

"They're listed in the phone book." He wagged his finger at the sergeant and added, "If anything happens to my wife because you public servants didn't want to be bothered, you'll hear from me again. And again. For the rest of your life."

When he was gone, the three policemen chuckled. Phelan suggested that Mrs. Krevek was probably in a bar somewhere getting drunk.

"Wouldn't you be if you were married to him?"

"I'd move and leave no forwarding address."

The phone rang. "Police. Cochran speaking."

As the sergeant listened, his mouth dropped open. "Did you say *Krevek*, sir?" He covered the mouthpiece and relayed a summary to his colleagues: "Sniper in Sonoma County . . . four dead, ten wounded . . . sniper dead, thought to be *Claudia Krevek* . . . "

All three officers rose to their feet. Cochran listened for a moment more, then glanced at the message that was emerging from the interagency teletype machine. "Yes, sir," he said into the phone, "the authorization is coming in. Gray hair, narrow face, about seventy

years old? Ernest Krevek, yes. He was just in here looking for her
. . . might still be in the lot . . .''

Phelan ran to the door. ''He's sitting in his car using a phone . . .
oh, oh, he's backing out . . .''

''Bring him in,'' Cochran ordered. ''It's an eight thirty-six. Sonoma wants him held for questioning. Armed and dangerous, all due
caution . . .''

Krevek's black Cadillac eased out of the lot and turned onto the
street. At the sound of shouts, the car pulled to the curb and stopped.

''Mr. Krevek, wait!'' Phelan called, running across the lawn with
Schaefer behind him. ''Come back! We have news about your
wife . . .''

CHAPTER TWENTY-SIX

Jack was reading the *San Francisco Chronicle*. "It says here that Krevek's defense is going to be that he had no idea what his wife was up to. Nobody will believe that. Sounds like desperation to me."

"It'll be a hard sell to a jury," Ruby agreed. "Who knew how the brakes worked, who owned the guns, who knew how to screw up the computer? The old s.o.b. should plead guilty. Look, the fog is burning off . . ."

They were on the deck of their cottage at Harbor House, a bed-and-breakfast inn on California's north coast. Ruby was on a lounge chair going through a shopping bag full of letters that had come in for them at the hospital and the park. Jack was catching up on newspapers with his leg cast propped up on a chair. Twenty minutes earlier the fog was so thick they couldn't see the beach below, though they could hear the muted thunder of the waves. Now the fog was thinning into mist and retreating out to sea. Like magic, dramatic headlands appeared, a curving strand of beach, blue-gray water, enormous rock outcroppings beyond the surf. They watched for long minutes in silence.

"Fantastic," Jack said at last. "Three cheers for Mother Nature."

"Beautiful, isn't it? This is my favorite place in the whole world."

"Better than my hospital room, that's for sure. I'm glad I'm out of there."

"They were glad to see you go. They had more security people on the payroll at the end than the park ever had. And the parking lot . . . half the spaces were taken by the press. I keep looking over my shoulder, thinking they're going to find out where we are."

"It's been a week and a half. You'd think they'd lose interest."

Jack turned to the business section of the paper. Ruby continued

190

looking through the letters, opening those that looked especially interesting.

"The paper is full of amazing stuff," Jack said. "Here's an article about Speedtech. The headline is 'Disaster Sells.' According to this, Speedtech is getting inquiries from parks all over the world about Thrill. Everybody wants a copy of what is now the most famous coaster in the world."

"I'm not surprised," Ruby said, ripping open an envelope. "You watch, a year from now Thrill will be rebuilt and the park will be busier than ever."

"Will you be there running the fireworks shows and the midway games?"

"I doubt it. I'll be with you, and it won't be at Wildcat Mountain and it won't be in Chicago designing foundations."

Jack smiled. "We can't live on love alone. One of us is going to have to work."

"Eventually, maybe, but not for a long time. Here's a letter from a guy in Hollywood who calls himself a 'celebrity agent.' He says we can make three hundred thousand dollars in one year on the lecture circuit, more if a movie is made. He says we're America's darlings and should cash in on it while we're hot."

"Save that letter."

"Lots of interesting stuff in this pile. Here's a scribbled note from St. James . . . twenty Bullwinkle dolls have come in the mail to replace the one you lost."

"How did anybody know about that?"

"I'm afraid I mentioned it to a reporter during one of the first interviews. Sorry. Say, here's a telegram for you from Brazil. I didn't know people still sent telegrams."

"My dad's in Brazil . . . he probably just heard the news. Open it. Read it to me."

"Let's see . . . well, it's just three words. 'That's my boy!' "

Ruby was surprised at the effect the message had on Jack. The newspaper slipped from his fingers and he looked stricken. His eyes glistened. She asked him if he was going to cry.

"No, it's just that . . . well, you'd have to know him. He's never said anything like that to me before. I guess he figures I finally did something right. He's stingy with compliments, and when he does give one he usually ruins it with an extra comment. 'It was brave of you to climb that ladder, son, but did you first make sure your insurance was up to date?' It's a breakthrough for him simply to say 'That's my boy,' and let it go at that.''

"Saying anything more in a telegram from Brazil would cost a dollar a word." Ruby took Jack's hands and pulled him to his feet. "We are America's darlings and we should be making love. Let's go inside."

"You know what, Ruby?" Jack said, hobbling carefully after her. "You are more fun than . . . a roller coaster."

In the picturesque town of Mendocino, fifteen miles north of Harbor House, the owner of a grocery store watched a couple pick out picnic supplies. She was an attractive woman with a slim figure and a wide smile, he was a square-shouldered chap with a walking cast on his leg. It was nice to see such happy people, the grocer thought. Probably up from San Francisco without their spouses.

At the checkout stand, the woman pointed at a rack carrying the latest tabloids and began laughing. The man laughed, too, and before long the two of them were laughing so hard they had to hang on to each other to keep from falling down. The grocer stepped from behind the cash register to see what was so funny. Apparently it was a headline:

ROCKET RUBY AND THE SPIDERMAN
ESCAPE TO SECRET LOVE NEST

Is it wedding bells for
the coaster crash couple?

192

Author's Note

If I've gotten something wrong, it's not the fault of Ron Toomer, President, Dal Freeman, Director of Engineering, and Herb Mudrow, Project Engineer, all of Arrow Dynamics, Inc., who did what they could to educate me about roller coasters when I visited their plant in Clearfield, Utah. My fireworks guide was Al Souza of San Diego Fireworks, Inc. My thanks to all of them.

Thanks also to American Coaster Enthusiasts of New York City for prompt attention to my requests for reprints of articles in *Roller Coaster*. Exceptionally helpful was *The Incredible Scream Machine— A History of the Roller Coaster*, by Robert Cartmell, jointly published in 1987 by Amusement Park Books and Bowling Green State University Popular Press. The magazine and the book would fascinate anybody.

For reading early versions of the manuscript and making many valuable suggestions, I am in debt to Cynthia Nelms, Knox Burger, and Christopher West Davis.